Praise for
# Platform Dwellers

"A civilization with a hidden past and an uncertain future...a land unknown, beckoning to be rediscovered...*Platform Dwellers* had me completely captivated and left hungry for more.
I loved every second."

—*The Little Book Bistro* Blog

"The intricately crafted world, unbelievably clever characters, mind-blowing plot twists, along with the ever so subtle romance between the protagonists are all the elements that take this dystopian story up a notch and make it unputdownable."

—Jasmine, *Life of a Simple Reader*

"*Platform Dwellers* is a high-concept story that definitely delivers. In the book's terms,
it's 'epically tidal.'"

—Diane Castle, author of *Black Oil, Red Blood*

# Platform Dwellers

Katarina Boudreaux

OWL HOLLOW PRESS

Owl Hollow Press, LLC, Springville, UT 84663

This book is a work of fiction. Names, characters, places, and incidents are products of the author's imagination. Any resemblance to actual people, living or dead, or to businesses, companies, events, institutions, or locales is completely coincidental.

Platform Dwellers
Copyright © 2018 by Katarina Boudreaux

All rights reserved. No part of this publication may be reproduced, distributed or transmitted in any form or by any means, without prior written permission.

Library of Congress Cataloging-in-Publication Data
Platform Dwellers / K. Boudreaux. — First edition.

Summary:
Though Land has been silent since the final revolution, Joe picks up SOS signals and leaves her home on a repurposed oil platform to investigate what remains of human Land society, uncovering secrets hidden for generations.

ISBN 978-1-945654-10-7 (paperback)
ISBN 978-1-945654-11-4 (e-book)
LCCN 2017963797

For Kuillin James. You are where love lives.

# Chapter One

"LIGHTS OUT IN TEN MINUTES," Dad says, his frame dwarfing the oval door to my room. "You know the drill." He stoops to prevent his head from scraping the ceiling.

"I know the drill." I make a big deal of paying attention to my schoolwork open on the virtual pad in my hand. I'm logged into the wireless LAN that connects me to our main Platform router, but I've already completed the assignments on power cogeneration, plus the extra credit on kinetic energy. The last day of school is tomorrow, so schoolwork was light. Dad doesn't know that. I doubt he even knows it's the last day. "They'll be shutting down the radio wave generator soon."

"All right," Dad says. "Leave the meter box for the cage farm open, would you? They're checking it tomorrow."

I nod, eyes still on my screen. "Will do."

Twenty feet beneath us, there's a circular cage farm tethered to our home like a big, bus-sized globe. Every house has one. The Planning Commission regularly sends a rep to check the meter on the side of the farm to prevent over harvesting. Honestly, I couldn't eat more redfish and speckled trout than we're allotted anyway. Thank the crusty barnacles for our deck garden that provides some food variety.

"Are you sure you're sixteen? Sometimes I think you're forty."

"Sixteen." I glance up and smile at him.

Dad's face softens, and he smiles back. "I know. I watched your birth. See you in the morning, Joe."

"Yes." Breakfast and sometimes dinner are the only times I ever really see him. His research takes up the day and often the night.

Dad swings my door shut, and I listen for the click that means it's latched properly. I log off the network by swiping my wrist across the screen, closing the diagram of a nuclear power plant I had pretended to be studying. I wonder for the millionth time what it would be like to really see, touch, and smell what we learn about. From the start of school at age three, practically everything is virtual. I'll never see a real power plant, so power cogeneration seems silly to study.

"The last day of school," I whisper. No more boring, useless assignments. I can focus strictly on the hands-on work necessary to make the models of large-scale communication projects connecting Platform to Platform into reality. Local LAN or VPN isn't good enough, not with families separated by projects on different Platforms.

*Like mine.* My stomach clenches, but I force myself to think about my final project. Once the models get final approval by the Planning Commission, I'll have free access to use Platform materials and build them full scale. The possibilities are endless.

The floor rolls to the right when a bigger wave hits, and my stomach lurches. Why Mom and Dad chose to live on one of the ten spar Platforms instead of the main fixed Platform, Nod, is beyond me. Unlike the steel and concrete legs of Nod, the spars are moored loosely to the seabed, so we move with the current and waves. Thick metal tethering lines connect to shackles on sunken ships buried under the seabed over two thousand feet below us. They're not visible through the muddy water, but moving with the waves is a constant reminder of how unstable we really are.

The main lights will shut off automatically in a few minutes. I want to be in bed when they do, as the secondary lights consist of two rows of dim, round track lights above my bed and one row over the door. They're just powerful enough to light the way to the exit.

I put my virtual pad carefully in my desk drawer and turn the handle until it clicks shut, then take off my blue school uniform. It's made from fire-resistant industrial coveralls. Textiles still has almost a hundred of them, as all oil workers were required to wear them on the Platforms pre-virus. I'd cut the sleeves and pant legs off to make it more comfortable—and more my size.

I remove pajamas from the single drawer beneath my bed that holds all my permitted clothing. Looking at my bed as I put on the threadbare, long-sleeved t-shirt and coarse pajama bottoms—more patches than original black-out material—I sigh. I need to redo the stuffing in my mattress. I have an allotment of disposables available from Textiles—I just have to collect it.

"For once, I'd like to sleep in a bed made of straw, or wood, or anything besides metal and unusable scraps," I say. I know I'm being childish; other materials are impractical for long-term usage. They deteriorate too quickly in our offshore environment. And the coldness of the room is partially my fault—I don't decorate my room with found objects. I like things simple. But I still hate the sound and feel of metal.

"Feathers. Feathers would be great to sleep on."

It's cool this time of year, and I never get warm enough. Being surrounded by metal doesn't help. I grit my teeth against the cold of the chair rim against my hands as I push it beneath my desk.

I toss my dirty clothes into the metal opening next to the sink that leads to the laundry room, anticipating my shower and clean clothes tomorrow. Like everyone else on the Platforms,

I'm only allowed a shower once every two days. We re-use our outer clothes as much as possible, so laundry day is on shower day.

I swipe my wrist against the meter on the mirror above the sink. As I wait for my allotted cupful of water for face washing and teeth brushing, I gingerly hop from one foot to the other to minimize contact with the damp floor. I quickly scrub my face with some of the water, then use the rest to brush my teeth after retrieving my toothbrush from a small drawer to the side. I make a face in the mirror and spit the water toward the back of the small bowl, creating a satisfying splat against the metal sink.

I swipe my wrist again and drink the eight ounces of water I'm issued. I put the cup back in its holder and study myself in the mirror. Wide-set eyes, perky nose, lips a little too full for pretty. No eyelashes to speak of and monolids. Hair the color of the sunset when there's a storm at sea—not quite red, not quite gold. I look like Mom and Dad, a perfect mix.

I turn back to my flat mattress and see the light on my phone blinking from the side table. My phone has seen better days. It's silver and clunky, half the size of my flattened hand, and some of the letters are hard to make out on the scratched screen. I need to take it to the PC phone repair station for screen restoration but don't want to explain its quick deterioration.

I jump into bed a second before the primary lights go out and grab my phone. The main radio wave generator is shut down by now, so it must be Drayton on the secret line I set up for us almost a year ago for after hours and non-Planning-Commission-approved messages. The software I wrote breaks several rules, so I feel sneaky using it. My virtual pad hotspot also breaks PC rules, as they can't track my usage. It's cool to hide something from the PC.

I unlock my phone with a swipe of my wrist across the screen and read Drayton's message.

I see them again.

I close my eyes and imagine seeing anything but my room, then answer.

It's after hours. I hit send and wait.

Drayton is my best friend. He lives two bridge viaducts away, which is why we can communicate on the secret channel. I haven't been over to his house in months, as our senior course load has been demanding. Plus, the PC has issued earlier curfews since the roads have been failing. The wood on some of the walkways to the main platform is getting sketchy, not to mention the metal bracings are rusting.

The screen lights up.

I know, but I see them again.

Drayton has been telling me for a month that he sees lights on Land. With the completion of the super powerful telescope he built over the school year, he can see things the rest of us can't. He's convinced there are people on Land trying to contact us—which I remind him is impossible since every scrap of technology on Land was destroyed in the Moralist revolt a hundred years ago.

I type the same thing I've always typed. It's part of the way Drayton and I get along—I remind him of reality, and he reminds me to think outside the box.

That's impossible.

I count to five, then look at the phone.

But it's not impossible. Some people stayed—there must be survivors. They could have rebuilt the entire infrastructure by now.

"Always the optimist," I say and type, If anyone was left alive after the virus.

I know Drayton will take the bait. His reply comes quickly. We don't know what happened.

It's a discussion we've had a million times. I pucker my lips and respond.

**We'll talk about it in the morning. Pick me up for school?**

School is on the main Nod Platform almost six kilometers around the ring road from my home. Mom took me until 184 days ago, when she was moved to complete research on Neft, a neighboring Platform. Now, Dad does sometimes, but more often than not, I walk or ride my bicycle. I can smell the heaviness of bad weather, and I don't want to ride—or worse, walk—in the rain. Plus, the lifts are scary when the weather is bad. And it's the last day of school. I add an extra please.

**Please. Come on. I hate rain.**

My phone lights up with Drayton's reply. **Yes. Be ready.**

I smile and turn the phone off. Drayton is dying of insane curiosity right now about the lights. But all I can think about is my future. I've passed all of the PC placement tests for the Technology track. Tomorrow, I finish my school requirements and start the next phase of my life: my senior project. I'll be considered an eligible adult researcher when the completed project is accepted by the PC. Once it's completed, I'll be assigned to an official research project. If I fail, the PC will move me into sorting or recycling, or teaching if I'm lucky.

I put the phone back on the side table and look at the satellite picture I've drilled with old fishhooks to the ceiling. "Long-distance communication," I whisper and turn to lie on my right side. "I have six months to make you work. Then a career to build."

Our Nod-issued solar generator on the roof above the kitchen powers down. It sounds like mad whispering. When it's silent, the secondary lights power off.

"Tomorrow, I begin," I say and put my hand on the wall in front of my face. I know it is there in the pitch black—solid, cold, and smooth. I imagine it rooted to the ground instead of built on top of the sea. I dig around for the bed strap and belt myself in.

I shut my eyes and dream of my mom—out there, floating on Neft.

# Chapter Two

THE RIDE TO SCHOOL IS SILENT as we cross our spar Platform and the adjoining one. Drayton knows I need time to wake up. Even after my shower, I'm groggy. Every building we pass is an exact replica of the building before it—one-and-a-half stories, drab, no yard, washed-out beige. In front of each structure, racks for drying fish climb like stairs to the sky. These buildings are all homes, but they look like metal boxes compared to the Land homes I've seen pictures of.

We reach the ring road closest to the lifts. The seas are choppy today, and Drayton has to concentrate on not driving us into the ocean. The scavenger ships have been out for weeks searching for materials to patch huge sections of roadways that are rotting away. Driving on the metal frame, the ocean visible thirty feet below through the grid, is harrowing. In rain or fog, you can't see what material you're driving on, and the exposed metal becomes slick. There are metal guards along the side of the road to catch cars that that lose traction, but they're rusty in some sections, and I don't trust them. Drayton is an experienced driver, though, and I'm not overly concerned.

I finally feel human enough to talk. "Excited about your speech?"

"Not really," Drayton says.

"What's it about?"

"How the PC sucks."

"Drayton! You can't say that. You'll get expelled from Nod!"

"Okay, so I won't say that. I'll talk about how we live on a dying structure. Stuff like, how long can we keep breathing new life into these Platforms? Will ingenuity alone save our homes? What new innovations will help us create new materials? I'll bring up the idea that the PC should allow island exploration."

"Innovation. That's a good topic. Stick with that. Cut the rest."

"Innovation of what? Roadway materials? I could talk for ten minutes about plastics on Babble. But who wants to listen?"

"Good point. Babble. What a stupid name for a Platform."

"What's wrong with Babble? What would you call it?"

"Platform Complex Number Six because that's what it is."

"Take it up with the PC. Start a naming revolution."

"You know they wouldn't listen."

"True. But seriously. I have to say what I think, and the PC is so stuck in the past that they—"

Part of the surface near the edge of the road falls into the ocean right in front of us. The railing it was holding up squeals under the weight until it breaks at two rusty points. Drayton slams on the brakes, and I scream. The back of the car fishtails, and Drayton throws the parking brake on. We come to a screeching halt five feet from the break.

"That was close," Drayton whispers. "Too close."

"That's never happened before. To me, I mean." Two years ago a whole family plunged into the sea because part of the roadway crumbled beneath them. The metal grid under the blacktop and wood had rusted out. Since we're elevated thirty feet, we aren't sure if they died on impact or drowned. The PC allotted more metal to road repair that year, but it wasn't enough to fix everything.

Drayton edges the car to the left of the ring road and turns the engine off. "I'll mark the breach with the spare. It's just a rim, but I can prop it up with debris. Then we'll get across and report it at the lifts."

He pops the trunk and squeezes out the car door. A car and a truck line up behind us. I grip the seat when a shrill horn blares. I see Drayton talking to Mr. Oron, our main metal worker, in the rear view mirror, then close the trunk and slip into the driver's seat. "Mr. Oron will mark the hole. He has a big metal sheet in his truck."

My heart is still pounding. "Maybe we should just all move to the main Platform."

Drayton shakes his head and guides the car carefully past our almost accident. "Not unless we magically receive materials to redo the upper ten stories of the Empire. There's no room."

Drayton pulls up to the lift line. We are four cars back, so we've got about a ten-minute wait. Ahead of and above us, Nod's main building, the Empire, rises in all its metal glory. It's hard to separate the metal piping exterior into forty floors. Inside, the pipes are different colors that distinguish various levels and purposes. The first ten stories are yellow to indicate maintenance and operations control. The next ten stories have red piping, and that is where we have classes, produce new cloth, and recycle small plastics, glass, and other reusable materials. Stories twenty to thirty are green and serve as housing units for maintenance and school workers. The last ten stories have blue piping, but they are unfinished.

The main Nod platform was originally set up for ease of movement for oil workers. All buildings circle the Empire, which housed offices, communication, food and clothing dispensary, and emergency items. Processing plants for water desalination, power generation, drilling, and refinery are stacked around the Empire. Two-story square buildings radiate from the stacks and originally contained trash recycling, a waste treatment facility, a school, medical and health facilities, and stores for anything else the workers would need for six-month shifts. It looks like a mother with her children around her. A partially-collapsed helicopter pad extends into the ocean like a broken arm.

When we are next in line, Drayton rolls down the window and pulls up to the lift basket. He swipes his wrist across the square scanning meter attached to a four-foot post and pushes the call button on the side. "I need to report a roadway malfunction."

I get out of the car to swipe my wrist across the meter and feel drawn to the edge of the railing. Thirty feet down is a seething body of dark water. Twenty feet up and a world away is Nod. Through the steel and concrete supports, I can see ships surrounding a ring Platform on the other side of Nod. There are two trawlers and one half-submerged barge ship. From the looks of it, they're sinking the barge. More infrastructure support.

Drayton honks the horn and I get back into his car. "Just processing."

Drayton drives the car into the lift basket and puts it in park. "I know. But we don't want to miss the last day of school. We're near-death survivors now."

"Speak for yourself."

The lift whirs into motion and hoists us up the remaining twenty feet to the main Nod Platform. It doesn't catch and bounce halfway up—maintenance must have finally fixed the hydraulics. The metal mesh gate opens, and Drayton drives out. Mrs. Pashce, the lift operator today, is waiting to take our statements. She goes to Drayton's window first and scans his wrist chip with a handheld scanner.

"Time of incident?"

Drayton gives her the details. The Nod walking promenade that skirts the entire main Platform ends at the lift, and the Rodri twins walk past us with their mother. They must be two or three years old by now. Mrs. Rodri worked with my mom. She was always nice to me, and Mom liked her. We didn't see much of her because she lives on the seventh spar Platform, but when she visited, Mom turned on the charm. So did I.

"Wrist please?"

I hold up my left wrist, and Mrs. Pashce scans it. "How's your father?"

"He's good, Mrs. Pashce. Thanks for asking."

Mrs. Pashce squints at me. "Haven't seen him at the fish fry lately."

"Dad's been working a lot."

"It's important to attend," Mrs. Pashce says. "The Council's noticed his absence."

"I'll tell him." Dad hates going to their open meetings. Though the Council's members are elected, they have no real power beyond organizing community building events, requesting supplies, and reporting grievances. The local Planning Commission has the real power.

"Do that. First Friday of every month. And at graduation next week, of course." She turns back to Drayton. "The information about road conditions has been delivered to the PC office. Once they review it, Maintenance will be out to fix the roadway."

"It's pretty serious," I say. "Someone else could not notice it and fall in before they have a chance to evaluate."

"It's already been blocked off. PC Gramble is on duty today, so it'll get repaired quickly. Now, off to school."

"Thanks. Have a tidal day." Drayton's voice is monotone, so I know he doesn't really mean it.

We pull away, and I ask, "What do you have against Mrs. Pashce?"

"Nothing. She's just a minion. Council this, Council that. PC Gramble, PC Fristhe."

"She didn't mention PC Fristhe."

"Because we all know he doesn't authorize any repairs. He just reports it and asks for more materials."

"That may be true, but that's not Mrs. Pashce's fault. And you really do need to be careful about what you say in your speech today. The PC will be listening."

Drayton touches his wrist chip. "I'm not worried."

I am, but I let it drop. We pass the main PC campus, originally security offices for rig workers and contractors that the PC has repurposed for their offices. Drayton slows down so the overhead scanner can read our chips, and the light at the end of the campus turns green. Drayton turns right in front of the medical compound where I was born. Maintenance recently repainted the outside, and it is a bright red.

Drayton takes another right in front of the elevator docks. Ships of all sorts are lifted for repairs—some towering out of sight, some barely ocean worthy.

There are only five other cars in the rectangular parking area across from the Empire's school entrance where Drayton parks. His car is the nicest—he always manages to find yellow paint to keep it looking new. I call it the Yellow Dream.

He pats the steering wheel. "I'll need a new wheel soon, and I have no idea how I'm going to find one. Now it would be easy to replace if—"

I roll my eyes and interrupt him. "If they allowed Land trips. Let's be realistic. We aren't ready by a long shot. They would have to run lots of tests. Complete soil and water samples, viral samples. We don't have the research staff to do that and keep the Platform going. Who knows how much time that would take."

"So better to survive as we are?"

"I like breathing. Don't you?"

Drayton pinches my arm playfully. "Whatever, Joe. You'll always argue the opposite. It's charming, really. See you at assembly? The Drop? Then we can celebrate. Better yet, you can come see the lights."

The Drop. I had almost forgotten about it. I don't want to think about it. "Saved up your questions until now?"

"Guess so. All that near death made me forget them for a while. Want me to ask them again?"

I laugh and swing the car door open. The cracks in the parking lot blacktop are like rivers running away from the car. "I heard them. Yes, yes, and maybe. Thanks for the ride. The car's running great…especially the brakes."

"Good thing I rebuilt them a few weeks ago."

Drayton is a whiz with building anything. He's rebuilt everything on and in his parents' house to function more efficiently. He doesn't have to apply for a research project because he tested into Maintenance on the Platform. Which means he could be moved. I try not to think about that, either.

"Yes. Can you work on the roll of the spar Platforms next? Hard to sleep sometimes."

Drayton points at me. "For you, anything."

"Get me something solid to live on that isn't fifty stories high."

He taps his head. "It's my next project."

I smile and get out of the car into the damp air. I'm surrounded by buildings and can't see the ocean, but I can hear the waves and smell the salt and pervasive fish odor. It smells like every day of my life. I wait for Drayton a few steps away.

"I think you need to see them," Drayton says. "Change that maybe to a yes."

"See what?"

Drayton bumps into me. His eyes, the color of the sky after heavy rain, are full of mischief and life. He has eyelashes to spare, beautiful, dark eyelashes. I was jealous of them when we were young. Maybe I still am.

"The lights," Drayton continues. "I'm going to report it as soon as we graduate. They're appearing more frequently…stop staring at me."

"I'm not staring. I'm examining. And I see how your mind is working. Report it after graduation so you can get credit for the find as a Maintenance adult? Smart. Sly even. I'm impressed, Mr. Valedictorian. But how do you know no one else is looking?"

"Good question. Except I have a better answer—no one has the telescope to see them but me. I checked the Commission's registry with a VPN sweep. Everyone just looks at what they have, not at what's out there. Don't leak the intel."

"Lips are sealed. And now school. So dismal."

"Are you taking the stairs or the elevator?" he asks.

"Since Juris was stuck in the elevator for eight hours? I'll take the stairs."

"Well, at least you'll get some exercise. It's a good thing the PC doesn't put up cameras in the climbing gym. You'd be on probation."

The climbing gym is in the empty thirty-first floor of the Empire. I go because I have to scan my chip at an exercise area every day, but I don't climb. Instead, I study the Platforms from the open areas and dream up new ways to connect them all with lightning quick communication infrastructure. I have a clear view in every direction between the pipes.

The sports fields are on the western spar Platforms, the docks, the eastern. The community gardens and social center are on the northern spar Platforms, and the southern ones, where I live, are all research facilities or abandoned oil system structures that can't easily be repurposed. Houses are interspersed between recycling dumps and processing centers on each Platform. At the thirty-first floor of each spar, raised roads connect the spar Platforms to Nod's central Platform. From the vantage point of the climbing gym, the whole system looks like an oyster shell with a gigantic, multi-colored pearl inside.

"Good thing they don't have the resources for cameras everywhere. We'd all be on probation. See you."

We part ways as Drayton heads to the elevator and I head toward a door labeled "stairs." The stairwell to school is an outdoor one, but there is a metal cage surrounding it, so I'm not scared. I scan my wrist, and the lock buzzes open. It's a long climb from floor 1 to 11, but Drayton's right. Exercise is good for me.

"Hey, wait up."

I hold the stairwell door open for Drayton. When he passes through an alarm buzzes, but it stops when he holds his wrist against the scanner.

"Line at the elevator's too long. I'll race you. Go!"

I pretend to hustle until Drayton is out of sight then slow down and climb at my normal rate of speed. I run my hand along the jagged outside wall. The Empire's insides are all turned out. The finished rooms in the Empire were oil maintenance and drilling rooms. The rest are open air crisscrossed by a maze of pipes. The PC finished some of them, then stripped the work crane to use as support for one of the spar Platforms. They built the rest of the existing walls and subfloors with parts from cruise ships. I'd have rather just lived on the cruise ship.

"Waiting for you!"

I smile. "I know."

I finally reach the landing where an eleven is painted on the wall beside the door Drayton is already holding open. He gestures that I should go in first and scan.

Not normal Drayton behavior. "Fancy today."

"Last day should be the best day," Drayton says and bows. Now that we are at school, Drayton and I won't see each other. Since he is moving into Maintenance, he's on a different track. "See you at the assembly. I'll keep my speech short. Non-expellable."

Drayton waves to a group of boys in the hallway. Most are from our grade, so I wave, too. Nod is an outpost research Platform Complex, so there are only sixty-two kids in my school. Everyone knows everyone. Most of them are my age or a year or two younger. All of our parents were assigned to Nod when several new research projects started simultaneously. A few families joined the research teams mid-project—like Mrs. Rodri—so there are a handful of younger kids. Once projects are completed, families tend to move to Platforms with better amenities. Both my parents have continuous research projects, so we've never moved. Or Mom did, but Dad and I didn't.

Empty rooms without solid walls line either side of the hall. Pipes run in convoluted squares and rectangles around me. It's like living in a red geometry proof with no discernible answer. I turn right into our school corridor.

"Ready for the Drop, Joe?" De'jon laughs and brushes by me. He's a year younger than me and lives three houses from me on my spar. His sister is from a second marriage and much younger. I babysit her sometimes.

"You know it." The fact is, I'm not physically ready for the Drop, but I am mentally—except for the water. I hate water.

I take my seat next to Lisette in Acoustical Physics. She's the only girl in school that I can actually have a conversation with. She doesn't talk about stuff that doesn't matter, which is great, because neither of us are good at small talk. I like how she looks right at me when she talks to me, and I like that sometimes her hazel eyes are green, sometimes blue. Today she's wearing a gold apron that matches her complexion over a full skirt with an embroidered waistband that has seen better days. I recognize it from seventh grade graduation.

"What do you call that again?" I ask. "It's traditional formal dress, right?"

"Yeah, it's a *dirndl*. My great-grandmother's. They were Bavarian, Mom says—that's where I get the medium height and solid frame. She made me wear it for last day of school."

"Cool. It's festive, I'll grant you that." I set up my virtual pad. "And I'd call the last day of school festive. For us, anyway."

"Josephine."

I hear the voice but pretend that I don't, hoping that its owner will just go away. Lisette pokes me in the ribs, and I sigh loudly.

Harriet, with her beautiful, heart-shaped face, is standing to the right of my desk. She is, to put it simply, my biggest rival. She is into communications as well. Both of her parents are top oceanographers.

"Joe. And what?" I reply smoothly.

"It's a shame such a pretty name was wasted on you. Josephine was an empress. She ruled a nation."

"She was also divorced because of her inability to bear an heir," I counter and offer Harriet a half smile. "If you had paid attention in Land history, you'd know that. So, I prefer Joe."

Harriet sniffs like I smell worse than shrimp nets hung out to dry after a big catch. "Suit yourself, *Joe*. What's your senior project about? I know that mine is going to be a success. The future of inter-Platform communication is safe with me."

"Let me know how it goes. I'm interested. Really."

"You can't compete, you know. There are the haves and the have nots when it comes to smarts. Mediocre never comes out on top."

Mr. Peterson enters the classroom, and Harriet brushes by me. Lisette rolls her eyes, and I forget the conversation immediately. Next week Harriet will pretend to be my best friend and try to weasel ideas from me. Which will never happen.

Lisette writes "idiot" on her virtual pad. I write "inconsequential" on mine and then pay attention to Mr. Peterson's lecture.

The rest of class passes quickly. I'm interested in Mr. Peterson's work. It's already in use on some of the transport ships for early communication with the docking Platform. He's one of the few teachers who both teaches and researches, and I've heard it's because he specifically asked the PC if he could teach. He's influenced my concept of underwater sound wave applications.

The bell rings, and Lisette and I go to our next class together. Although Lisette's emphasis is terra farming, we have a similar schedule this semester because she tested into the Technology track, too.

"I like your hair like that," Lisette says.

Lisette always says something randomly nice before something that I won't like. I narrow my eyes at her. "It's normal. What's wrong?"

"Oh, I thought it was…different. Any news from your mom? The mail ship was in port yesterday."

"No," I say flatly and walk into our next class.

"Sorry," Lisette says softly.

Mom hasn't contacted us since she left for Neft. It's like she forgot about me and Dad. "I'm sure she's busy. She probably has stacks of letters she hasn't sent. Once we can connect immediately to other Platforms, she'll write more frequently."

We sit in adjoining desks for Land art history. The PC mandates that we take this non-technological class as seniors to ensure we are well-rounded graduates. Most of us are completely uninterested, but Miss Maldres valiantly tries to keep our attention. She really loves teaching and believes in the PC's requirements.

"Since it is our last class, and I will miss you, I would like for us to have a free art period today," Miss Maldres says. "Draw whatever you want, and remember, the beauty of creativity is as important as our technology. It's all about balance."

"Ugh," I murmur, but take out my light pen to draw on my desktop's built-in light board. I try to imagine holding a paintbrush and using real paint for art instead of a computer input device, but I can't. We need all the remaining paint in storage for building maintenance. I sigh and start my drawing by writing my initials at the bottom.

"Never good to start at the ending," Miss Maldres says from behind me. "Think about something you find to be beautiful. Create first, then claim, Joe."

I wait until she moves away, then mimic, "Create first, then claim" under my breath as I erase my initials. Lisette smiles at me encouragingly.

*I hate art*, I mouth at Lisette, then look back at my empty board. I think about what I like, what I find to be artistic.

Definitely not the ocean. And I can't draw my mom.

I draw the only thing I have ever been able to draw besides stick figures: a flower. Class drags on, and I add different layers to the flower like never-ending fish scales. Eventually, the lights blink, indicating time is up, and I sign the bottom of my flower in relief.

I peek at Lisette's work. It's a series of circles in a mound shape. "Is that dirt? Like for terra farming?"

"Or bubbles? I don't know. Maybe it's silly, but I think dirt is artistic. I wish we had more of it. I think it's…"

"Beautiful," I say at the same time she does.

Lisette gives me an awkward thumbs-up.

The bell rings. Miss Maldres claps her hands. "All right. Time for the annual graduation address. Report to the twelfth floor, main square. Assembly formation. Congratulations, students!"

We file out with the rest of the students. A buzz of chatter follows us, and Maritza from the northern spar bumps into me.

"Ready for the Drop?"

She has the quietest voice of anyone I know. "Yes. Of course."

"I knew you would be. I'll have to come over after graduation. I want to see how your mom set up her fish drying rack. Is that okay?"

I cringe but get over the reference to Mom. Mom's fish drying rack is made from recycled tarpon bones. It's scary to look at but highly functional. "Sure. It's pretty cool."

Maritza hugs me quickly, and we continue up the stairs to the twelfth floor. I whisper to Lisette, "Why is everyone asking me about the Drop?"

"Harriet has a betting pool going that you won't do it," Lisette says. "You don't even climb; why would you do the Drop? She put up an entire bolt of cloth and one metered meal on it. Drayton took her up on it and bet you would—two rebuilt, functioning motors. No one else bet."

"She would do that," I mutter. "Well, she's going to lose. I'm going to do it."

Lisette puts her arm around my shoulder. "I don't doubt it for a minute. Neither does Drayton. Let's get a seat."

The main square on floor 12 is filled with old oil barrels that have been cut in half to make seats. The barrel lids serve as rollable legs. Lisette goes to the area designated for Resource Technology, and I share a barrel with Juris in the Communications Technology area. Maintenance and Teaching specialties make up the other two seating positions. All told, there are eighteen of us graduating today. There is a raised platform in the center made from two barrels with a long, flat piece of metal laid across them. Everyone settles and our school principal, Mr. Deneri, climbs on top of the platform.

"Soon to be graduates, congratulations. You are the 103rd class to complete your coursework and placement tests at Nod."

We all clap politely.

"And now, a word from the administration." Mr. Deneri opens his virtual pad and begins reading the PC's address to us. "Congratulations, seniors. As you embark on new journeys in your research and careers, let us take this moment to remember our forefathers and their achievements. The original twenty-four founders, visionaries from Hermeneutics Labs, brought almost two hundred researchers and technologists to our network of Platforms during the Moralist revolt. On Land, children were exterminated because of genetic abnormalities. The Bones virus gripped the population. The zealot Moralists made the call to arms, and the Day of Salvation was planned. All technology was to be eradicated.

"Our twenty-four founders saw the need for an alternate path. They salvaged technology and key people to create a new life for us here on the Platforms. These founders made up the first Planning Commission, our council of twenty-four that provide us with a logical means of sustaining our families and Platforms in the greenest, most equal way possible."

Mr. Deneri coughs uncomfortably. We are all silent, but I swear I can hear Drayton seething from across the room.

"We are strong together, in the use of our resources and the technology of our minds. We know that you will use the knowledge you have gained here to create the next generation of technology. And now, a word from your valedictorian."

Drayton rises and approaches the Platform. I don't know what he is going to say, but I have a bad feeling about it.

Drayton shakes Mr. Deneri's hand and climbs on top of the makeshift podium. "Classmates. It is an honor to speak before you. But perhaps I should scan my chip first."

Several of the teachers chuckle, and all the students laugh. I laugh but hope that Drayton doesn't say anything treasonous.

"I would like to read the open letter that I am sending via the next mail ship to the head Planning Commission, our PC, as is the custom of all valedictorians."

A few students clap. I snap and smile when Drayton looks at me. I raise my eyebrows and mouth, *Don't do it.*

Drayton opens his virtual pad. "Planning Commission members. First of all, thank you for continuing to be our founders and for handing your positions down within your own families. But I wonder—have any of you ever been to Nod? I would like to suggest an election so that your outlying Platforms can be responsibly represented. We also appreciate the standards of conservation you have instituted to maintain us—water, cage farm, exercise, schoolwork. We have become more equal with the metered chipping system and abolition of currency. And yes, we appreciate you sending us supply ships and trash barges, even more so when you inflict embargoes on us because we have not complied with your standards."

Everyone starts to whisper. We all know he is referencing our friend Bryce's father, Mr. Leery, who was removed from the Platform for not taking care of the family's cage farm. Mr. Leery was wrapped up in his research and forgot to repair one of the outer ribs of the cage farm. Sharks got in, and his stock was eaten or released. He claimed exhaustion and requested a trial. The Council sided with him because the PC had instituted overly rigorous deadlines for his project. The PC ruled he needed to repair his cage farm and perform thirty hours of community work. When he refused and the Council supported him, the PC enacted a supply embargo until the Council changed their minds. Bryce's father was removed to the Hades Platform. The embargo went on for two weeks. Bryce and his mother stayed on Nod and were given a new cage farm.

Drayton raises his hand for silence. "But perhaps these standards need to include colonization? Our Platforms are disintegrating."

"Thank you, Drayton," Mr. Deneri says and almost pushes Drayton off the makeshift podium. Some of the students start to hiss, but Mr. Deneri dismisses us. "Visionary statements, indeed. Lunch."

# Chapter Three

GENERAL PANDEMONIUM ENSUES as lunch is first come, first served. We get to leave the dreary inside of the building and collect our PC-issued lunch from Duritz's Place. The whole class pushes down the stairway and spills into the common area on the ground floor. The elevators are inoperative because the PC wants us to exercise on our lunch break.

I find Lisette in the crowd.

She is flushed and worried. "Drayton is going to get himself removed. I didn't see the PC reps, but they could've been listening remotely. They'll be at the fish fry after the graduation ceremony next week for sure. Doesn't he have any fear?"

"Apparently not."

"Did he read that to you before today?"

"No." A group of kids rush by us, and I slow down. "I don't want to wait in line for lunch. Or talk about this. It's depressing."

"We can take the long way," Lisette says. "And no problem, because I have news. Guess what? The project I applied for—they've accepted me! I found out at assembly!"

Lisette and I walk the three blocks to Duritz's Place. Duritz provides PC-approved meals for our school lunch, and also food for any visitors from other Platforms that don't have access to a cage farm or garden. His cage farm is quadruple the size of our personal ones…and where the Drop ends. The walkway there isn't in shambles because it is strictly for pedestrians.

"—and the new soil is reclaimed from one of the outlying barrier islands, uninhabited, so it isn't just sand we will be trying to enrich. It's the real deal. The message came through on my pad during assembly."

"Of course they accepted you. You're awesome!" I say. "Even though pads are supposed to be off during assembly."

"I didn't open the message. I just saw the word 'acceptance.' I read the rest on the way down the stairwell."

"I'm teasing you." We pass a break in the pipe walls that creates an overlook. Mom and I would come here when I was a child to count ships. I still count them. "I count six trawlers, two barges, and some serious rain clouds."

"And a couple of cruisers, look there!"

I do, and Lisette is right. "I missed them."

"They're smaller. You have to be looking for them. Think what they would look like from the barrier islands. They would be eye level—specs on the horizon." Lisette continues talking about barrier island soil reclamation until we stop in front of Duritz's Place. Racks of non-gutted catfish are drying in the front of the restaurant. They smell terrible.

"—I get to start in a month," Lisette finishes. "They're making plans for possible habitation barges. Nod is shallow, so it's not unthinkable that one could be tied to our Platform. Land, like you've always wanted."

"That's great, Lisette. But don't you want to travel farther away from Nod? Join Drayton on his colonization crusade?"

"No. This is home."

"Is it?"

Lisette throws her arm around me and squeezes. "It is. Just look around."

"I know. It just never feels permanent. I guess in my mind, home shouldn't float. You know how Mom always talked about the family farm." Mom passed on stories from her grandmother about the family citrus farm in Florida. Those stories mean everything to me. They connect me to the past, the present…

Where Mom is too busy to write.

I shake Lisette's arm off and look at the pink plaster building in front of us. It is the brightest building in Nod. Sometimes I wonder if Duritz got lost and really meant to end up somewhere else, like the Abkutun Platform across the ocean in the Caspian Sea, instead of here in the Gulf, next to the brown water of the American peninsula.

We walk through a small maze of makeshift tables and the legs of other students to get to the door of Duritz's. I jerk to a stop when Harliss, one of our fellow graduates, jumps in front of us and holds a plate of seaweed under Lisette's nose.

"You're late, so I saved you some." Harliss has had a crush on Lisette since second grade. His hair is like a spiky sea urchin on top of his head, which matches his personality—awkward. "End of the pan seaweed is soggy."

Lisette chuckles. "Thanks, but I don't mind soggy."

Harliss shrugs his shoulders and withdraws his arm. "Suit yourself. See you at the Drop, Joe."

"Yeah, see you," I say and wish there was no such thing as a Drop or betting or a Harriet. I plow toward the door of Duritz's, hungry now.

Glancing back, I catch Harliss giving Lisette a shy smile before the door swings shut behind us.

"Are you ever going to give him a chance, Lisette?"

"Nope. Not my type."

"He tries so hard."

"So did the Moralists, and look where that got us."

I chuckle. "Word." The inside of Duritz's Place is almost deserted. Most of our classmates are eating outside, legs pushed through the walkway slats. "Inside?"

"Sure," Lisette says and picks a corner table. I follow her. There are no menus, and the plastic surface of the white table is sticky. Duritz makes his way over to us. He favors his right knee, and I've never seen him hurry. He places our standard issue eight-ounce cups of water on the table. His face looks like it was flattened with a shovel at birth. The sun has bleached his hair almost white, and it's matted into long dreads. He scans our wrists, then stores the scanner in a patch sewn onto his pants to make a large pocket on his right thigh.

"Dining in?"

"Late start?" I ask at the same time. Duritz is still in his fishing gear and stinks like he's been swimming with several different species of deep-water fish.

Duritz winks at us. "Slept a little late. Adults can do that on school days."

Lisette giggles, and I roll my eyes at her. "Right. How about the seaweed? I heard it was at the bottom."

"I've got some fresh coming out," Duritz replies. "And there's some eel left, sponge. Not as fresh."

I make a face. "I hate farmed sponge. It's still a sponge no matter what you do with it. I'll have seaweed, straight up."

"Eels for me!" Lisette giggles again. "The PC is going all out today."

"They order the healthy, sustainable lunch," Duritz says. "I merely stock and serve it. Coming right up."

"We can go through the line," I suggest.

Duritz holds his hand up. "Let me get it. You're my last mouths to feed for the day. Plus, I already have the eels on ice."

"Eels," I say and shiver. Duritz disappears behind the counter, and I turn to face Lisette. "Why the weird giggling?"

Lisette leans over the table. "I'm giggling because Duritz is cute. In an off-limits, way-too-grown-up sort of way."

"Ew, Lisette. Just ew. He's my dad's age."

Lisette takes a sip of water. "He cooks. And his jokes are corny."

"His face is...unique."

"I know, I know." Lisette sits back in her chair and crosses her arms. "Fine. I want to know more details about this project of yours. What gives?"

"I'm trying to keep it under water. The Clinical Board finally gave me permission to pursue my long-range communication project before I join a team."

"By yourself? That's heavy."

"I'm ready for heavy. To be honest, the heavy part is having advisors. And the PC to report to."

"It's a lot of work on your own. What about your dad?"

"Dad is not on my Clinical Board. It never even came up as a possible conflict of interest."

"Have you talked to him?"

I am saved from answering by Duritz. He puts two plates on the table. "I'll have it out in no time. Fresh is best."

Lisette thanks him. I look more closely at my plate. The paint has been scrubbed off, but I know the shape. "Is he seriously using old signs as plates now?"

Lisette picks hers up and holds it in front of her like a shield. "Fresh *is* best."

"Stop. No, really. What has salvaging come to? We're eating on Yield signs."

"Well, how many real plates do you have left?"

My great-grandmother hadn't thought to bring plates, just scientific equipment. So my father had grown up eating out of whatever his mother could find that was serviceable—shells, Styrofoam cones, or with his hands from the cooking vessel. But my mother had brought almost twenty plates to their marriage. She didn't take any of them with her, so there are eighteen left. Most of them are patched, but two are in pristine condition.

Lisette is still waiting for an answer. I don't want to bring my mom back into the conversation, so I say, "Enough."

"Oh, okay. Sorry. I forgot about how your mom left. I mean, I didn't, but sometimes I forget the circumstances. It's hard not to talk about her." She stumbles over her words.

It's not her fault. Everyone knows everything about everyone on the Platforms. Every building is connected to the next by the same steel and wood walk or roadway, every home is connected to the same wave-powered generators, every family works in the same research or resource facilities. We are so inextricably intertwined that it makes my head spin.

"It's okay," I say and redirect the conversation. "So, your seeds. What seeds do your mom and dad have to distribute in the PC program this year? I'm wondering what I'm going to be eating for the next year since I sure didn't keep any."

Lisette starts talking about her parents' seed inventory immediately, and I pretend to listen, but I think about Mom. One week after she left, PC Fristhe had come to the house and explained that her research on Neft had been extended indefinitely. Stunned, I had asked why she hadn't told us her research trip would be long term. PC Fristhe had replied, "official business." Dad didn't ask any further questions. I did, but PC Fristhe kept giving me the same response. He never blinked when he answered and kept his arms stiff by his sides, like he was jumping off a tall Platform.

Lisette nudges my arm, and I jerk in my seat. Duritz scoops an interesting seaweed salad onto my plate. The seaweed has been sun baked in a light yellow sauce. I don't even look at Lisette's plate. I'm not fond of eels.

"Bon appetite," Duritz says happily and backs away from the table.

I don't mind the taste of seaweed, so I take a big bite. The yellow sauce is tangy, but I can't place the flavor. Whatever it is, it's much better than the plain sea grass that I had for dinner last night.

"Not bad," I say between mouthfuls. "Yours?"

Lisette makes a face. "Should have gone with the farmed sponge. Going to have to force this down."

We don't waste any resources on the platform, including food. We save bones, recycle waste water, and use every scrap of material that we have until it goes in the permanent scrap pile. Even then we keep it to stuff beds.

Lisette gags and gulps down her water.

I push my glass toward her. "Have some of mine. At least it isn't octopus. That would be a real mess before our last classes. Indigestion on a plate."

Lisette manages to finish the eel, and we chatter about graduation until I remember that I need new stuffing for my mattress. "Want to stop by floor 14? I need to visit Textiles."

"Sure. I need some thread, anyway."

We return to school the short way, so we pass the LAN processing center with its huge spiky tower and the original rig post office, which now serves as a personal technology repair center. Our friend Aaron who graduated two years ago works there, and we wave to him through the window.

We scan our wrists at the school stairway, then trudge up to floor 14. Piles of recycled cloth, ready-made clothes, shoes, string, fishing nets, hammered plastic bottles and cans, and other items stretch across one half of the room. The other half is packed floor to ceiling with equipment for stripping fiber, reweaving natural fibers, and general fabric recycling.

"Can I assist?"

Lisette and I turn around quickly. Mr. Thres has beady eyes like a crab. His shirt is made of shaped fish bone and dried shark skin. He is a genius at converting everyday items into clothing.

"Mr. Thres. I need filler for my mattress."

"We have plenty right now, so you came at a good time." Mr. Thres scans my wrist. His fingers are long, every fingernail filed to a point. "You can take two bags—no, wait. You are in Overuse."

I look at my wrist. There must be something wrong with my chip. "I can't be. I haven't received any textiles in months."

Mr. Thres motions for me to follow him. He reaches behind the counter, and the bones on his shirt rattle. "I've been having problems with that scanner. Let's try this one."

He scans my wrist with the second scanner and smiles. "You're right. Take your pick, Bin 342. Lisette?"

"I'm just looking for thread," she replies. "Any color. How are your tomato plants doing?"

"Fine, fine," Mr. Thres says. He scans Lisette's wrist, and I drift away to check out Bin 342. Bin 340 has some really nice fishing net shoes with thin rubber soles, and I'm tempted to try them on, but pass it up and hit Bin 342. I find two bags of decent filler and bring them back to Mr. Thres. "Can I have these as distribution?"

Mr. Thres scans the barcodes on both bundles, then my wrist again. He puts the bundles into a frayed fishing net and hands them to me. "Done. Anything else, young ladies?"

"No, thank you," Lisette and I chime together.

"Unless you want to throw in some hammered plastic…" Lisette trails off.

Mr. Thres raises his right eyebrow, which makes him look pretty scary, so we hustle out of Textiles and head back to school to attend our last two classes of the day. Ocean Dynamics isn't difficult, and Language Arts is a sleeper class. We only have one bilingual speaker on Nod, and he wants to teach us Japanese about as much as we want to learn it.

Most foreign languages were phased out on the Platforms after the first generation. English was the language of choice, but a few continued their native tongue in their family units. Now, the PC is trying to revive multi-lingualism, but I'm not interested in participating in their programs, and so far, they haven't required chip-scan attendance.

❧

"On Neft, there are three different foreign language speakers."

The final bell is still echoing, and I had really hoped to get through my last class without hearing Neldres talk. He sits in front of me and Lisette, and his face reminds me of a puffer fish about to burst. His body and ego, too. "It'll be like I'm living in a different universe. A cultured one, instead of this floating trash rig. Real linguists instead of virtual, dead voices."

I gather my light pen and storage device. Did Mom feel like that about Nod?

Neldres continues to brag. "In two weeks I'll be studying languages in paradise."

"Seems superfluous," Lisette says. "I mean, English is the primary Platform language."

Neldres laughs snidely and looks Lisette up and down. "Some of us have a taste for finer things."

Lisette's cheeks turn red, and I give Neldres a hard look. "May you sail in smooth waters, Neldres. Very smooth."

I grab Lisette's arm and pull her behind me. When we are out in the hall, she takes several deep breaths.

"Don't worry about him. He's a fool," I whisper. "Like he'll ever be able to say hello or goodbye to anyone, much less in another language. They'll have him translating old books for our pads."

Lisette still looks upset, so I don't press her to talk. We ditch our bags at the base of the stairs and climb side by side to floor 31.

We scan our wrists and enter the climbing area, panting a little after the twenty floors. There's an obstacle course made of unusable tires and old fishing nets, a wall of pipes to boulder across, and patched up sails to climb. Some kids use the next level up as a parkour course. Everything smells damp and moldy since there are no real walls, and the wind is stronger this high up. Sometimes, we find feathers stuck in the pipes, and we turn them in to recycling. I've always wanted to keep one—for the feather mattress of my dreams.

All the students in my year have exercise period now, and I see them broken into small groups. The anxiety and excitement in the room is like an electric current. They're all clustered around the Drop in the center of the room. It's an enclosed chute that snakes down thirty stories and dumps into Duritz's cage farm. The good news is you won't get eaten by sharks or barracuda. The bad news is it's a long, convoluted thirty stories down in the dark.

The PC has forbidden the Drop, but floor 31 has no cameras, the Council doesn't seem to mind, and Duritz built a ladder from his cage farm back up to the Platform. It's become a senior tradition—or obligation, depending on how you look at it. Every senior doesn't jump, but those who do get a little extra respect, and not just from other seniors. Word gets around.

The bell rings, indicating that we are supposed to be exercising. Instead, Andrew, one of the biggest kids in the class, steps up to the Drop.

"Well, are you or aren't you?" Neldres yells, his puffer fish face turning red.

Andrew steps into the chute and plunges into the darkness.

Several of the boys high-five each other and jump through the chute screaming. A few girls jump through. Maritza, our soft-spoken classmate, backs away. So does Lisette.

"Not for me. I'm fine living my whole life without doing that."

Harriet is with Kay and Darby, who always follow her like shadows, and I feel them watching me. Sweat pools beneath my armpits. Part of me wants to back out—respect is not something that motivates me—but the other part of me says *do it—don't let Harriet win.* Plus, I'd planned for this chute drop. With Mom gone, it's like any other year. I want to mark this senior year, this final year of school, by doing something I would never normally do. But on my own terms. Hitting the deep, dark water with that much speed would give me a heart attack. So, I had come up with an alternate plan. I'd done a dry run of it while everyone else was climbing a month ago. It hadn't been pretty, but it had worked.

Three other kids from class jump. Drayton joins us. "So, I was wondering..."

"Don't," I say confidently and move calmly to the chute drop. Lisette gasps behind me. Bile is rising in my throat, but I ignore it. I put both hands on the opening. My fingers are stiff and splotchy, and my wrists shake, but I jump through.

The first floor isn't a straight shot down, and since I carefully studied the rig diagrams, I know that the chute intersects a second pipeline on floor 29. It's my only chance for escape, and I'd made it out on the dry run. That's the only reason I don't throw up. I create serious friction by star fishing my arms and legs, and when the pipe takes a hard right turn, I thrust my feet to the left and force my body to make a U-turn. My head hits the wall, but I grab for the pressure wheel and hang on. I right myself, then crawl another two hundred feet and kick out the exit panel on the twenty-ninth floor.

"And done," I mutter. I scoot out of the pipe carefully on my hands and knees. I consider kissing the floor, but I'm in the middle of the glass recycling area. Most of the glass is amber and green, but there are a few shards of blue. I hear several pieces crush beneath my weight as I gingerly move across the pile.

"Joe?"

Lila, who is three years older than me, is standing in front of the pile of glass. She handles the glass sorting on Nod, though I know she tried to test into the Technology Resources track. She lives on the northwest spar Platform and is constantly smiling.

"Careful. Those are small pieces of glass. Where'd you come from?"

I look around but can't think up a plausible route to explain my presence. I tell the truth. "I crawled out of the Drop. It intersects on 29 with this horizontal pipe."

"The Drop?"

"Yeah, graduation." I step off the glass pile.

"Okay," Lila says. She pauses. "I'm not sure I understand how exactly you got here, but okay. I should scan your chip for all these broken pieces."

I gulp. That would tip my family's glass allotment way into Overuse. "I'm not asking for distribution."

"No, but they're much smaller pieces now."

We look at each other. Lila's eyes are a beautiful deep green. I had never noticed before.

"I didn't jump," Lila finally says.

"Sorry."

"Glad you did." Lila walks back to the glass controller's booth. Since she doesn't say anything else, I tiptoe out of the glass recycling area and walk purposefully to the stairwell. I have twenty-nine flights of stairs to run down and an ocean to jump into.

Or climb out of, as the case may be.

# Chapter Four

I TAKE THE STAIRS TWO AT A TIME and cross the Empire square to the center of the Platform in record time for me, but I'm not quick enough. Before I can climb down Duritz's Place cage farm's ladder, Drayton is climbing up. I'm relieved it's only him. My plan hinged on no one seeing me.

"Dove off somewhere?"

I don't answer him. Instead I grit my teeth and make myself drop the remaining fifty feet into Duritz's cage farm. The water is cold, and I hate the feel of fish swimming around me. Their bodies are slick and ticklish against my skin. I kick hard to get back to the water's surface, then climb the ladder up after Drayton. I spit salt water out and wring my hair.

Drayton is waiting for me at the Platform. We can still see into the cage farm, and fish fins break the surface of the water. "I don't think anyone else missed you, so your secret's safe. I was going to tell you not to jump, but I'm glad you did. You knew about the betting pool?"

"Yep."

"I thought you might. Chanko did the same thing last year, by the way. He hates enclosed spaces."

"I didn't know."

"Yeah, he didn't tell many people about it. So…pretty brilliant move."

I shake my head and wrap my arms around myself. It's cold now that I'm wet. "So was your rebellious speech."

"We'll see what happens. I'll revise it before I send it out. Promise."

Maritza screams past us and lands in Duritz's cage farm.

"I can't believe she jumped."

Drayton points at me. "You gave everyone courage. I mean, if you could jump…"

I finish Drayton's sentence. "Anyone could."

"You jumped!"

I turn to find Lisette behind us, still dry, and she hugs me fiercely. I hug her back. "Not really. I'll tell you about it later."

"Well, Harriet thinks you jumped. And she didn't! Score!"

"Thanks, Lisette."

Drayton helps Maritza onto the Platform. Several kids come up to us and congratulate me. It's a nice feeling to get away with being resourceful. Lisette gives me my bags. I smile gratefully—now I don't have to hike back up to the climbing gym to get them. I feel light even under their weight.

"So, we're done. Ceremonious speech complete. That's that."

"Are we really done?" I mean it rhetorically, but Drayton answers anyway.

"Yes and no. No more classes. Rudimentary education completed. Now it's onward to the glory of the official graduation ceremony, then our specialties and continuing to fix the hunks of junk we live on."

Lisette walks to Drayton's car with me while Drayton jogs toward the stairs. He still has to get his bags.

"So, how'd you do it?"

"Rerouted on the twenty-ninth floor. Landed in glass recycling. I broke some glass, but Lila let me go."

Lisette shifts her bag to her left shoulder. A light rain starts to fall. "Only you. Good thing it was Lila. She's always been nice. I'll see you around?"

I realize that I rarely see Lisette outside of school. I've taken her for granted. We never had to plan to see each other—she was always sitting next to me in school. She lives on the farthest spar Platform, near the last bridge viaduct on the north side. Her back door is the ocean on the rough side. I've walked there a handful of times, but I'll only see her at the fish fries once a month from now on.

Then I remember something. "Will you be coming into town with your sister when your reclamation project begins? She's on floor 14, right, in materials?"

"Yes! Maybe we could get together early? Before I ship out each day? Until your project works. Then you'll be able to talk to me directly. If anyone can make cross Platform communication work, it's you."

"I'll make it happen."

"Okay. See you soon."

Lisette throws her arms around me again. I hug her back, and for a minute, I forget we are seniors. My mind filters through memories of Lisette throughout our school time together. Then the reality of how everything is changing comes back, and I force myself not to cry.

Lisette breaks away first and waves goodbye, turning away before I can wave back. Though I am sad, I know I will see her again. I'll just have to make time for it and plan it out. Maybe not tomorrow, but soon. Nod is so small. I will find a way.

"Ready?" Drayton is still sopping wet, but he's retrieved his bags and he looks happy. He salutes the Empire then dances stiffly across the square. A Maintenance truck honks then drives around him. Mr. Quannstram, the driver, shakes his fist at Drayton. We laugh. Xander, a kid a year younger than us, calls Drayton's name. Drayton hollers back at him.

"I'm ready to go, but if you want to stay and say goodbye to your friends, I know where the spare key is hidden…"

"And let you drive my baby? I think not. I'll catch up with them later. Maybe at the fish fry."

"You're so lucky. You have real transportation and can actually get around. It'll be tough to see Lisette now even though we all live on this Petri dish of an island. I'm going to have to bum rides—probably from you—every week over to her house, and vice versa. Dad always needs the car."

Drayton opens the door and motions for me to get in. "You want to see Lisette every week? What about her car?"

"You aren't my only friend, Drayton. And they share their solar-powered cart. You'll have to help me make it happen. It's important."

Drayton raises his eyebrows and starts the car. "Sorry. You're always buried in your books and projects, so I thought you wouldn't have time. We'll figure it out, long as you remember I'm your only *best* friend. Come on, get in."

I climb in and shut the door. I smell like fish and brine. I sit uncomfortably in the seat, my wet clothes sticking to everything. "You don't let me forget it. Thanks for the lift home."

"No problem. I know you hate walking in the rain. Best friend privileges." Drayton starts the car and pulls out of the parking lot. The traffic is light because the work day isn't over, and the younger kids are still in class. Rain plinks against the windshield. The clouds are low and heavy, so the sky looks like it has a dark eyebrow across it.

I eye Yellow Dream speculatively. Everything on the Platform relies heavily on sun power. We're working on wind and wave alternatives, but it's been cloudy all day, and I know Drayton's car doesn't have the best panels for storing power. "Will we make it on the solar reserve?"

Drayton pats the dashboard. "She'll hold out before this storm hits."

We travel through the PC buildings and stop in line behind a repair truck at the lifts. Mrs. Pasche is still at the control booth, and she waves us through, eyeing our wet clothes and hair. Drayton swipes his wrist at the scanner. I roll down the window and do the same. The lift closes around us, and we sink back to the ring roadway. The chop on the ocean is higher than it was this morning. Weather is definitely rolling in. I hate storms, and I'll be happy when I'm in my house and we aren't driving on the rickety ring road.

Drayton starts the motor as the lift locks click loudly into place. We scan our wrists across the scanners and drive onto the first bridge viaduct on the ring road. He chuckles. "I knew you had something up your sleeve. I didn't even want to do the Drop. It was intense."

"The whole day was. Your speech—maybe you'll be removed from the Platform by the end of the month."

"No one's removing me. The goal was to shake things up a little bit."

"And our near wreck. Now the storm—those clouds mean business. It's already rumbling. And it smells…"

Lightning streaks across the horizon, and the wind picks up. The last hurricane almost knocked out some of the piles that hold our Platform in place. It was scary for a few days, and I don't want a repeat experience. "It smells like big trouble."

Drayton *pshaws* and waves his hand dismissively. "It'll pass. You worry too much. Don't talk about the weather. Let's talk about the lights instead."

"You talk about your lights. Maybe I'll listen."

"Look, it's the last day of class. Come over and see the lights. Celebrate the end of an era. I'll take you to Lisette's tomorrow. You don't have to bum a ride. I'm offering."

I decide to accept Drayton's offer because it's real. And I don't want to let go of seeing Lisette almost every day yet. "All right. In the late morning, though."

"For Lisette, your friend whom you care deeply for, yes," Drayton says. "The lights, tonight. For your best friend whom you care even more deeply for."

"Until he is shipped off to another Platform for treasonous ideas."

"Not happening. I'll pick you up. Is your dad working?"

"I don't know."

"Well, find out. My mom can officially invite you over if he's around."

I can see my house over the next viaduct. It doesn't seem any more welcoming than school. "I get tired of scanning into a tin can sometimes. Don't you hate how metal feels when it surrounds you?"

"Your house looks more like a Cracker Jack box than a tin can. Imagine scanning yourself into a box of delicious treats."

"Have you ever seen a Cracker Jack box?"

"Every day," Drayton says. "Dad has one in his museum."

"Oh! A new relic?"

Drayton stops in front of my house. "No. Just not an important one. He keeps it in storage. I like the smell of the box."

"You are borderline crazy. See you later, assuming the weather clears." I slam the car door before he can reply and run into my house.

The scanner is skewed, so I have to scan my wrist at a weird angle to get the front door unlocked. It finally unlatches, and I'm glad that it is warm inside.

"Hello?" I yell.

No answer. I put down my bags in my room and peek upstairs. No lights, no sounds. Dad is probably out on the far docks looking for functioning satellites. This morning he had said,

"Have a good day" and hurried out the door with lots of equipment. The weather gets rough on the far docks, and I hope Dad has on his life preserver and is strapped in. I don't need both my parents gone.

I shut the thought from my mind and return to my bedroom. I need to re-stuff my mattress. My phone is already blinking.

**Well? Well? Well? 19:00?**

I smile and reply to Drayton.

**No Dad. Better hope there are lights to be seen.**

I put the phone down carefully on my desk. The Platform is steady for now, but I still feel the room moving. The walls are closing in. Since Mom left, the house is eerily quiet when I'm by myself. I don't like it. All I want to do is sleep. Or work.

I untie the end of my mattress and dump out the rag filler. I put the new bundles in and fluff it. Hopeful, I lie down in the center of the bed.

It still feels like metal.

"Fail," I mutter and turn to face the wall. I could sleep, but I have to eat. There's some leftover catfish that Dad harvested from our cage yesterday, and I warm it up on the stovetop. I take bite after bite mechanically. It tastes like nothing. A nothing life.

I shake my head. The storm is raging outside, and I hate everything about my current situation—especially how much the house is rocking around me. I feel like a fish swimming in a swinging bucket. But it's okay. My life will change as soon as I make my communications project work. If it will work.

I tie the old stuffing from my bed together and use it to dust the house. When I'm done, I attach an old fishing pole to the bundle and sweep up. A text from Drayton alerts me that he's arrived to pick me up, and I write a note on the light board in the kitchen for Dad, and shut down the power early when I scan myself out to see Drayton and his lights.

# Chapter Five

IT'S STILL SPRINKLING when Drayton parks in front of his house, but the heavy rain from the storm passed earlier. I jump over a puddle and follow Drayton to the front door. Drayton's house is different from every other building in our Platform Complex. There are two rusted metal and glass cages filled with herbs and spices sticking out from the upper story like eyes. A neon green cistern sits on the roof like a hat, and a fire hose stretches from it down to the garden area. I count ten weathervanes sticking out from the sides of the house like multiple ears. The gray exterior is splashed with bits of black paint so it looks polka dotted.

"Home sweet home," Drayton says and passes his wrist over the scanner. I do the same, and we take our shoes off at the front door. The hallway is lined with red, green, and yellow buoys. Plastic swimming separators cut the living room in half. Fishing lures and crab pot floats are piled in one corner. A carousel horse is propped up next to a rectangular pinball machine. The walls are covered in old advertisements. A shiny red vacuum, paper shredder, and several flat screen TVs covered in nets and wires block the back door.

"Thirsty? We have some freshly collected rain water," Drayton says and indicates a pitcher made from an old watering can.

"No, I'm good," I murmur.

Three speckled trout are hanging from hooks above an open drain in the kitchen floor. Spears of varying lengths hang from the wall behind the hooks. Orange Styrofoam floats cut in half are lined up beneath the fish with leaves in them. I sniff. Sage. It covers the odor of the fish.

"Looks like I missed the spear fishing."

"Yeah, did it earlier."

"Ugh. I would have puked. All that blood in the water."

"That's why I did it earlier. Come on."

I follow Drayton down the hallway to his room. It's as eclectic as the rest of the house. His walls are papered in posters of old music bands and movies. His collection of Land treasures includes clocks, shiny telemetry instruments, surveying equipment, rulers and tape measures, and several telescopes. I love being in Drayton's space—I already feel less tense. It's comfortable and interesting.

"It's like found objects multiply in your house. You'll have to add another wing soon."

"Not likely," Drayton says and puts something smooth and cold in my hand. "No materials to build with. Look at this."

I turn it over curiously. It is convoluted and beautiful, even though it is made of metal. There are measuring devices on it, and a cylindrical part to look through. An inscription in cursive is on one side, but I can't make out the lettering. "Is this an old telescope?"

"Even better. A sextant."

"Sextant. Which is…not related to anything I'm thinking it's related to, is it?"

Drayton snickers, then gets serious. "No. It's an antique instrument for celestial navigation."

"Of course it is." Drayton loves any gadget, but he loves gadgets that have to do with the stars the most. It's one of the things I like most about Drayton. His mind is always on what isn't right in front of him. "Where'd you get it?"

Drayton takes it from me carefully and returns it to the drawer. "I pulled it out of an old vessel docked by Lisette's that no one has claimed."

"Foraging in someone else's property? Is that wise? Or legal?"

"Don't have to scan my wrist to enter a vessel."

"True," I say. I touch the bell jar clock by his bedside. It's stopped at the wrong time, but I hear it ticking. "Is this still working properly?"

"Since last time you were here?"

"No, since my doppleganger was here. Of course since I was last here."

"Joe, you're getting mean in your old age. Mean and sensitive. And it's been so long since you visited…"

I roll my eyes.

"Fine. It stopped a few days ago, but I repaired it again. I set the time, but it's running slow. I'll figure it out."

I laugh. "You're a collector of strange, beautifully broken objects."

"Some things you can't collect." Drayton puts his hand on my shoulder.

I knock his hand away reflexively. "Don't even think about putting me in a jar."

"Wouldn't dream of it," Drayton says softly. He steps around me and pulls out another banged up piece of machinery. "Now this—"

"You kids okay?"

We both jump at the sound of Drayton's mother's high-pitched voice. She's standing in the doorway like a small fairy, a tray held between two hands. She's a petite woman, and her hair is piled on top of her head in a complicated series of knots.

"Yes, Mrs. Coleman," I say in my polite voice.

"Just dandy, Mom," Drayton chimes in. "Showing Joe my prized possessions. She's intrigued."

"That's lovely," Mrs. Coleman says. She looks from me to Drayton then back to me. Her long shawl is dark purple and sparkly and accentuates her figure as she enters Drayton's room. Her pants are made from sail cloth, and her shirt is recycled plastic. Not many could make the ensemble look classy, but she does. "Drayton, you should have cleaned your room. It's unspeakably messy."

Drayton rolls his eyes.

"Don't roll your eyes at me, young man. I birthed you."

Drayton groans. "Thanks, Mom."

"You're welcome." Mrs. Coleman winks at me. "You'll understand when you have children of your own."

Drayton saves me from answering by gesturing at the tray. "What's that, Mom?"

"I've made a nice treat tray for you two kids."

"Thank you, Mrs. Coleman," I promptly respond.

She places the tray on Drayton's huge upside down bathtub table. The tray's handles are ceramic with painted flowers. Two yellow cylinders wrapped in plastic are arranged parallel to each other.

"Your father is back from the salvage mission. They found a floating trash barge."

"Unmanned, I assume?" Drayton asks.

Mrs. Coleman nods. "Yes, and filled to the brim with artifacts and scrap."

"We totally need the scrap for supplies," I say. "That's wonderful news."

"Anything exciting?" Drayton asks excitedly at the same time.

"Not to me," Mrs. Coleman says and puts her hand on Drayton's arm. "But to you and your father…"

"Those artifacts help us understand more about—"

Mrs. Coleman interrupts Drayton. "Talk to him about it at breakfast, dear. You have a guest. Whom, I might add, has beautiful manners though you do not. Now, eat your treats and bring that tray back in one piece. It was your great-grandmother's, so be careful."

"All right, Mom," Drayton says.

Mrs. Coleman smiles brilliantly at me, then leaves the room. She doesn't shut the door.

Drayton points to the door, then at his ear. "She's got plans for us."

"Awkward…" I'm embarrassed, so I study the treat tray. "Are those—what are those?"

"This is tidal for her," Drayton says and picks up a cake. "Twinkie. Still in the plastic from when great-grandfather brought them over from Land. She only breaks these out for special guests."

I feel warm inside. I like Mrs. Coleman. "She's so generous. And sweet."

"Yep. She must have big plans. She'll show you great-grandma's wedding dress next. Maybe her preserved flowers coupled with the story of how she had the first Platform wedding. No officiant or Council. Just an 'I do' and done. It's one of her favorite topics of conversation lately."

Mom liked to tell stories, too. I wish I had paid more attention during our mother-daughter dates. Especially when she told me about how she met Dad and when I was born. What her grandmother had told her Land was like.

"It's nice how she talks to you," I say softly. Drayton hands me the Twinkie ceremoniously. "Thank you."

"You do have good manners, Joe," Drayton says and opens his Twinkie. He holds it like a glass and toasts. "To the power of preservatives."

I open mine carefully. It smells sweet and ripe, like some of the flowering vegetable plants that Lisette grows. I put a small bite in my mouth, and I revel in the flavor. "Tastes like sunshine."

Drayton finishes the last bite of his. "On a cloudless day. Come on, eat up. It's almost time."

I shake my head and take another small bite. "I want to enjoy this. Savor each bite. I don't have these every day."

"Neither do I. But what's the point in drawing the pleasure out? It's there, then it's gone. Great while it lasts."

"I hope that isn't how you feel about people, Drayton."

"Some of them."

"Stop teasing." I take the last bite of Twinkie and swallow it. "Delicious. Let's go see these lights."

"Finally. Show time. We have to avoid my mom—she'd want to chaperone—but that should be easy. She's doing lesson plans."

Mrs. Coleman trains the upcoming medical students on all fifteen Platform Complexes. She creates virtual lesson plans based on PC standardized testing material for the mail ships to distribute. They take forever to get to the complexes across the ocean.

Drayton snaps his fingers. "You're zoning out on me."

"Sorry. Thinking about my project. We could transfer information so much quicker underwater."

"No more school thoughts for the night." Drayton leads me down the main hall. "We can't work all the time."

"Right." Drayton has modified the hallway lights to be brighter than what I am used to. Mechanical levers that open storage spaces or impromptu tables stick out randomly from the walls. There are several old photographs tacked onto light shades suspended from the ceiling, and two crawfish boil pots serve as chairs near the garden entrance. Strings of light bulbs arch over the doorway. They're all on.

"Those are new. How do you not go over your electricity allotment?"

"I manipulated the gain on the wave sensors. Sneaky, but legit. Mom likes them."

"Impressive that the meters don't detect the drain."

We turn the corner, and Drayton puts his hand over his lips. He rolls back the carpet. It's covered in wide circular patterns, and is barely worn. He steps hard on the corner of one of the pretty tin tiles beneath it. It pops up, opening a space a little larger than my shoulder width.

I look in astonishment at Drayton. He points down, and I peek into the hole. Wooden steps nailed to the supporting beam lead into a space enclosed by metal caging. It looks like a large black crab trap hanging from the entrails of Drayton's house.

"When did you have time to do this?"

Drayton puts his fingers over his lips and nudges my arm.

I don't want to look scared, so I put my foot on the first step even though the underside of Drayton's house looks like it's about to fall down. The stairs don't cave in, so I keep going. Motion sensors pick up my movement and lights attached with handmade metal clips turn on as I descend. I stop at the landing and wait. It's made from a piece of ship hull and slopes toward a cabin door from a cruiser.

Drayton jumps down next to me, and I look above us. The tile is back in place. "How'd you get the carpet back down?"

"Shh," Drayton whispers and gestures for me to follow him. He moves the latch of the cabin door aside, then swings it open. "You are entering a non-PC controlled zone. No scanners here. Watch your step."

I smirk and saunter through the door. The sea is right in front of me, and a small, single-engine fishing boat with a sleep-in cabin hangs from the exposed beams and plastic plumbing of Drayton's house. It's weird to see the guts of a building upside down.

"How'd you build this dry dock? And where'd you get the boat? It's a relic."

"The dry dock was already here. I just restored it. Everyone has forgotten about it, and it isn't visible from the ocean because of the rig leg. I noticed it when I was spear fishing a few months ago. And I reallocated this boat from the far docks. It was my grandfather's."

I look at Drayton in horror. "Reallocated? Drayton, that's stealing. The PC will issue you a citation."

Drayton cuts me off. "Family property. Dad can claim legacy. And they aren't going to go looking for this one. Too small."

I nod, impressed. "All right. You've been busy. And you didn't mention any of this because…"

"You've been more busy with your projects."

I know I look guilty, and I definitely feel guilty. "Sorry. This is really cool. How'd you cover the tile? Magic?"

Drayton jumps into the boat. "Not quite, though I'm almost to that level. A double-hinged tile. Remove the bottom lock. Fix the carpet, replace tile, re-lock tile. Voila."

"Clever," I say and visually examine the boat. Even though it's dark, I can tell Drayton has made sure it is weather proofed and in top-notch shape. He's painted it red. "Was it rammed? Why's there a patched hole in the side?"

Drayton moves around the boat comfortably while he answers me. He picks up ropes and rearranges rigging and gear so there is a clear pathway to the cabin. It's like he was born to the sailing life. "Don't know. My grandfather was a rebel from all accounts, so maybe he got into a fight. Dad says he lived life on his own terms. He had a record number of citations and was detained on Hades for a few years. The hole—maybe that's why grandfather abandoned it in the end. It took some serious work to get it repaired so it's watertight. You coming?"

"Coming where?" I feel bile rise in my throat and swallow quickly.

"Onto the boat," Drayton says in pretend confusion. "To see the lights. That's why we're here."

Panic is creeping through my body. I don't like boats. "I know that. What do you mean, on the boat? Wait. Where is the telescope?"

Drayton points to the cabin on the boat. "In there. The boat's docked. We aren't going anywhere."

"Can't you bring it here?"

"Nope. You'll barely feel it rocking; it's anchored really well to the beam joists. Trust me. Everything will be fine."

I don't trust anyone when it comes to water. I'm an adequate swimmer, but I hate it. It feels like the water is waiting to pour into my lungs. It's a horrible thing to fear water when you are surrounded by it.

"What, like the time you told me it was all right to just put my feet in the water and then you pushed me in?"

"That was years ago, and I was trying to get you to remember that you actually can swim. You swam today—remember the Drop? No games. Promise."

I did swim, but only because I had to. "Fine. But I want a personal flotation device, and not another word about the water."

"Fair enough." Drayton hands me a life jacket, and I take my time putting it on securely. It smells musty, like shoes left out in the rain.

"It stinks," I say and step into the boat. It dips and rolls and my stomach turns. "You said it wouldn't rock!"

"I said it would barely rock. This color looks great on you. Really attractive."

Since the life preserver is a dingy red, and my hair is the same color, I know that Drayton is being facetious. "Thanks. Perhaps I'll salvage it and make something from it. Like a hat."

"You couldn't salvage it if you tried. Who knows how long it's been in storage."

"Thanks. Glad to know you think so highly of my crafting skills." I take a deep breath and pick up a new scent that gets past my musty-shoe life jacket. "What's that smell?"

Drayton opens the door of the boat cabin. "Gasoline. There may have been some gasoline stored aboard for the motor."

Gasoline is strictly forbidden for personal use on the Platforms. The Platform oil reserves were drained and are now held at an undisclosed location in case we have future need. The PC would pack Drayton off to Hades for a year if they knew.

"May have been?"

"Don't worry. I'm not using it. Already set up a solar motor. But it's good to have some around just in case, no matter what the PC says."

"Drayton, you're becoming a criminal." I imagine Drayton all in black, slinking into people's homes and raiding their tool supplies.

The cabin door is small, and I have to duck when I follow Drayton in. He uncovers the telescope that takes up half the cabin space. The glass is missing from the cabin windscreen, so the ocean stretches out before us. It sounds more like a shout now that we are right above it. On the Platform, it's more of a murmur. Two stripped bunks are on either side of me, and two huge laundry buckets turned upside down serve as chairs. The bunks are repurposed back seats from cars.

"Wow."

"Remarkable. Ingenious. Yes, I know."

The boat shifts, and I get queasy. "Ugh."

"Sit down a minute and get your sea legs under you. You won't feel the motion as much."

I sit on the bunk, and I do feel better. One of Drayton's arms is wrapped over the telescope. His elbow is at a weird angle, and it looks like his arm has no bones. The telescope's optical tube is almost the size of his torso and twice as wide.

"What are you doing?"

"Showing you the magic. Prepare yourself for some tidalness."

He presses something on the boat's main navigational console, and the lights shut off. "Come and look."

It's incredibly dark, so I stumble to the telescope. Drayton positions me, and I look through the eyepiece. The image is fuzzy at first, but clears. Giant shadows flank a large open space.

"Is that the Land? Dauphin Island?"

"Yes. The real deal. Now watch carefully."

Shapes become more defined as Drayton turns the focus knob. The fan shapes are trees, and the square, taller ones are structures that look like ours on the Platform but more massive. One building looks like it has lights on in it, but they blink off. There's so much information to process. The Land is flat and spreads away from the water smoothly. The bridge connecting the island to the mainland isn't visible, but I see the definition of the shore. I refocus on the trees and see flashing lights in a consistent pattern. I take a sharp breath and step away from the telescope.

"Did you see them?" Drayton asks excitedly and takes my place. "Let me see." He moves the levers on either side of the telescope. "Now we have crisp focus. That's six of them. More than last night. Look again."

Drayton steps aside, and I press my eye to the eyepiece. I see the lights clearly. I blink and count again. "I count seven."

"Seven!" Drayton pushes me aside.

The boat rocks, and I stumble back to the bunk.

"Hey," Drayton says and motions wildly with his left hand. "There's a pattern, Joe. I'm sure of it."

The Twinkie I ate is churning in my stomach, and I take several deep breaths. "A pattern?"

Drayton moves excitedly around the cabin like a flying fish. His eyes are bright. He mumbles to himself and backs away from the telescope. "Three. Three. Three. I think it's an SOS signal."

"What?" I return to the telescope. "SOS signals are communicated via sound. Not lights."

"But if you don't have sound, lights are the next best thing to communicate with. Joe, it's definite. Three. Three. Three."

An alarm rings. Lights out.

"Damn. We only have thirty minutes," Drayton says irritably.

"You haven't built a generator for that yet? Illegal lights?"

Drayton gives me a dirty look and turns the boat lights back on. He covers the telescope while he talks. "Even I have my limits. Aren't you excited about this? I mean, the Land people could be trying to communicate with us. We're the only Platform that can be seen from shore. This is epically tidal."

"Maybe," I say and follow him when he leaves the cabin. "But what do they want from us? To steal from us? Have us rescue them? Infect us with whatever they may have?"

Drayton hops off the boat, and both it and my stomach roll with the motion.

"Take my hand, Joe." Drayton reaches for me, helping me off the boat and holding my hand for what I think is a moment longer than necessary. Then he's unzipping my life vest and throwing it into the bottom of the boat. "We'll talk in a minute."

I follow him down the corridor, up the stairs, and back through the hole in the floor. We stop in front of the heavy, closed door that Mrs. Coleman uses as her work area. Pretty painted flowers decorate it.

Drayton calls through the door, "Taking Joe home, Mom. Lights out soon."

We put our shoes on and scan ourselves out of Drayton's house. "Now. Let's think bigger than what we've been told. The complete picture. The PC is just a bunch of people like us. They have no way of knowing if all technology was eradicated on Land. Or if the Bones virus is still viable. I bet it would have played itself out by now."

"Played itself out?"

Drayton opens the car door for me, then gets in the driver's seat and puts the car in gear. "Yeah, either killed everyone who was susceptible, or the people left found a cure. So, let's say you're a survivor of a militant religious revolution and a nasty virus with organ-cooking fever. Would you start trying to rebuild or just rely on sticks and stones in the jungle?"

I chew on my lip. "I guess if I were on Land with no technology, I would at least try to have running water and electricity. And a shelter."

"Exactly. It's human nature to create a sustainable living environment. Now, what if these lights are an attempt to gain our attention? Ask for help? Or invite us back to the Land?"

"Invite us back to the Land." I laugh. "Drayton, you are the quintessential optimist. What do you expect? A written invitation?"

"Why not? I would send an invitation, like these lights. I mean, surely some history has survived, and they know that a fishnet full of people evacuated and took what technology they could with them before the Days of Cleansing when everything went boom."

"Nothing manufactured," I quote.

Drayton drives over the next viaduct. "Now that's a thought. Everything manufactured was destroyed, right? That's what we've been told. But did they keep their weapons? This could also be a security risk."

"Maybe. Probably. If I were a Moralist trying to get a bunch of people to do what I wanted, I'd keep my weapons. But the PC has a cache of weaponry, too. All of the weapon-laden ships that the Moralists didn't sink, the PC appropriated."

"All of them? It's a wide ocean. It took years for the PC to organize the salvage expeditions. Let's not be naive. The ocean is vast."

Seventy-one percent of the earth. "Okay, true."

"What is this?"

Car lights arc across the viaduct. A PC vehicle—a white truck hauling a sturdy power generator—blocks the road. Drayton slows and stops. PC Gramble is standing on the viaduct looking down at the water. His reflective PC sash glows in the light.

Drayton waits. "What is he doing?"

"Nobody would be out night fishing. It's too rough after that storm."

PC Gramble turns and looks at Drayton's car. He walks over to my side and taps on the window. I unroll it.

"Wrist, please."

I stick my wrist out the window, and PC Gramble scans it. "Out late tonight, Joe. Almost curfew." PC Gramble leans on the window and looks at Drayton. His handlebar mustache casts long shadows on his face. "Drayton."

"Good evening. As you know, Joe's home is directly across the next bridge. I'll get her and myself home before curfew, sir. Unless I have to go all the way around."

PC Gramble smiles. "I know. Heard you had a near miss today on the ring roadway."

"Yes, we did," Drayton replies.

PC Gramble checks his scanner. He taps the hood of Drayton's car and then scans the meter on the side. "You aren't in Overuse. That's good."

He walks to Drayton's side of the car. Drayton slowly rolls down the window.

"Maintenance fixed the problem. Thanks for reporting it so quickly."

"Doing my duty," Drayton says.

PC Gramble spits, then rests his elbow on Drayton's window for a moment. "Good to hear. Be careful getting her home. These roads are tricky in the dark."

"I will be."

PC Gramble nods at Drayton and walks slowly back to his truck. He gets in, starts the motor and drives away. He comes very close to the passenger side mirror.

Drayton edges the car to the side then drives forward. "I'm not sure what I think about that."

"Sounds like he was checking on us. It was pretty scary this morning."

Drayton slows down and rolls over the bridge carefully. "More like snooping. Things are changing. And those Land lights are the biggest change."

The outline of my house appears. In the darkness, it looks like a collection of dried bones. There is nothing alive, nothing green around it because Dad and I don't care for the plant boxes Mom created from old ice chests in the front yard. They're full of dried up plant stems. Mom was the gardener.

"Are they?"

"This change is," Drayton says. "Look, I want to follow up on this before we report it. Can I see your communications project tomorrow?"

"But the See-Saw's not complete. I have months to finish it."

Drayton parks in front of my door and raises his eyebrows at me. "You're a terrible liar, Joe. I know you. You've had a prototype ready for weeks. Maybe months. Don't try to fool me."

I see the set of his jaw, and I know Drayton will be at my house tomorrow whether or not I want him to be. I sigh and open the car door. "Fine. But it really isn't ready. I still want to modify some things."

"It's as ready as it'll ever be, I bet. I have to get back before lights out. I have a feeling PC Gramble is itching to give me a citation."

Drayton drives away, and I run up the twelve steps to my house. I look at my watch. All of the lights are off, and it's seven minutes until lights out. Dad isn't home, but the PC allows him a curfew pass. He's probably still tracking satellites.

I scan my wrist and slide down the inside of the door. I'm exhausted. The house is cold and the floor damp. I'm cold and damp, too.

Nothing to do but wait for tomorrow.

# Chapter Six

DAD IS HOLDING one of our hard-hat mixing bowls. Mom liked to be creative with found objects. She wanted a warm kitchen, so bright pieces of beat up old flags are tacked to the walls. They're faded now, but neither Dad nor I have taken them down. Several pots hang from hooks to the left of the stove, and all our utensils and plates are stacked neatly on a shelf made of driftwood. My mom's indoor bone drying rack for fish is built into the wall. I'm glad that there aren't any gutted fish on it. I can barely eat when the kitchen smells like raw fish, and Dad and I let the sage die last month.

"Breakfast in the making!" Dad sings in an off-key, warm voice.

It isn't fair. This is the first morning I could have slept late, but Dad, the cook, wanted to make us breakfast.

I stretch my arms over my head and yawn in protest. "For the record, I should still be sleeping."

"I found an active signal."

I stare at him with wide eyes. Finding an active signal is huge for future satellite communication between Platforms. I don't think it's as promising as our underwater capabilities, but it's still big news. "That's great. From which navigational satellite? *Galileo* or *Glonass*?"

Dad puts a plate stacked with water cakes in front of me. "*Galileo*. Still in MEO—it hasn't fallen from its orbital path at all. Think of what we can do if I build a reference station that can communicate with the existing program."

"Eyes in the sky," I say and take a bite. It's pretty decent, so I take a second bite before I swallow. Mom used to tell me not to stuff my face, but Dad hasn't made water cakes in a long time, so I do. I love the fluffy consistency and how it tastes like nothing but expands in your mouth and fills you up.

Dad turns off the electric stove and slides his plate on the table. "It means more hours, more work."

"No problem. It's important work." I stuff more food into my mouth.

Dad cuts a piece from his water cake and looks at me. "Look, I know we haven't talked about…"

Not only am I up early when I don't have to be, but now Dad wants to talk. About Mom. I can't handle it. "No need to."

Dad pushes his fork around the plate. "You've always been mature. Only child syndrome, right?"

The scraping noise makes me shiver. "Right."

Dad wavers. "Then I'll be working more the coming weeks. If you need help with your communications project, let me know."

"I'm all good," I say and pick up my plate. I take the pan off the stove and put my plate in it. "Thanks for breakfast. I'll take care of these."

The back door is directly across from the table. It's held shut with a small hook, which Dad unhooks for me. It's only six steps to the wash area. I start pumping. The plastic piping extends thirty feet to the water's surface, so it takes a few pumps to get the water flowing. The PC doesn't meter our round sea holes, so I can pump as much seawater as I need. A basic filter gets rid of most of the salt, so we can use it for tasks like dish and clothes washing. The sea holes aren't ideal. A child fell through one on Neft and drowned.

The pump jams. I look down at the water, and it looks like it's ready to drown me. "Not today," I whisper, take a deep breath, and climb a few rungs down the ladder that drops into our cage farm. Our patio is made from an old barge, metal bars protruding from the bottom all the way back to the Platform like a jungle gym. I kick the pipe and hear a hum, then water pours into the white plastic mortar bucket.

I climb back up, wash the pan and plate, then place them in the old box spring we use as a drying area. Mom used to spend time every day listening to the sea and tending her patio plants. Now, it just looks like abandoned space. Most of the pots are broken from the last big storm we had, and I haven't planted anything new. Her gardening tools litter one corner, and a large blue tarp covers the last soil bed she had worked on. The net screens have two large tears.

"Dad," I yell over my shoulder. "The screens are ripped up again. Birds."

"They sure are at it again," Dad says from the doorway. He hands me his plate, and I wash it as well. "I'll fix them this week."

"Okay," I say and walk around him. Dad always says he'll "fix it this week," but it ends up being next week, or the next, or never. He forgets. Mom and I always picked up his slack. "I'm going back to sleep. Thanks for breakfast. Happy signal hunting."

I return to my room and lie in my bed until I hear the front door open and close. I imagine the sound of Dad's feet padding down the stairs and into his beat-up blue work truck. I hear the motor roar to life a few seconds later, then silence.

Peace.

I turn face down on my pillow before I twist to my side and will myself back to sleep. I don't even buckle myself in.

Nails are pounding into my brain. I sit up and hit my head on the metal bar above my bed.

"What? What?"

I look around my room, but no one is in it but me. A sharp knock comes from the outside wall. I crawl to the end of my bed and move the flat No Parking sign I have hung over the small, square window that looks out to our walkway and patio.

Drayton smiles in at me.

"No," I say and crawl back to my pillow and pull the covers over me.

A minute later, Drayton opens the door to my room. "Your dad didn't shut your front door, so I let myself in. The scanner went berserk, but it finally recognized my chip. You need to invite me over more often. Why are you still in bed? Are you sick?"

"I'm sick of you. And fish."

"No, you're not. We live on fish." Drayton sits at my desk. "I see what you mean about too much metal, though. Looks like the inside of a sardine can in here. Feels like we're in a sardine can. Sounds like we're in a sardine can. Has it always been this plain?"

I had taken down two pieces of Mom's artwork a few weeks ago. I couldn't sleep with them leering at me from the walls, reminding me she was gone. "No."

"Redecorate. Get some fishing lures. That'll brighten things up."

I pretend to go back to sleep.

"No joke, this room is depressing. No wonder you're still sleeping. It's almost 9:00. Shouldn't we get started?"

"A-E-I-O-U-A-E-I-O-U," I say into my pillow then turn my head to glare at Drayton. "That means leave."

Drayton is rifling through the plans for my underwater communication satellite—the See-Saw. "Vowels are nice. They have no meaning without consonants. Totally safe to use them as a sentence." He shakes the papers. "You have a model built?"

"Yes," I hiss. "Leave. You're invading my space, and I need to re-brush my teeth."

"You can brush your teeth in front of me. I knew you when you were in diapers."

I grimace and drag myself to the sink. I need two more hours of sleep to feel human. "I got out of mine before you did."

"Keep telling yourself that," Drayton says and picks up my latest technical drawing of the See-Saw from my desk. "Router and modem all in one. This is brilliantly ambitious. I wish I'd thought of it."

I pick up my toothbrush, swish it around in my mouth, then spit. Water cakes are good, but they stick in your teeth. "Thanks. I think it'll work."

"Totally. Maybe a tweak in the casing to make it more pressure resistant, but it will work. Are you wearing that today?"

I look at my pajama bottoms and realize they were my mom's, which were her mom's, so the pattern is of really robust bouquets of flowers popular a hundred years ago. There are several patches made from denim and lime-colored cotton. "Yep. I haven't done laundry."

"Harsh."

"Just give me a minute." I try to flatten my hair. The humidity is high, and it is a riot of curls today. It could be its own Platform Complex.

"Your hair looks fine. It's the best part of your ensemble."

I sigh dramatically and finally manage to tie a triangular piece of sail cloth around my messy ponytail. "What I wouldn't give for just one day of flat hair. Trying to control this mess is tedious."

"It wouldn't suit you. Where'd you hide the model? Come on, I can't stand a mystery."

"I'm not hiding it. Why should I? It's in Mom's room."

Drayton follows me across the kitchen to the opposite side of the house.

"Isn't that your dad's room as well?"

"No. He moved into the loft after she left. I wanted to, but he made the move first."

"Joe…"

I don't want to talk about my family, so I slide the door open and switch on the overhead light. My great-grandmother's collection of traditional Kabuki masks look like they're laughing at me. Colorful art made of driftwood breaks up the masks, and a long piece of transparent red fabric covers the wall next to the window. It reminds me of a river of blood.

Mom's car hood work table is jammed into the corner. It's where she did her craft projects because she felt this room had the most creative flow. Me too, so I'd cut a hole in her table with a ten-gauge nibbler. Now, my See-Saw, my baby, looks like a gigantic egg resting in it. It's the size of a four-foot flotation buoy with side ridges that remind me of a sea cucumber.

"Ta da. May I present the See-Saw, a self-generating sonar relay station. I used most of the functioning parts from the rig's existing communications system, like the microphone and receptor. I re-worked all the circuitry and programming and wrote the software. I developed a super sensitive hydrophone. Like an ear with a built-in eye."

Drayton pokes around my satellite. "Of course you did. And I bet you wrote one hell of a program to decipher all the data. You've been working on it, what, since winter break?"

"Yes. It's only complete because I got lucky with the casing and just used an old underwater drone. Which is why you should leave it alone."

Drayton drops to his knees, then pats the side of my satellite. "It needs to be tweaked."

"Tweaked how? I double checked everything."

"Pressure balanced. Don't worry, I'll fix it. How are you going to sink it? Is it anchored or free…oh, I see."

"I'm sinking this prototype here," I say. "My second model will be for the moon pool." The moon pool is the central sea opening of Nod, right in front of the Empire.

Drayton selects tools from the collection on Mom's table, and I get nervous. "I ran the numbers for pressure and temperature at two hundred yards below surface. I don't think the casing needs any work."

Drayton dives underneath the satellite. "Just a little tweak. I know what I'm doing."

"Look, I don't feel comfortable—" I hear a snapping noise, and I cringe. "Drayton!"

"Fixing it! It'll be better than it was, promise. Just hold on a moment."

Drayton's body contorts around the satellite. It looks like he is holding the satellite above his head.

"What are you doing?"

"Securing the weight system to the casing. Tidal action will rip this off. Hand me the torch."

I grab the welding torch and protective facemask and hand them to Drayton. He grins at me. "This is going to be revolutionary. We could communicate to the next Platform Complex using a predetermined alphabet code and repeating stations— maybe even floating repeating stations, though we'd have to secure them in deeper waters. Challenging, but not impossible."

"Yes, I know. I built it," I say. Drayton puts on the mask, then turns the torch on. "Don't catch my See-Saw on fire. Or yourself. Or the house."

Drayton continues working. Smoke fills the room, so I slide Mom's work area window open. The scanner on it doesn't function, and Mom never reported it. Neither did Dad. They thought it was nice to feel the breeze on windy days or late nights and not have the PC know about it.

After several minutes, Drayton hands me the torch and flips up his visor. "Let's go sink your baby."

"Now?"

"Why not now? We may sink into the ocean tomorrow ourselves."

"What a pleasant thought." I make sure the torch is turned off and examine my See-Saw. "Glad I piled all the old signs underneath it for fire safety. It was hard to come by that many, you know. Metal isn't easy to find when you don't steal it."

"That's why I repurpose it." Drayton's eyes are bright and his energy fills the room.

I start to feel excited. "All right, smarty pants. I've thought of a couple ways to get this to the sea hole. We can use the signs to piece together a flat gutter, or a net that we spin around—"

"We'll carry it to the sea hole."

"Carry it?" My See-saw doesn't weigh tons like the aerial satellites, but it's heavy.

"Sure. Rope-and-pulley system. I have something we can use in my car. I'll get it."

"All right. I was thinking something more grandiose…but you're right. We'll go simple. I'll clear a pathway on the porch."

The back door latch falls off when I move it, and I put it on the stove. "I'll fix you later," I say and step outside. Making a pathway isn't hard, as there are only pots and planters to move. I pile them in front of one of the torn screens. I touch one of the plants Mom loved—its flowers were white and smelled delicious. It hasn't bloomed since she left.

Drayton makes a bunch of noise in the hallway then sticks his head through the kitchen window, which is right above the pile of pots. It doesn't have a sensor because it opens onto the patio. "I've got ropes and pulleys."

I mentally calculate the distance between the See-Saw and the sea hole. Numbers move through my mind effortlessly. "I've got a plan."

"I knew you would." Drayton notices the screens. "I'll fix the screens for you later."

I follow Drayton into Mom's room. "Thanks. But you don't have to. Dad said he would."

"I'll fix them. Let's get this done."

The next hour is filled with me explaining and implementing my plan. Together, we tie the ropes to create an intricate counter-balance system. It's annoying and tedious, but we make progress. Mom's room looks like a rope octopus exploded in it.

Finally, we get the satellite in position above the sea hole. It will rest in the bottom of our cage farm. We stand at the edge of the hole, and Drayton holds the rope to keep the See-Saw out of the water.

"The rope is at two hundred feet," Drayton says.

I pat the side of my See-Saw. I know she's ready to go. "It's now or never. Let her go. I can't do it."

Drayton lets the rope slide through his fingers, and I watch my See-Saw sink beneath the water.

"I should sing a song to commemorate this epic launching. There once was a girl named Joe-Joe…"

"Completely unnecessary," I say and cover my ears. Drayton has a terrible singing voice.

"Almost there," Drayton says and shows me the rope. His fingers are lightning quick as he lets the rope out until it suddenly stops. "Maximum length reached."

I feel a strange combination of elated and emotionally drained. If the prototype See-Saw doesn't work, a year of building and planning will account for nothing. I don't have time to think up and build another project. Not a good one, at least.

I pick up the pruning shears and cut the rope. "Well, it's in the cage farm. So that's done."

Drayton puts his arm around my shoulders, then drops it awkwardly. "I'll free dive for the rope later."

"Thanks for lending it."

"No problem. You have a clear view of Dauphin Island from here. I'd never noticed that before."

"Yes, of course I do. So do you. So what?"

"Making conversation."

"You never just make conversation. Come on. Why's that important?"

Drayton squints. "The lights are centered on one particular area of the Land. The tip of Dauphin Island. It makes me wonder who else on the Platform has noticed them."

"Stop wondering," I say. "Let's clean this up, so I can check the reference station."

"Where'd you build the reference station? In the broom closet?"

"Don't be an ass. It's under the laundry I haven't done in my room. Who has a broom closet?"

Drayton chuckles. "Go. I'll clean up."

I curtsy playfully. "My knight in shining armor."

"Yeah, yeah, yeah." Drayton starts to untie the intricate knots in the last counterweight we set up. "Don't trip on…oh, that's right, you don't like dresses. Did you ever like dresses?"

"No, that was Mom dressing me. I never thought the damsel in distress outfits looked good on me. Get it? Distress? Dress?"

Drayton claps his hands slowly.

I know my jokes are terrible, but I tell them to Drayton anyway. He never laughs, but that's kind of the point. I smile all the way to my room. The reference station is set up in the corner. I pull the clothes off of it and pat it. It's just a little taller than I am and looks like a small scale model of the Space Needle that I've seen in Land history class. I check my laptop. It is processing data and…

"Picking up a signal," I whisper and type in code directions via the software program I created. I ask the reference station to locate the See-Saw and start receiving data through the transducer. I start with a series of pings at different distances. Information returns to the See-Saw, and my software program organizes the returning data.

I lose track of time and am just starting to evaluate the long-range potential for my satellite when Drayton comes into my room.

"The pings are traveling consistently. I don't know who to give the software to in order to complete long-range viability testing. I did load it onto Lisette's pad a few weeks ago. She doesn't know what it's for, but who else? There aren't that many people I would trust."

"Set up a broad range signal, and see if anyone answers you."

"Don't be silly," I respond and show him the screen. "That will never work, see? I have to input a specific address to ping." I pull up a map of Nod. "I need to connect to these points. They are random but identifiable distances from the home receiver. Then I'll know if everything is functioning properly. We won't have to go through the PC's central receiver anymore for cross Platform communication."

Drayton puts his hand on my back. "So you'll be able to talk to Lisette without the PC snooping. Awesome. Now, if I'm no longer needed…"

I swivel in my chair and look up at Drayton, surprised. "What? Where are you going? Don't you want to look at the raw data the See-Saw is collecting?"

"You need to map out those coordinates and find people to connect to, and I have to go."

"Yes, I do. But why? You said we could go to Lisette's this morning. Remember? Lights, Lisette equals trade off? It'll just take me a few more minutes to finish this data sweep."

"I have a lunch date," Drayton says miserably. "I won the bet."

Harriet. I wonder if she made the bet knowing that she would lose and get to have lunch with Drayton. I turn my chair back to the laptop. "Thanks for betting on me."

"Thanks for jumping. Sort of. I'll come back and fix the screens?"

I'm aggravated, and I want to be difficult. "Dad will fix them."

"I'll be back to fix the screens."

"Suit yourself," I reply. I triangulate communication points on my laptop so that I don't have to keep talking. I know Drayton is still standing there. I hate it when things are awkward between us. "Scan yourself out. I don't want the PC here."

I hear the front door close, and I push my laptop away. I'm unsettled and pace around my room in circles. Eventually, I open my laptop back up and refuse to feel anything but success.

Harriet's project won't stand a chance against mine.

# Chapter Seven

"All right, the screens won't be going anywhere for a while," Drayton says and sits on my bed. "How's it coming?"

"Thanks. It's coming." I hadn't asked about his lunch with Harriet, though I can tell he hated it. Drayton hates wasting time.

"Look, Joe…"

His voice sounds serious, and I don't want to hear serious. I interrupt him. "Want to ping Lisette? Since we didn't go there today because of your lunch."

"Sure. About the lunch—"

"Don't want to know about it." I instruct the See-Saw to ping Lisette's virtual pad.

Lisette. This is Joe.

I wait, but nothing happens. I ping again.

Lisette. Look at your pad. This is Joe.

I wait.

Joe? Are you on this side of the platform?

I giggle. "She answered! It works! I just made my first contact with the See-Saw!"

"And the revolution begins. Congratulations."

I sunk my project. Working so far. I'll tell you about it later.

I wait, and Lisette replies. Congratulations. I want to hear all about it. I can come over tomorrow with my sister. My project doesn't start until next week. Are you busy?

"She can come over to this side tomorrow," I say to Drayton. "At least she doesn't make empty promises."

"You two should have…should get together."

I raise my eyebrow at Drayton, then get an idea.

**Meet me here. We'll go to Drayton's. 8?**

Lisette responds immediately. **OK.** Man that was a quick response.

I chuckle and type the command to disconnect on my laptop.

"What's funny?"

"Nothing," I say and imagine the look on Drayton's face when both Lisette and I wake him up at 8 a.m. He hates surprises.

☙❧

Dinner is a non-event of leftover grilled jellyfish. The texture is worse than eel, chewy and bland, but I choke it down.

Mr. Jinks, our next-door neighbor, drops off some tools he borrowed from Dad. Since his wife died, he comes by every few days. I listen to him talk about flattening wire trash cans to make flooring for his patio addition for almost thirty minutes. When he finally leaves, I sigh and retreat to my room. Dad isn't home, so I keep fiddling with my communications program.

So far, I've transmitted local pings and received feedback, but I want to know how far my See-Saw's sonar can actually reach with its current power and amplitude. I've read in the virtual records that whales can hear each other from Nova Scotia to Bermuda—almost 1400 kilometers—so I'm hopeful that my LFA, 90 Db, 200 Hz sonar will be able to reach the next Platform, Shiloh, which is only eighty kilometers away. My software uses its active mode to package words into sound waves. Short phrases at first, but eventually letters, conversations.

But I don't know anyone on Shiloh to target. I bet Dad does. I'll ask him if he gets home before lights out. I direct my See-Saw to switch from active to passive mode and prepare to spend the next thirty minutes listening to the invisible communication underneath me. Maybe I'll hear whale song. I've always wanted to hear live whale song.

My phone blinks. It has to be Drayton. An image of Harriet and Drayton eating lunch sticks in my mind, even though I didn't see them. It makes me sick, so I force myself to focus on the phone. It isn't after hours yet, so it could be important.

**Dad's home. The trash barge didn't yield a lot of usable repair materials.**

I frown. We need materials.

**Thanks for the update.**

I hear a series of pings. Data is coming into my laptop from the reference station, but I pick my phone back up when it blinks.

**We'll have to take metal from the abandoned platforms soon. If the PC allows us to disturb the reefs.**

There's been a few scuba missions to determine if salvaging sunken Platforms could work for our needs. I hadn't thought much about it, but it could yield—

A second, then third series of pings hit my laptop in rapid succession. A series of streaks and dots cover the program's graphing chart.

"It's a school of whales, or dolphins. Maybe a tarpon," I mumble and run the time and ping frequencies through my software. The data doesn't show the normal shallow trajectory of moving mammals. Something is wrong.

Three pings hit the reference station again, all at the same depth and the same frequency. I must have miscalculated the input of the hydrophone, or perhaps there's a glitch in my transducer or receiver.

Three pings hit the reference station again.

"Stop. This is getting scary." I switch the See-Saw to active sonar. Nothing. After several seconds of listening for echoes, I power it down completely. There is no moving object in the See-Saw's range.

Dad knocks on my door but doesn't open it. "Everything okay? I'm back."

I throw dirty clothes on top of the reference station and pull my shirt off. I hold it in front of me and crack the door open. "Everything's fine. Getting ready for bed. Changing for lights out."

Dad backs away from me. "Oh, sorry. I'm exhausted, Joe. Thinking about going to bed."

"Good night."

"See you in the morning, then," Dad says.

"All right," I reply. I remember about Shiloh but don't ask him because if the See-Saw is malfunctioning it doesn't matter. I shut the door and wait several seconds. I put my shirt back on and look at my laptop.

Whales don't initiate communication waves in groups of short, steady threes. I can't think of any ocean creature that does. I consider every bit of programming, every piece of the See-Saw. I am sure there is nothing wrong with my software. Someone, or something, is sending signals unrelated to my sonar scans directly to the See-Saw.

A flurry of pings registers on my software. Disorganized dots light up the graphing chart on my screen. I input programming to filter the dots into a recognizable matrix. I wait for the results.

Morse code.

*COME*

I read the words on the screen then shut my laptop. Someone is targeting the See-Saw.

I pick up my phone.

Drayton. I need to talk to you. Now. In person. Tap on the window.

# Chapter Eight

THE TAPS ON THE WINDOW MAKE ME JUMP, even though I'm expecting them. I haven't moved since I typed the message to Drayton. I have a million thoughts rolling through my head, and I can't focus on a single one.

I move the flat sign covering my window. Drayton's face is pressed to the glass on the other side. His brow is furrowed, and he looks worried. I hold up five fingers. Drayton nods and disappears. When we were growing up, five fingers meant that one of our parents was approaching and to be on our best behavior. Now, it just means that my dad's home.

I open the door to my room quietly and wait. I don't want to explain about the See-Saw or the signals yet, or detract attention from Dad's work. He's searched for an active satellite signal his entire career and deserves to have the spotlight for the find. Dad doesn't sleep much when he's in the thick of research, so there's a good chance he is already asleep now that he is home and in bed.

I tiptoe out the door and down the hallway to the kitchen. I stop for several seconds beneath the doorjamb but hear nothing. A heavy wire skeleton of a chair is in front of the porch door. Dad must have noticed the latch was broken and put it there so the door didn't swing open and closed all night. The chair squeaks when I move past it on the way to Mom's room. The floor above me creaks, and I panic. Dad. I slide the back window open and squeeze myself through it before I remember that

Drayton fixed the outside screens on the porch. I can't crawl out the side of the enclosure and down the gutter to the Platform. And I don't have anything to cut through the netting with.

"Damn," I whisper softly and look uncomfortably at the sky. It's clear, but the stars barely break the darkness. The sea hole looks like a gaping mouth ready to swallow me whole. I kneel beside it and look through. It's a twenty plus foot drop into dark, swirling water. "Stupid water."

I think of a million ways to disarm the front door scanner, but none of them would work without tipping off the PC, and it's close to curfew. "Double damn," I swear. I haven't used the jungle gym under my house in years. I don't want to now, but this is important. I feel around for a life vest on the wall but can't find one. Dad probably has them all on his research float.

"Don't fall in," I whisper and take a deep breath. I bend over the sea hole and find the bar mounted underneath the far edge. I grasp it with both hands and swing myself through the hole. I remember approximately how far apart the bars are and reach awkwardly for the next bar. My fingers start to tremble.

"Stop that. Hand over hand," I tell myself firmly and focus on making it to the last bar. I finally reach the corner of the house. I kick my legs hard and land on the concrete edge of my house slab.

"Joe," Drayton whispers and reaches out for my hand. He pulls me securely onto the Platform, then hugs me. "I thought you'd remember the jungle gym was there. Too bad I fixed the screens today, right?"

"Right," I say and exhale.

Drayton hugs me a second time. "No life jacket? And without getting wet. Impressive. Risky, but impressive."

"Why are you all wet?"

"Scanner avoidance plan A. Took my chances and swam from the cage farm to the dry dock lift. That chain was tough to scale. Rode my bike the rest of the way."

He shows me his hands. They're all cut up.

I wince. "Sorry."

"It's okay. What's up? Your message scared me."

I grab Drayton's hand and drag him with me until we are away from my house and the two others next to it. We climb under the first tier of the viaduct and get into the abandoned builder's rig. It has a partially beamed steel floor and is suspended by twisted cables beneath the metal and wood bridge. The brake keeps it from moving down the track beneath the viaduct. We used to play pirates here when we were children. Several make-believe swords made from long florescent bulbs are still stacked in the corner with old doorknobs we used for pretend cannon fire.

I take a seat on one beam and hold on to the steel of the tier above me. "Okay. Where'd you leave your bike?"

"On the other side of the viaduct," Drayton says and sits across from me. "There's a deep depression, so I don't think Gramble or Fristhe can see it if they patrol."

"Good thinking." I take a deep breath. "I turned on the passive sonar, and I was pinged."

"Dolphins? Not the right season for whales, if we ever even get them. If I were a whale, I wouldn't mess with these shallow waters. Not worth their time. Can't remember seeing any last year."

"Not dolphins. It was a direct ping."

"Okay. What then? Oh! You think it's from Shiloh?"

I shake my head.

Drayton's eyes widen, and I nod.

"Three in a row," I say emphatically. "Three times in a row. And I don't believe in coincidence. Not this much of a coincidence. Plus, there's more."

Drayton expels his breath in a low whistle.

"A message in Morse code. *Come.* That's why I wanted to talk to you in person. It's scary."

"This proves my hypothesis even more," Drayton says in excitement. "People on Land want to get our attention."

I put a finger over my lips. "The signals could be from anything—an old beacon, a bad weather buoy that was activated when I used LFA instead of our normal mid-range or high-level sonar. Maybe the old sonar surveillance system. Those were ocean wide. But not the message. That was deliberately sent."

Drayton claps his hands. "This is seriously tidal. We could be the first Platform dwellers to be contacted."

He continues, but something is bothering me. Like when an item is out of place in your room, but you can't quite put your finger on what it is. Or you forget where you put your virtual pad, but you can almost remember.

Then I recognize the feeling. We're being watched. Or listened to.

"—and we can offer them technical know-how. It would solve the problem of non-renewable resources for us, and I, for one, could use a change. New materials to work with. New projects to imagine and build."

"Whom did you tell you were coming here?"

"Whom? Or is it who?"

Leave it to Drayton and his super grammar to correct me. "Doesn't matter. Did you tell anyone?"

"No one. Why?"

The PC. I'll take full responsibility and tell them we were getting fresh air, that I was having a nervous breakdown over my mother's extended leave. I get on my knees and peek through the space between the viaduct and the rail.

There is definitely someone standing at the edge of the viaduct—but not Gramble or Fristhe. I recognize the figure and smirk. I scoop several snails from the viaduct post, stand on the tier, and throw them right at her.

"Ouch! Oh, gross!"

"That's why," I say to Drayton and sit back down beneath the tier. It's the only time I've been glad to see Harriet. "I thought it was the PC."

"Stop!" Harriet says in a high, whiny voice. "I'll report you both."

I don't care what Harriet is saying. It's Drayton I'm thinking about. He told her he was coming to my house.

Drayton leans forward to peer up onto the viaduct. "What are you doing, Harriet? You need a PC permit for night fishing."

Harriet stomps her foot. "You know I don't fish. The real question is what are you two doing? This has to do with your project, Joe; I know it."

"Everything does not revolve around you, Harriet," I reply and swing myself to the top of the viaduct. Harriet reminds me of that fishy smell in clothes that even Lisette's fancy plant soap can't get rid of. "Or communications."

I take off toward home but stay on the periphery of the road, in case Dad looks out the window or the PC rolls by. I take my time, as I want to finish the conversation with Drayton, just without Harriet or the PC in tow. I want to know why he told Harriet he was meeting me.

I hear running footsteps behind me. "Joe, wait. I know what it looks like, but I didn't tell her anything about the See-Saw. I swear it."

I turn around and look at Drayton. He is super serious. "You want me to believe that she randomly knew that you were leaving your home and coming here?"

"Not me, you. I think she's stalking you. It's kind of creepy."

I look hard at Drayton, but his sincere expression doesn't change. Serious. I know he's telling the truth. "Like watching me?"

"That's what stalkers do. She saw you leave and followed you."

It makes sense. "All right, I believe you. Did you send her home, or is she still lurking around?"

Drayton points at the house and road, then at the viaduct. I follow him back to our original location in the abandoned builder's rig. After a moment of uncomfortable silence, Drayton clears his throat.

"She's gone. I mentioned I knew where she got the raw information for that last oceanography paper. She won't be back. At least not tonight."

He sits next to me and I wait. He doesn't divulge the info, so I have to ask. "Well?"

"Curious? Or searching for leverage? I thought you didn't care about Harriet."

I look at Drayton as if he were a plate of eels. "Caring and curious are two different things."

"All right, I'll tell you. She lifted the wave data action results from her parents' research. Dad told me."

I purse my lips and chew on the inside of my cheek. Harriet wasn't good at oceanography. If the school found out she cheated, they'd have to revoke her completion record and report it to the PC. There'd be a formal inquiry. "She won't talk."

"Nope. Now, back to business. I think we need to respond. Let them know we are here, and we are listening. That we're open to the possibility of communication."

"Are we? Do we really want to communicate with them?"

"Of course we do. The break happened decades ago, but we're still extended family—same species. We should at least reach out. It's the right thing to do."

"It may be time to involve the PC. I don't want to, because I'm going to have a hell of a time explaining my illegal network, the See-Saw, etc."

"No PC. The PC will analyze and analyze, and we might miss this opportunity to reconnect."

I consider Drayton's words. "Fine. Let's say we respond and start a conversation. Then what? Tell the PC we didn't know who we were responding to?"

Drayton looks out across the water. I know the look, and I cringe when he says the words. "Then we follow through. Go to Land and meet them."

"Which is insane. Totally insane and unsafe. The Bones virus could still be viable. They may take one look at us and kill us. They could be cannibals. Not to mention the PC would expel us to Hades when we returned."

"Come on, it wouldn't be so bad. Just think—I could build you whatever you needed. Stimulating conversation every moment of the day." Drayton chuckles. "Cannibals? Really, Joe, that imagination of yours. You know that is highly unlikely, given they were being led by religious zealots."

I study the water beneath us. It's never still, always going somewhere. In the dark it looks like the oil the Platform used to suck from the seabed. Sinister.

"We don't know who we're dealing with. Some were of different faiths." We don't have organized faith on the Platforms, though some people practice in their own homes. The PC has no restriction on faith; it's just not something most people participate in. "How could one visionary sway *all* of the world's people to eradicate technology? Don't you think someone besides us holed up and stockpiled?"

Drayton hops from the main beam to a secondary beam. "All right, I'll admit that some of the history is fuzzy. And let's face it, there's no one left who can tell us exactly what happened. Our ancestors took their technology and ran—or sailed, as the case may be. But you've received a direct message. Maybe from the people who did hole up. Let's find out."

Drayton turns and spins on the second beam. One wrong step and he could slip through the spaces between the steel. "Sit or stand. You're making me nervous moving around like that. It isn't safe. Neither is going to Land."

Drayton extends his hand to me. I take it, and he looks me in the eyes. "All right, Miss Naysayer. Take my joy. But let's talk tomorrow and figure out a plan to make first contact."

"Carefully. We could be opening a can of worms."

"We've never even seen a worm, Joe. Don't you want to?"

I tilt my head. Drayton's hair is straight and dark. One lock falls over his right eye, and he looks very mischievous.

"I'm not so sure."

"I'm sure. You'd love worms, in the can or out. Think of all that wriggling."

"If you say so," I respond neutrally before bring the conversation back on track. "Documentation. Everything needs to be documented. Let's try not to completely ruin our records doing this. Or our credibility."

I climb out of the builder's rig and put both hands on the Platform. The fake ground feels real, but I know that beneath me is water and all things that live in water. We live on beams of metal and concrete and call it reality when it's actually just manufactured habitat.

"I would like to see real ground," I say wistfully and straighten. "I'll admit that."

Drayton is right beside me, and he puts his arm around me. "Think of it. No more sea sickness. No more life jackets."

"Yeah, yeah, yeah," I say and shrug his arm away. "Everything about our lives is fake. What if I don't like real?"

"It's just a different kind of real. Our lives are real right now. What we feel is real. It's just the surroundings that are fake. We're trying to recreate what it was like on Land. So let's reach out to them and go there."

I imagine what standing on real ground would feel like. Supported, rooted. Like each step was connected to the core of the planet. "I'm on board for the reaching out part. Going to Land—that's your crazy talking. Let's walk back before we get picked up for breaking curfew."

"All right. Let me tell you about real." Drayton recounts the story of me falling into the sea and almost drowning because we were doing something we shouldn't have been doing. He begins another one with a similar story line. Drayton was always there to save me and explain exactly why I had to do whatever forbidden activity I epically failed at doing. The stories make me feel real and connected, and I appreciate that Drayton is telling them.

"Good times," I say and chuckle over the story of me getting caught in the crab traps on the far side of the island because I believed they were unethical. "I still won't eat crab, you know. Their eyes give me the heebie jeebies."

Then it hits me. Since Mom left, I haven't had any good times. I'd stopped having fun and started working on project after project to make myself feel busy and important. Relevant. Anything was better than having to deal with the fact that we weren't connected.

Something distracts me from my thoughts, and I look around Drayton. A light in my room blinks on then off after a second. Probably just the See-Saw's receiver blinking.

"Two groupers for your thoughts."

I laugh. "Having an epiphany. I need to have more fun. See you tomorrow. Give me a lift up, please."

"To where?"

I point to Mom's window. "Broken scanner."

"Still?"

I nod. "Mom liked it open. You can't see it from the road, and the PC has never done a full house check on us. I think they're afraid of the masks."

"I'm afraid of those masks." Drayton threads his fingers together to make a basket, and I step into it. I slide Mom's window to the side, and scramble up to the ledge. I reach for the red fabric and pull myself in the window. I drop to the floor, lean over and whisper, "Don't get caught," then slide the window shut.

The house is pitch black, so I feel my way through Mom's room and find the door handle. I push it gently open, then stay against the wall until I get to my room. I trail my fingers across the cold metal kitchen table as I pass. I enter my room and prepare to…

Harriet is leaning over my laptop. Papers are shuffled around on my desk. "Harriet," I whisper furiously. "You fink. How'd you get in?"

She looks at me from the corner of her eye. "I have my ways. You've been busy. This looks to be—"

"Beyond your capabilities," I say and snatch the papers from my desk. I look at my laptop, but Harriet wasn't able to get past the password. And hopefully she didn't understand my diagrams. "Fishing for ideas? Get out of my house."

"Or what? You'll wake up your daddy and tell him about your clandestine little tryst with Drayton? I'm sure he'd love to hear all about it."

I stare at Harriet and wish her into the deepest depths of the darkest areas of the sea where there are fish with large teeth that I can't even imagine. "Get out."

Harriet shrugs her shoulders daintily. "Sure. Your ideas will never work. And it's so cramped in here anyway. Like a jail cell—or Hades, for example. Which I'm sure you'll be on soon."

"For what, Harriet? Consorting with you? Because you being in here equals entering my house illegally. Your chip isn't on my scanner's guest list."

Harriet laughs snidely and looks at the reference station in the corner of my room. "Don't point fingers, Joe. I'm thinking you didn't scan yourself out. Or in."

Since I don't want to defend myself against something sort of true, I decide to confuse her. "Oh. You think I stole the prodigal hytense cohexive ingram capacitor?"

"That junk you're building? What a sorry senior project."

"Well, it affects change," I say with assurance. "Big change. And I did not steal it. I repurposed it. Now get out the way you came in."

Harriet looks like she may spontaneously combust in the center of my room, but she turns and leaves. Instead of going through the front door, she goes into the bathroom. I watch in awe as she stands on the toilet lid and hoists herself through the window. A grappling hook holds her weight as she climbs down the ten feet to the Platform.

"I'll be damned," I say and grab the grappling hook from the window ledge. I pull it in and wind the rope around it. I recognize it from the climbing area at the Empire. "Maybe I should have tried climbing."

I close the bathroom window and test the scanner. It works. I don't know how Harriet got past it.

"Was that Harriet? Joachim's girl?"

I whirl around and put my hands behind me, dropping the grappling hook into the recycling bucket. Dad is standing in the kitchen.

"Yes. Not a friend," I say. I pick up one of our drying rags and put it over the grappling hook. "More like a disease."

"Why'd she go out the window? Last time I checked we had a front door."

"She was snooping around my project. We're both in communications."

"Oh." Dad pauses. He understands. The PC assigns research based on the quality of our projects. "Well, it's late for her to be traveling on the Platforms."

Of course Dad would be concerned about Harriet's safety. He's a dad. And of course Dad wouldn't know that it is technically now after curfew—he doesn't have one. "She'll be fine. It's only three viaducts, same spar."

"Okay. She has a bike?"

I don't know if Harriet has a bike, but I nod.

"But the window?"

I don't want to have this conversation. I move around Dad and across the kitchen. "It's a senior thing," I say like that explains everything.

Dad pretends to get it. "I see."

"So, good night."

Dad looks everywhere but at me. "Look, Joe, I know things have been difficult. I'm not good at everyday dad stuff. But if you need to talk about, well, anything, I can talk about it. I'd want to talk about it. Your future. Our future."

For a moment, I think about telling him about the See-Saw. Asking about Shiloh. But I notice the circles underneath his eyes. His projects have always been the center of his life, even before Mom left, and there's no reason to change that now. He's so close to a break through.

"Everything's fine. Harriet's just silly and jealous for nothing. She's not worth your time or mine. I don't think she's even worth her own time, that's how bad it is. Sorry she woke you up. Good night."

I squeeze past him on my way out of the bathroom, walk the two steps to my room, and shut the door. I hope Dad returns to his and gets some sleep. I flop down on my bed and think about empires. And broken scanners.

# Chapter Nine

MY LEGS ARE WRAPPED UP IN THE SHEET, so I kick it off. I struggle to turn over. The security strap pulls against me.

"Hey," Lisette's voice says. "Your dad let me in after he asked if my name was Harriet. It was weird."

I sit straight up in bed and put my fists up in front of me. My room is a haze. Five seconds ago, I was sleeping. "What?"

"He asked if I was Harriet, and when I said no, he let me in. Really weird. He's met me before, you know."

I put the pillow over my head. This is the second day that I haven't been able to sleep in. "We all look the same to him. Why are you here?"

"You said to meet you here. I've got the car. Well, the cart."

I lie back down. Nothing makes sense this early in the morning. "What time is it, Lisette?"

"A little after 6:15. I'm early."

"Yes, early," I manage to say. I hate when my sleep is cut short. My human software does not compute. "Social hours haven't started yet."

"I can wait outside. I don't mind."

Lisette sounds sad and embarrassed. I pull myself together and shake the sleep away. "No. Early is good. Early is fine. The plan is to go and surprise Drayton—catch him off guard. I just have to wash up. Today's Thursday, right?"

Lisette nods and walks to the pile of gear in the corner. "What's all this?"

"It's a reference station for my project. It picks up signals. It's how I contacted you yesterday."

"Oh. I bet it's spectacular, genius stuff," Lisette says and rolls her eyes. "Maybe I can check your mom's plants while you're washing up?"

"What we have left is on the back patio. They're struggling."

"Understandable. We haven't had much rain this month until a couple days ago. Sometimes they need a little loving care to get them back on the right track."

Lisette leaves, and I am relieved. I don't understand why my dad just let her in. I'm not a child anymore. I would never do that to him if one of his colleagues came by.

Lisette's head appears around the door, and I stifle a scream. I know she's leaning into the door, but it looks spooky and reminds me of decapitated fish.

"Your dad went to work. I forgot to tell you. He said to make sure and eat breakfast. It's the most important meal of the day."

"Will do."

Lisette's head disappears. I stand up and stretch. I didn't brush my teeth last night, so I drink last night's allotment of water. It tastes delicious, and I'm glad I still have the morning allotment to drink with my meal.

As I move to the washing station in the bathroom, I remember the grappling hook and panic, but it's still in the recycling bucket. Sighing, I relocate the hook to underneath the mattress of my bed. Returning to the bathroom, I notice that the wash bucket is half full. Dad must have collected our metered portion from the cistern this morning and taken his shower. "Just enough," I say brightly and take off the clothes I hadn't taken off the night before.

My hair isn't short, so the majority of the water goes to it. The rest I use sparingly with our plant soap. Unless I use sea hole water, I won't be able to wash again for two days under PC regulations.

I dry off with an old pair of Dad's pants that can't be patched anymore and amble through the house with my pajamas wrapped around me. Lisette is probably entranced with my struggling plants, but I don't want to risk it. I close the door to my room behind me, then gasp.

"Oh, oh!" Drayton says and flushes.

I grasp my clothes tightly. "You!"

Drayton runs out of my room.

I grab a pair of leggings and one of Mom's t-shirts that I salvaged from her closet. It's my favorite—the color of the sky on a bright day. I want to kill Drayton in something I like wearing. I grab the brush from my sink and storm after Drayton. "Drayton Coleman!"

"I'm so sorry," Drayton says and backs away from me. "Lisette said you were inside."

I smack Drayton on the arm with my brush. "This is my house, or did everyone forget that? My house! I live here!"

"Ouch." Drayton rubs his arm. "I didn't know. Lisette didn't mention that you weren't dressed. I'm sorry, that was messed up."

"Messed up?" I brush my hair and supply a different word for Drayton. "How about unnecessary?"

"Yes, I'm sorry. I should have waited outside. But I couldn't sleep, and I knew Lisette was coming here this morning. I saw her contraption she calls a car and thought you'd be…"

"Decent?"

He nods.

"Well, I wasn't, and I don't appreciate you barging in like you own this place because you don't." I finish brushing my hair. "What is with these early mornings and you people? We don't have to be anywhere."

"I know. You like your sleep. Sorry."

"And we were coming to surprise you."

He flushes. "Oh. Double sorry. But not."

And then I'm not angry anymore. My anger usually blows itself out—especially when Drayton looks so guilty and sorry. I give Drayton another quick chop to the gut with my brush and return to my room. I put the brush on the sink and search for a pair of shoes.

"Can I come in?" Drayton asks.

"Why, yes, thanks for asking," I say and pull on a pair of really worn polka dotted rain boots.

Drayton walks to my desk and studies my laptop. "Anything new?"

"How could there be anything new? I just woke up. Literally. But last night Harriet graced me with a surprise visit. She was trawling my room. Good thing the See-Saw plans are in code. She woke my dad up when she climbed out the bathroom window. She inexplicably got past the scanner."

Drayton whistles. "Did you lay into her?"

"She left quickly."

"Good for you. She's floundering for project ideas."

"Want me to make you some breakfast?" Lisette says from the doorway. "Your potato vines are actually doing quite well, so I harvested what was ready. I can't say much for the rest of the plants. Have you even tried to keep them alive?"

Lisette is smiling and has dirt under her fingernails and on her right cheek. I smile back at her. Her happiness is contagious. "Not really. And yes on breakfast. Thanks."

Lisette disappears into the kitchen. I breeze by Drayton but he stops me.

"Before breakfast—let's answer the message. Let's say okay."

I sit in front of my laptop and open it. Lisette sings a nonsensical song in the kitchen. "It's a crime to be so happy this early in the morning. Nice, but a crime."

"Focus. This is important."

"If it's so important, why don't you come up with something better than 'okay' as an answer?"

"Okie dokey?"

"Ha ha." I set up the link to the See-Saw, then translate "why" into Morse code. "I'm sending back 'why' in active mode."

"That feels defensive, like you already have your mind made up about them."

I close my laptop. The message is sent. "I think it's logical. If this is for real, their transducer will pick it up." I put my watch and my grandmother's ring on. It's blue and sparkly and reminds me of my mom. I motion to Drayton. "After you. Guests first."

I follow Drayton to the kitchen. Lisette is still singing when I sit on the stool at the kitchen table. The stove warms up the kitchen, so Drayton opens the window. The whole scene reminds me of when Mom was still here. "Smells good."

Drayton joins me.

"You can't have any of my potatoes. Ever."

Lisette giggles. "That could mean a totally different thing."

I don't laugh.

Neither does Drayton. "Did you tell Lisette about the SOS yet? The message?"

I shake my head.

Lisette turns off the stove and puts the skillet of potatoes in front of me on an old dishrag. "That way you don't have to wash an extra plate."

"Thanks. I'm going to remember that. I hate doing dishes."

Drayton steals a potato and eats it. "Are you going to tell her?"

"You tell her. I'm going to eat *my* potatoes."

Drayton tells Lisette about what happened with the lights and the See-Saw, and I chew one delicious bite after another of really well-cooked, well-salted potatoes.

Lisette asks Drayton questions, and I listen to his answers. We are like a little subset of a family, and it makes me happy to have them both in my kitchen. The room feels inviting.

"A Land expedition is the next step," Drayton concludes. "We'd have to roll the dice on virus viability."

"You could ask my sister Drees about the virus," Lisette offers. "She's been studying it for a few years. It's her specialty."

"Isn't she stationed at Canaan?" I ask. Canaan is the Platform where the majority of historical research work is done. It's even farther from us than Shiloh. It rests on top of a sunken cruise ship in the shallows near the outlying Caribbean islands.

Lisette looks at her hands. "She is. Or she was. She arrived yesterday and will be home for a few weeks. She took the most recent Transport ship over. Sorry I didn't tell you about it, but it's hush-hush. Dad's embarrassed. She's on medical leave for exhaustion."

"That's okay." I say. Research is everything on the Platforms, and if you have to take a leave of absence, it's not good.

"Lucky for us, unlucky for her," Drayton says. "Let's ask her."

"Okay," Lisette agrees amicably. "She's been quiet since coming home, but she loves her work, so maybe it will be good for her to have company and talk about it. Are you going to formally report Land contact to the PC? I have a feeling you're supposed to. This is big news. Nothing like this has ever happened before."

Drayton and I exchange a look. I scrape the very last bite of potato from the pan. "No PC yet."

"Here's the problem, Lisette," Drayton explains. "The actual PC is on Neft. It would take at least a week to get a message from our PC office to them and another week to receive permission to proceed. So we answered—not the answer I wanted, but an answer. We'll present it to the PC later so that they have to do something about it."

Lisette looks thoughtful. "Fair enough. I guess there's no harm in answering. What about your dad?"

"What about him?" I ask defensively.

"He could counsel you about the best way to proceed with the PC."

I shake my head. "This is my senior research project. I'm not giving it up, not even to Dad. Besides, he'd tell me aquatic transmission won't work long term. He's too into *Galileo*. He's never been interested in underwater applications."

Lisette looks at Drayton, then at me. "Let's talk to Drees and see what she thinks happened to the virus. It'll be good for her to socialize a little. And she definitely knows all the latest theories. We'll know if Land is even an option before you approach the PC."

"Great," Drayton says. "I'll drive."

# Chapter Ten

LISETTE'S HOUSE IS MORE GARDEN than building. Any object that can possibly hold soil is stacked in odd arrangements in the yard—gas cans, tackle boxes, drill casings. Plants and soil spill from all of them, and some are wrapped in nets or coarse tablecloth. It's like a living salvage yard.

"You've expanded the garden. Do you care for all of these?" I ask as I get out of Drayton's car.

"Yes. Mom and Memie start them, but I care for them. I'm good with seedlings."

"You're amazing," I comment. "You create things that grow. So much better than metal and circuitry."

Drayton chimes in. "I'm all for plants. They feed us, which is important. I'd hate to just eat seaweed and seafood day in, day out."

Lisette laughs nervously. "Yes. That's the goal. It's getting harder, though. The soil we have needs replenishment. It's from the gardens that the Platform workers originally made by the soccer fields. I have to keep finding new ways to add nutrients. Sometimes I dream about farming real fields."

"Lisette."

We all turn and look in the direction of the voice. A tall girl with white-blonde hair approaches us. Her face is full and circular like the moon. She's dressed in a loose fitting jumper made from sun shade material. Her wide hat is made from an old plastic light fixture. She squints at us. "I was looking for you. You and Memie left super early."

"Drees! These are my friends, Drayton and Joe."

I met Drees when I was younger and know she's albino, but I'm still fascinated by her lack of color. I try not to stare and stammer, "Pleased to meet you again."

Drayton says something to the same effect, and Drees looks at me with interest. "I remember you. Communications, right?"

"Right."

Drayton gets straight to business. "Lisette said you were working on the Bones virus. We were just talking about it."

"You were?" Drees asks.

"Yes. We were just curious. We know it wiped out millions, but do you think it's still active on Land?"

Drees looks at me, then Lisette. Lisette gives her an encouraging nod. "Just hypothetically, of course. I told them you were an expert on it."

"Let's go inside," Drees says. "The sunlight hurts my eyes."

We follow her into the house, and Lisette starts saying sorry for this or that being in the way, or not clean, or broken. "We don't get many visitors."

I pat her on the back, seeing we're stressing her out being in her space. "I've been here before, Lisette," I say and duck underneath a large vine held up with metal hooks nailed into the cement like spines. "Your house is lovely. Charming, really. Like a cottage in the woods in some of the old fairy tales we read in grade school."

"Thanks. But those stories always scared me. Everything was always a mess at the end. Or everyone died."

The interior of her home smells like dirt and gutted fish. Plants and dried fish hang from a coaxial cable that runs from the kitchen to the front door. Various pots and vegetation cover a small boat hull functioning as a sofa and two suspended chairs made of fishing nets. A mister is set up over the kitchen table, and several plants are submerged in the sink.

"Wow," Drayton comments. "There's so much vegetation."

"The PC gives us a double water allotment or none of this would be possible," Lisette explains to Drayton. "We cook in the bathroom—Dad set up a second kitchen there. I'll get chairs. They're in the back."

Which leaves us with Drees. She is clenching and unclenching her fists around the fabric of her dress. "Did Lisette tell you about my breakdown?"

"She said you were unwell. Exhausted," Drayton responds carefully.

Drees' hands relax. "Oh. So this is unrelated."

We both nod in unison.

Lisette returns with three folding chairs that screech when she opens them. Lisette sits on the floor and motions for us to sit down.

Drayton and I sit. Drees walks around the room, then eventually sits, too. "I study the virus. It's my specialty."

After a few seconds of silence, I prod Drees. "At Canaan's research station?"

"Yes. I researched the origins of the virus. It's a long process, but my preliminary findings indicated that it had mutated and jumped species from apes like other hemorrhagic viruses of that timeframe."

I nod. "We learned about them in health. They were nasty."

"So it would no longer be in the population?" Drayton asks.

"No," Drees says. Her face crumples like she is about to cry. "But there's more to it than that. I'm not supposed to tell you it was manmade, but it was."

Lisette gasps. I look at Drees blankly.

"Manmade as in it was genetically engineered?" Drayton asks.

Drees sobs. "Yes. The PC doesn't want anyone to know." She bows her head, and we can barely make out what she says next. "It came from Hermeneutic Labs. The genetic-splicing work was patented by the original Platform migrants. I was told to stay silent about it until my conclusions could be verified."

Lisette wipes the tears from Drees' face and hugs her. "Let me get you some water. You can have my ration today. I don't need it."

Drees takes a deep breath and continues. "No, no. Water won't help. The PC forced me to take a leave of absence, so I came home. I've been keeping it inside, but you asked, and I had to tell someone about it."

"Why didn't you tell us? Your family?" Lisette asks.

"You're embarrassed that I've been sent home."

Lisette shakes her head. "I'm not embarrassed. I'm glad you're here."

"Dad isn't."

Drees' voice is shaking, and I hate to ask more questions, but I need more answers. "What are they going to do with your findings?"

Her eyes fill with tears again. "Nothing. They say my testing was faulty. That I'm making it up. They'll never verify any of it. My career is ruined. But I know that I'm right. I tested and retested everything. The results were clear every time. I was first in my class here, and when I did my after studies on Canaan, I was second. I know what I uncovered. You can't hide where a virus comes from. It's like a signed map."

Lisette pats Drees' arm. "Of course you can't. It's like seeds that are developed for certain qualities—you can trace the breeders, the parent plants."

Drees begins to sob violently. "I'm not crazy."

Drayton stands and motions for me to stand as well. "I don't know you well, but I don't think that at all. I believe you."

"Maybe we should look at the gardens now," I add and mouth *sorry* to Lisette.

"You know where they are," Lisette says and holds her sister.

"Out the front door, around the back," I say to Drayton and drag him along with me. The back of the house looks much the same as the front, except that there is an enclosed greenhouse to protect more delicate plants from the wind on the rough side of the Platform. Lisette's dad is working on a tier of plant clippings inside. I smell the nearest flower.

"What are you doing?" Drayton asks.

"Smelling the flowers."

"How can you look at flowers when the biggest—" Drayton starts.

"Isn't this one beautiful," I say loudly. "I wonder if Lisette's mother or father worked on this project. Or Memie." I make a big deal about examining another plant. "Memie is the middle sister. Lisette dropped her off before coming to my house this morning. Her dad is working right there, in the greenhouse. PC Fristhe eats here with him regularly. Look at the garden. Don't miss your opportunity."

Drayton finally understands. He leans over the nearest plant container. "Why, yes. This plant should be edible if it isn't. It smells good enough to eat."

"It is. Mint is definitely edible."

Drayton smells the next plant. "This one, too. I can't imagine what we would do without edible plants."

"Starve." I move closer to Drayton. "Look, keep pretending. Her dad is tight with the PC."

"I already figured that out, super sleuth. I'm not an imbecile."

"Hmph." I lean over a box that has cactus-like flowers poking out of the dirt. "I wouldn't eat this."

"If you were hungry enough you would. Or sick enough."

I shoot Drayton a warning look. "Perhaps we should check out the progress of the hybrid plants. Lisette's parents were working on them last time I came." I casually take Drayton's arm in mine and lead him to the back of the yard. I feel how all the muscles in his body are clenched with pent-up rage. "Looks like they were successful at small scale hydra-farming," I say, pointing to the floating plant pods. "Which is important for our long-term continuance here in the middle of the ocean."

"We've been lied to," he whispers furiously.

I trail my fingers in the water. "Not here. Hold it together."

"Hey, guys. Father doesn't want you to poke around our projects too much. They're fragile."

Drayton and I spin around. Lisette is standing near the hydra pods that haven't been seeded yet.

"Sorry," we both say.

Lisette cuts us off. "I think you should leave now. Drees is in bad shape. Can you let Memie know that the car is at your house, Joe?"

"Of course. I'll send a message."

Drayton grabs my hand. "We're leaving. Thank you for the visit, Lisette."

We tromp through the garden and around the side of the house. When we get to the car, he opens the door for me and makes a flourish with his free arm when he shuts it. Two seconds later, he slides behind the wheel. He shuts his door and starts the engine.

"What the hell was that? Charades?"

Drayton puts the car in drive and pulls away. "Give me a minute."

"For what?"

"To get my head together."

I cross my arms across my chest and count to sixty. "All right, one minute. That was a whole lot of crazy. But we can't jump to conclusions. What if—"

"What if nothing." Drayton shakes his fist at the meter antennae in front of the Platform's cement mixing facility. "All these tracking meters, and the PC is a sham. We have to see Flox."

Flox was a key part of our protocol class. His botched fish experiment is the biggest "don't do this" we study. His experiments in DNA splicing in fish led to the death of a girl. I've seen him once or twice on the Platform but never up close, and I'm fine with that. He doesn't socialize, and I've heard stories. "Why?"

"He knows things about the history of the Platforms no one else does, and I'm ready to listen. We need to talk to him."

"When did you become close friends with Flox?"

"Salvaging."

Drayton turns off at the next viaduct. My house is only two viaducts away. "Drop me off and you go. I have to send a message to Memie anyway."

"Send it from here." Drayton hands me his pad. "We're still in range of the school. Don't worry. What you hear about Flox isn't half as bad as how he really is."

"Great," I say sarcastically and pull up the messaging application on Drayton's virtual pad. Everyone on the Platform is listed in the pad, so sending anyone a message is easy as long as you are in range, which at maximum is about four viaducts away. I find Memie's name, hit send, and wait for confirmation.

Drayton rolls his window down. "Coming through!"

Ms. Rastgou is in the middle of the road with her fishing gear. She wears tan-colored netting head to toe to protect her from the sun. I can barely see her face.

"Don't yell at her. She's an elder."

"She's deaf," Drayton says and waits for Ms. Rastgou to clear the roadway.

"She has to fish off the low docks. She can't climb down to her cage farm anymore. I bring her extra fish since Mom's gone."

"We all do."

Drayton turns off the road. After a quarter of a kilometer or so, he downshifts to get over a narrow bridge made of shells. I've never been over the shell bridge in this area, so I look around. Frames of old ships and other transportation devices dot both sides of the road. Oddly shaped pieces of rubber, signs mixed with plastic bottles, and other non-recyclable discarded junk are sorted into sizes and piled neatly in various areas. No one wants this stuff. "This is the junkyard for non-metered items. Trash."

"Yes. I come here to dig for scrap metal. That's how I met Flox. He started a conversation with me."

Once the space between piles gets too narrow for the car, Drayton parks and gets out. I'm tempted to stay behind, but he raps on my window, so I open the door. "I'm going to haunt you for eternity if anything happens out here."

"What a pleasant thought," Drayton says and shuts the car door.

We trample over piles of junk. Some of the mounds are unidentifiable, but I'm pretty sure we walk across a pile of bird bones. "This is creepy."

"Not much farther."

The narrow path opens into a small clearing. A house made of every kind of material and shape I can think of is built in the north corner. The roof is made from the side of a ship, and the door came from a rig control room. Stacked tires comprise the front and back walls, and the side wall nearest me is made of plastic containers with rags stuck between them. Stairs attached to a fourth wall made from mismatched orange and tan metal sheets lead to nowhere. Pieces of fish and seaweed in various stages of drying hang from most of the plastic containers. I have never seen—or smelled—anything like it.

"Holy hell."

Drayton stops at the edge of the clearing. "We need to wait here for permission to enter his yard." He cups a hand around his mouth. "*Hello!*"

A loud screech fills the clearing and I jump. The sound comes from a bullhorn attached to the front door.

"Drayton? Is that you?"

"Yes, Flox. I want you to meet my…" Drayton falters and looks at me. He clears his throat. "My girlfriend, Joe."

My mouth drops, but before I can say anything, the door of the house opens and Flox emerges. He's a spindly man with a cane fashioned from a seven-centimeter-wide metal pipe. He walks toward us with surprising speed and agility.

"A girl," Flox says.

Flox's hair is a shock of white, and his beard is long and filthy. His right eye is squinted permanently, and his left is wide and pitch black. A long feather is stuck in his hat, and his clothes are from the 1880s. He reeks of body odor.

"My girl," Drayton says defensively and puts his arm awkwardly around my shoulders.

Flox looks at me, then back to Drayton. "Then she is welcome."

"We have something to discuss with you."

"We, or you?" Flox asks.

"We," I say in a firm voice and remove Drayton's arm from my shoulder. "For the record, I'm my own girl."

"Ah, she speaks," Flox says and smiles. "Like a flower opening its petals. The sound of a woman's voice is such sweet music. Speak again."

Drayton nudges my arm.

I don't know what to say.

Drayton nudges me harder, and I look at him irritably before refocusing on the hermit before me. "Do you bathe, Flox? You should. I imagine there are water meter rations even out here for such a purpose."

Flox chortles. It's high pitched, like two shells scraping against each other. "Mellifluous even when the words are not. Enter."

Flox returns to his home and Drayton follows. I trail behind them. "Why can't we just hear what he has to say from out here?"

"Because he's paranoid," Drayton says under his breath and ducks to walk through Flox's front door.

"He stinks."

"We all stink, Joe. Some of us just hide it better. Scan in. Flox has the sensor scrambled, so the PC thinks Flox just went in and out of his house a bunch of times."

# Chapter Eleven

FLOX'S HOUSE IS EERILY SIMILAR to Drayton's. Every nook and cranny has some object lying on it in the process of being built or taken apart. Piles of metal and plastic create obstacle courses in each room. Various machines without their insides line one wall. Large sheets of glass and mirrors lean against another. Several tables have piles of parts like bones on them.

"How'd he scramble the sensor without tipping off the PC?" I whisper.

"Same way Harriet did, I bet. I'm still trying to figure it out. He won't tell me."

"Sit, sit," Flox says and cleans off an old piano stool.

I examine the stool before I sit on it. It is covered in fancy red tapestry. "Someone brought a piano stool from Land? Why not just bring a regular chair?"

Flox laughs so hard that he coughs violently. He takes out a stained, pale yellow handkerchief and wipes his lips. He folds it carefully and returns it to his pocket. "Please. I can't abide people standing around."

I sit cautiously on the piano stool. Drayton moves a pile of wire connectors and sits on a bench next to me. "The piano is right next to you underneath all of those gears and clock parts. The stool came with it."

"Oh," I say sheepishly.

"Many things were brought, many things were caught," Flox says in an ominous voice. "A lady in the house."

"Whose name is Joe."

"I have no pretty things to offer you. Trinkets, baubles, beautiful colored things. But you are here for a different purpose?" Flox smiles at us. There are gaping holes where teeth used to be, and the ones that are left look like rotting, jagged dock posts. I guess no one tells him when the PC dentist visits our Platform every six months. Or he just doesn't go.

"Yes," Drayton says. "I've researched your story about why you were discredited. It bears weight. There are holes in the case."

I look in shock at Drayton. "How? The PC doesn't release trial details."

"It's pretty easy to hack into the system if you know what you're looking for."

Flox pulls his goggles down over his eyes and ties a long paisley scarf around his neck. "But that's not why you're here."

"What do you know about the Bones virus?"

Flox stands up and crosses his hands over his chest like he is dead. "The Bones virus."

"Yes. Its origins. Can you shed some light on it?"

A light suddenly shines right on Drayton. I scream.

Flox laughs and waves a black remote around. "There you are. There's the light on it."

I stand on the piano stool and manually turn the light above Drayton's head off. Multicolored wires and ropes are attached to the ceiling. Lights and fishing pots dangle from them like fruit. Trawler arms provide the supports.

"I'm impressed that thing still works," I say and sit back down. "Remotes are hard to salvage."

Flox turns and leaves the room.

I look at Drayton. "Well, this is helpful. I've already used all my water for the day. I'm taking some of your rain water for another washing. This place is filthy."

"Patience. You can have the water. I've never believed him until now, but he knows about the PC. I blew him off last time he tried to show me."

Flox reappears with a stack of photographs. "I brought these from the other house. The PC doesn't know they are still in existence."

Drayton takes the photographs from him. "The one you were born in that you allege the PC burned?"

"Yes, yes, indeed. The only fire on Platform record, one day after my trial." Flox looks at the ceiling and makes an awkward cross-like motion. "My father, the unwilling migrant, kept these notes. They forced him to move here because he was a drilling expert. My mother never liked it. She was young and needed space. She had me late in life, then died."

Flox's face looks like it's melting. I don't want to see him cry. "I'm sorry. How old are you, Flox?"

"Ageless, my dear. Ageless."

Drayton hands me the photographs. "These carry heavy implications. Tidal."

I look at the photographs. One is of a lab, the next two of a group of people working in a lab. There are names underneath each figure. Many of the last names are on my class roster at school. The last photograph is of a viral structure labeled "*Di Bona.*" And Hermeneutic Lab's name is at the bottom.

"Di Bona is the scientist who…"

Flox jumps up and down. "Bingo! Founded the Platforms. Coincidence that my fish work was condemned and my house burned to the ground when I referenced the Di Bona method of DNA clipping and splicing at my defense? Coincidence? I think not."

Flox coughs himself into a fit. Drayton pounds him on the back. "Careful, Flox. Don't get so excited."

I'm confused. "I thought your work was condemned because of a human death."

Flox sputters, so Drayton answers me. "Flox worked in fish genetics. The project had promise, and we'd probably be eating more varieties of fish if he'd been allowed to continue his work. A colleague's child not related to the experiment visited his lab and died."

"The girl was allergic to shell fish," Flox says in a loud voice. "There were several species in the tanks with my fish, and her allergy was acute. I didn't ask her to put her hand in the water and touch them."

"That's terrible, Flox." I look at the picture again. This time I scan for my last name and my mother's maiden name. I don't find either. "So, the builders of the Platforms, the founding mothers and fathers of our society, were part of the creation of the Bones virus. Flox, why didn't you bring Hermeneutic Lab's involvement to the Council?"

Drayton answers me. "Flox left."

I look up. Flox had indeed slipped out. "Where'd he go?"

"He disappears sometimes. His social skills are almost nil now that he's been out here so long. I'll answer for him—because the Council has no real power. Not then, not now. Recognize any of the names of those who do have power?"

I look at the photograph again. "Lisette's last name—Theron. Some kids in our class. Chanko. Is that Chanko's last or first name?"

"Last. He won't answer to his first name—Reyansh. He hates it."

"You hang out with him still?"

"Yeah. He's working on his senior project here before he moves out to Bethany to reorganize their free spaces. He hits me up for spare parts sometimes. Besides that, he's a hermit."

Flox thrusts a cup in front of me, and I jump. I recognize the sweet scent from a special party my parents had when I was young. My dad's father had died on Neft, so the PC issued a special meter permit for a fish fry and celebration dance. Mom made me wear a dress. Nod's drum core had come with their plastic buckets and spoons, and Mr. Visco brought his guitar. It was one of the best nights of my life, dress excluded.

"For the lady," Flox says.

Drayton takes the cup from me. "That's very generous of you, Flox. But…"

I take the cup back and smile. "The lady won't be sharing it. Thank you, Flox." I tip the cup and take a sip. The liquid pools in my mouth, and I relish the sensory overload—sweet but tart. I swallow. "Like summertime. Completely tidal."

"What is that?"

"Apple juice. Which I'm happily drinking because I'm a lady."

Drayton shakes his head. "You old fox. Where'd you get apples?"

Flox whistles. "Around. They hang from the trees if you know where to look."

"Obviously," Drayton says.

I hand Flox the empty cup. "Thank you. That was dreamy. And generous. We've taken up enough of your time. Listen, if you need anything…"

"I will find your reference station and contact you," Flox says and winks at me. "I'm ahead of the game."

Drayton clears his throat. "Sorry, I told him about our after-hours channel. It just slipped out."

I wink back at Flox. "That's okay. I don't mind. Thanks for the apple juice."

Flox makes a low bow and almost falls down. I follow Drayton to the front door, and we both scan out. I shut the door firmly behind me. "I hate to leave him here. Why didn't you bring me to visit him before?"

"I didn't think you'd want to meet him."

"Hmph," I say and walk two steps ahead of Drayton. The sun has disappeared and large clouds are rolling in from the west. "Why's he coughing so much?"

"Pneumonia."

"Has he received any medical care? Pneumonia is serious for someone his age."

"I brought him medicine from Mom last week after I heard him rambling about the PC's culling. I thought it was just the fever talking. I should have asked more questions."

"There's no doubt it's all connected. This is a mess." A strong gust of wind whips across us, and I wrap my arms around my upper body. "Drees should know that there is photographic evidence. She'd feel better."

"I bet her parents already know. Her ancestor was on the original team. It's interesting that one generation uncovered a past generation's atrocity."

"It's ironic. But why the secrecy? They're all dead. Maybe we can go back to the Land, maybe not, but no one alive now would blame them for having ancestors that developed the virus that killed everyone."

Drayton open the car door for me. "You're assuming that they released the virus into the population. It could have been stolen and released."

I nod in thanks at his gentlemanly gesture and sink into the seat. I buckle my seatbelt, considering. "Why the hush-hush if it was stolen?"

Drayton slides into the driver's seat. "Exactly." He presses the gas and the front tires spin. "I'll need to change the tires soon. Again. Without new blacktop, the roads will be impassable in two years even if we can keep rebuilding the wood supports."

I roll my eyes. "Which you know we don't have access to. And I bet tires are getting hard to come by."

Drayton narrows his eyes and looks in the rear view mirror. "Yep. We have to go back to Land soon if we are going to maintain the infrastructure out here, no matter what this conspiracy is or isn't."

"Now it's a conspiracy."

Drayton turns the car on and puts it in gear. "Could be."

"Said the shark to his dinner." I close my eyes and let my mind drift away from the mind-shattering revelations I've learned today from Drees and Flox. I think about my dad, the See-Saw. What it would be like to finally hug Mom again. How awkwardly Drayton calls me his girlfriend.

# Chapter Twelve

"RISE AND SHINE." Drayton's voice cuts through my half sleep like a bucket of cold water.

"What?"

"We're here. And you snore. A lot. It's kind of cute."

I poke Drayton's arm. "I do not."

"Do too," Drayton says and laughs when I poke him again. "Just kidding. You don't. Come on, let's go."

I open the car door and realize we are at the sports complex. It's a deserted clearing on the last spar in the Complex. There are no houses, just two small original buildings that now serve as a toilet and changing area. Tall poles with lights on the top are every twenty yards or so, and two basketball hoops mark the edge of the nearest perimeter. The ground is made of worn-down turf, and there are lines carving it up. No one uses the complex for sports anymore, but during the summer, some kids Platform jump from the edge.

But it smells like decay today. "Why does it stink?"

"There's a big red tide on this side."

"So why are we here? I assume it's not to Platform jump. Because I'm not going to."

Drayton looks over my shoulder. "Chanko. And you do snore."

I spin around and Chanko is right behind me. He is carrying a plastic bucket full of wadded blue tarps. He is taller than I remember, and his face is leaner than it was in school. He is very much in shape and has the kind of dark, curly hair that always looks good. His green eyes seem vulnerable and kind, which make him even more intriguing.

"Oh, hi. How are you, Chanko?"

"Fine. You grew up."

"She did," Drayton says irritably.

"How's communications going?" Chanko asks me.

"Good. What are you doing out here?"

"I want to give new life to our existing community structures. Playgrounds. Soccer fields."

"This is a soccer field?" I ask. "Do people play soccer here?"

"No, but once I finish cleaning it up, I hope people will."

I know nothing about soccer, and less about fields, but say, "It's nice" because Chanko looks so hopeful.

Drayton interrupts us. "Let's get down to business. Did you see them?"

Chanko nods. "Moving lights, Land based. Eight or nine at a time. Didn't notice a pattern, but I don't know what to look for."

"You saw the lights from here?" I ask. "With what?"

"Binoculars. I did what you said, Drayton. It's super dark at night, so I set up the tripod right on the Platform's edge. I wouldn't have noticed them if I hadn't been looking for them. But they're out there."

Drayton exhales loudly. "Thanks for verifying. Did you get my message about your family and Di Bona?"

"Yeah, I remember some of that stuff from when we cleaned out Grandpa's house. Lots of photos on flash drives, so I'm directly connected. I can dig. Mom and Dad left all that here when they relocated."

"Okay. I'm going to need help."

Chanko nods. "I'm in." Drayton and Chanko shake hands.

"Stop talking around me," I say. "What are you in?"

"Chanko and I are going on an expedition."

I drop my jaw. "What?"

"Just a small one. To Land and back. We'll scan out and use Chanko's trawler. I'll tell the PC I have an interest in the mechanics of the arms and want to work on the hydraulics before I join Maintenance. PC Gramble will buy it. We can go there and back in two days, three tops."

Fear wells in my throat. "Absolutely not. Are you both insane? What a terrible, half-drowned idea. I don't know…"

Drayton lets out a yell. I jump, then follow his line of sight. A worker drone flies over the field. The size of a small outboard motor, it's gold and glints in the sunshine. It lingers in the center of the field.

Chanko throws a wadded up tarp at me. I catch it against my chest.

"Run!" Chanko yells.

Drayton takes the tarp from me and starts running to the end of the field. Chanko runs after and tackles him.

Sports. They're playing a game. I start running in a zig-zag. Chanko and Drayton run past me to the other end of the field, so I turn around and run in the same direction. The fake grass crunches beneath my feet. Drayton and Chanko toss the tarp ball back and forth.

The drone passes over us and flies toward central Nod. It isn't moving very fast.

"Catch!"

The tarp ball hits me square in the chest, and I sit down hard on the field. But I catch it.

"Great catch!" Chanko says and helps me up. He takes the tarp ball from me and throws it over my head to Drayton.

"It's gone. We can stop now."

Chanko grins. "But we're having fun."

"I'm not."

Drayton runs into Chanko, and they both fall on the field.

I shake my head. "Play time over. When's the last time you boys saw a drone?"

Drayton stands up. "Last storm. The PC used them to identify damage."

"And now. Let's go."

Chanko takes the tarp ball from Drayton. "I'll dig. Message you through the secret channel."

I frown. "Did you tell everyone?"

"Chanko isn't everyone," Drayton explains. "Good job acting, by the way. Much better than the third grade play."

"That was a terrible play. No one could have pulled that part off. The revolution leader had the personality of a raw crab claw."

"Truth," Drayton says. "Later, Chanko. Go to Flox's if in doubt."

Drayton and I get in the car. I let my emotions go, not realizing until this moment how they've been building up inside me since last night. "Drayton. I'm scared. Really scared. I don't want to go to Hades. Dad will be so disappointed. And there is no sleeping in, no running water. Prisoners mold metal all day. I hate metal."

Drayton enters the roadway carefully. "Don't worry. I'm out thinking the thinkers. First order of business is your See-Saw."

"My See-Saw?"

"Yes. It isn't safe. If the PC is hard scanning the Platform Complex with drones, the signal will be picked up. You left the receiving station on?"

"Yes, in case we get an answer. It'll record it."

A cement work truck passes us on the left, and Drayton presses the Yellow Dream against the side rail. It's too close for comfort, but the truck gets around us. Drayton honks and waves at the driver. "Mac never drives the speed limit. Claims his sensor's broken all the time. I need to see how he's rigged it."

I could care less about Mac or the speed limit. "Focus, Drayton. I'm taking the See-Saw off line. The PC will ask for a record of findings. I don't know if I can delete the records from the transducer."

"They haven't found it yet. Let me think."

Drayton's words rub me the wrong way. I'm not a moron. "I'm thinking, too. I'm not good at being super sneaky."

Drayton stops at a viaduct that has a drawbridge. A tall ship moves though, and the bridge looks like a mouth with its jaws opened wide. Fasoul, the drawbridge operator, comes to the car and scans our wrists. Drayton makes small talk with him, and I keep thinking about my See-Saw. So much work down the drain.

The tall ship passes, and Fasoul returns to the control enclosure. He closes the bridge. The gears screech, and I put my hands over my ears. Fasoul waves us through.

"He's a pleasant fellow," Drayton says. "Strange ideas about hydraulics, but nice enough."

And that does it. I'm annoyed. "My See-Saw is on the line because of your stupid interest in Land, and all you can talk about is Fasoul and hydraulics?"

Drayton looks surprised. "No. I said I would think about it, and I'm going to. I'll figure out a—"

He stops in front of my house, and I don't let him finish his sentence. I get out of the car. I don't tell him goodbye before I take the steps two at a time, scan myself into my house, and slam the door behind me.

"Who does he think he is?" I yell and kick my shoes off.

I'm mad, and I'm hungry. I walk into the kitchen and rummage around in the dried goods. The choices are slim, but at least there are choices.

"He thinks he's some kind of awesome," I say to a handful of dried seaweed.

The front door opens, and I spin around to tell Drayton how un-awesome he really is. Except it isn't Drayton. It's PC Fristhe. I have a major flashback to the night he told us Mom was on extended assignment but hold myself together.

"Can I help you?"

"I rang the bell," PC Fristhe says and looks around the living room. His hair is cut too short for the shape of his head. His sash fits snugly over his chest, and one shrimp boot is shorter than the other. "You didn't answer, but since I saw you enter, I took the liberty to scan myself in. Your scanner is no longer level."

PC Fristhe picks up one of Mom's pottery vases. It's a knick-knack, but I hate that he touches it.

"It still functions. I know the PC has more important things to attend to."

"Indeed, we do," PC Fristhe says. He studies the living room wall. Mom had arranged dark, plastic junk salvage to look like the night sky. She outlined the constellations that represent our birthdays. "But you should still report it. That boy, Drayton, drove away fast. I thought something may have happened. Like another almost accident."

I put my hand around the skillet on the kitchen stove. I try to sound high schooly. "No accident. He's just a stupid boy doing stupid boy things he shouldn't do around girls. Especially not best friend girls."

"Well, those things happen with boys. And girls." PC Frithe puts his hands in his pockets and stares at me.

A shadow cuts across the front door, and I know Drayton is waiting and listening. I sigh in relief. I am not alone. "Thank you."

"No word from your mom yet?"

PC Fristhe has access to all the communication pads that come through the mail ship, so I know that he already knows the answer. "No."

"What a shame," he says. "I'll send Maintenance to fix the scanner." He scans his wrist and closes the door behind him.

I let the handle of the skillet go and wait ten seconds before I run down the hallway to my room. I push the sign over the window out of the way and press my face to the glass. Drayton's face is serious and his eyes dart from me to the side of the house. I hold up my index finger. One finger is Mom; Dad, two. I run to Mom's room and slide the window open. Drayton is waiting, and I throw the red fabric down to him. He grabs the end and walks up the side of my house.

"Sneaking around was easier when I was smaller," Drayton huffs and lands in a heap on Mom's floor.

I help him up. "Everything was easier when we were smaller."

Drayton pulls me into his arms. He holds me tightly for a moment, then lets me go. "Let's lock every window and the emergency lock on the door. You take the back, I'll take the front. Don't leave anything unsecured. Those worker drones are versatile, but they can't neutralize locks yet. Or record through the window tint. Neither can the PC. Meet you in your room."

Drayton's voice is urgent and it frightens me. "All right," I say and methodically lock each window. We've never locked the windows before—they all have monitoring scanners—so some of the latches are hard to turn. I finally clean enough rust off the bathroom window lock to turn it and return to my room. Drayton is waiting by my laptop.

"It's going to get hot."

"Better hot than cold. I need to check the See-Saw logs."

"Exactly. I couldn't get past your password. What is it?"

I step around Drayton and type my password. It's my mom's name spelled backwards with Drayton's initials interspersed between the letters. "None of your business."

"Secretive. Someone should know it."

I open my See-Saw's program and command it to filter the collected data. "Someone does."

"All right, fine. Did you notice Lisette's sister's excuse for a car is gone, and it isn't the end of the work day yet?"

"No. I didn't notice. I was…wait. Where's your car? PC Fristhe said you drove off."

"Two houses down behind the Grafs'. They're both at work. I know you were mad, Joe, but you have to think. You can't just storm off like that. Something is going on. Something big. We need to stick together."

"I'm sorry." I put my hand on Drayton's shoulder. "You and Dad are all I've got, Drayton."

"Thanks. But don't forget about Lisette."

"And Lisette." I let my hand drift down Drayton's arm. It's comforting that he is solid and present and real.

"Any reply in the data?"

I shake my head. "I'll take it off line."

Drayton's phone buzzes. "I've got a message."

"That is why phones buzz."

Drayton makes a face and reads. "Whoa! Hold up!"

"What?"

"Chanko hit pay dirt. Pull this up on the laptop."

I switch programs and pull up Drayton's device. I search for the message log, then display it on the screen.

Drayton leans over me. "He attached files. Full screen, please."

I select the files and start a slideshow. The pictures are blurry, but they explain why things are getting messy. Dr. Di Bona kept a lab journal, and his assistant, Dr. Chanko, didn't throw it out when he fled to the Platforms. He created digital files of each page.

I read entry after entry with Drayton. I feel sicker and sicker as I read about results from animal, then human trials. I quit reading after the entry where Dr. Di Bona modified the viral load so only the strongest immune system could survive viral contraction. This journal is black-and-white proof that the Bones virus was developed and released by Hermeneutic Labs.

"He wanted to wipe out young children and the elderly," I say to Drayton. "Anyone with a repressed immune system—any disease at all, asthma even. Simple allergies."

"But he made sure his employees and their offspring were the best stock possible. Linked up with laboratories near all major Platforms in the world. Arabia, Azerbaijan, the Gulf. The man was a genius. Maniacal, but a genius."

I sit on my bed. A warped idea develops in my mind. "How did they take the Platforms over?"

"They were *supposed* to already be deserted. The Moralists emptied them and planned to blow them up. But we're thinking the same thing, I bet. The inhabitants were shipped back to Land or told to walk the proverbial plank."

I gulp.

"All right, it's a theory. Doesn't mean it's true. But at least we know what's up. And that maybe the PC knows what's up. And it's only three in the afternoon."

"Should we tell Lisette?"

"Lisette…" Drayton drawls out her name. "No. She's too close to the center of this."

"Okay. I'll check the signals again tonight. Document."

"Then Chanko and I will make the Land trip and blow the whistle. The PC needs to be brought down."

I shut my laptop. "I think you need to slow your swim down. If we take out the damning parts, we can tie this to my research and come clean with the PC. The Council…"

"Will not think twice about turning us into the local PC. No, we have to go on this. Be ready with the See-Saw to document any communication after lights out. Drones can't operate at night. Not yet. Don't let anyone in except your dad. If the PC comes, get out of here. Go to Flox's."

"You're leaving?" I ask. I don't like the idea of being home alone. Not now.

"I have to plan this Land expedition, which won't be easy with drones on the loose."

I shiver. The PC could be watching my house, watching me. So is Harriet. There's no escape when you live in a metal can. I pull out the grappling hook and rope from under my bed. "Okay. I'll help you out. Harriet left this."

"Good to have."

We return to Mom's room. Drayton scans the sky before he slides the window open. Clear. He sets the grappling hook and tests his weight. "You know the safe word, right? Remember where to go?"

"I do," I say. Drayton and I had developed a safe word after I almost drowned in case anything happened and we needed to find each other without the adults knowing. I know he thought it up originally to make me feel better. "Because it'll help me not drown, right?"

"No, but…"

"Teasing. Eiffel. I remember."

"All right. Later."

Drayton rappels the ten feet and drops to the Platform. I pull the rope in, slide the window shut, lock it, and lean on the sill.

I'm alone. I turn around and look at Mom's masks. Even the walls have eyes.

I scurry back to my room and lock myself in. I look at my laptop, then at the receiving station in the corner of my room.

"What have I done?" I whisper.

# Chapter Thirteen

MY ROOM FEELS LIKE AN OVEN. "Damn," I say and look at my wristwatch. It's set to my pad's timer, and it's only 7 p.m. It isn't dark yet, so I can't activate the See-Saw.

I hear banging. It's coming from outside my room.

"Who's there?" I ask. My mouth is dry, and I wish I wasn't scared. I also wish the door had a peephole, but it doesn't.

I hear a muffled response, then a loud *"Dinner."*

I open the door and Dad is standing in the hallway. He really needs a haircut. Mom used to do it for him. "Why is everything locked up? I had to find the key to get into my own house."

Dad's voice is uneven, which means he's perturbed and trying not to show it. I shrug my shoulders nonchalantly and try to play it off. "I thought we could use a little security, especially now that you're working so much."

"On Nod? Whatever for?"

I think quickly. "Harriet."

"Why is this girl a problem? Do we have to lock this home down because of one of your—"

"Not friend," I cut in. I make a joke. "Drayton's mom keeps the Twinkies they have left under lock and key."

Dad raises his eyebrows. "They still have Twinkies?"

I nod.

"Well, we don't. Dinner. Not Twinkies. A dinner a day…"

"Keeps hunger away." It's the same phrase Dad always uses. "Sounds great."

"The potatoes are mysteriously harvested," Dad says.

"Lisette, the girl you let in this morning, looked over our plants today. They were ready to be cooked, so she dug them up for us."

"Oh. I wondered. You do your chores, and I'm grateful, but domesticity is not something you enjoy. Your mom spoiled us."

She did. And deep down, I know she loves us. "You need a haircut, Dad."

"I know."

Dad prepares a solid meal—greens from the garden and the leftover potatoes that Lisette harvested this morning. He makes crab for himself. I help out by handing him ingredients and cooking utensils when he asks for them.

"Dinner is served." Dad puts a bowl made from a car headlight in front of me. He puts a matching headlight bowl in front of him.

My stomach gurgles. "I'm hungry, and this is great. Minus the crab." I take a few bites of food. The potatoes are dry but tolerable. The greens are overcooked and wilted. "I do like potatoes."

"You hated everything except potatoes when you were a baby. It was a sad day when we ran out of potatoes."

"I didn't know I was a fussy eater."

Dad looks at me fondly. "You still are. Always have been. Your mom used to say you inherited that from me. She'll eat anything."

The table feels really empty. I shovel food in my mouth. Dad clears his throat and talks about *Galileo* and preliminary testing strategies. It's interesting, so I understand why he is so excited, but I don't offer any opinions.

"When is graduation?"

"Next week. You don't have to come. You should make it to the fish fry afterward, though. Mrs. Pasche was asking about you."

"I want to come."

"Okay, but you don't have to. I understand. Your research is important."

Dad puts down his fork. "Look, I know I've been distant, but I care about you and what you do. I'm your dad. I love you."

"Thanks, Dad." The conversation is beyond uncomfortable. The way we function without Mom is so complicated I don't even know where to start. I feel like I'm drowning in the shallows. "I love you, too." My words sound like "I love you but I miss Mom," and I feel expressively inadequate.

I have to get out of the kitchen. I push away from the table and put my dish and fork in the sink. "I'll clean up later, okay? I need to work on my senior project."

"I'll get them. Go ahead."

I know he'll forget to wash the dishes. He always does. "Thanks for dinner and the conversation."

Dad looks at me sadly but doesn't say anything.

"Okay then," I mutter and retreat to my room.

"Wait. Did you write to your grandmother that you were graduating?"

I lean against the door to my room. "I did. She can't come. It's mid-rotation."

"Oh. I'll see her next time she's in. Talk to her."

"She hasn't heard from Mom either."

Dad looks away. "She must be busy."

"Yes." I close the door softly. "Heavy," I say and sit at my desk. I haven't seen grandmother since Mom left. She lives on a deep sea research vessel that docks at Nod every three to six months. She always brings clothes for me and fruit for Mom. I miss her, too.

"Eye on the prize," I say and shake myself out of the doldrums. I open my laptop and set up a series of pings, then wait. I receive three signals in a row, three times in a row, almost immediately.

"And there's your answer, Drayton." Other pings start coming in before I can analyze the time and frequency. I'm filtering them through my Morse code application when my phone starts buzzing. I pick it up and read the text.

*Eiffel.*

Safe word. I don't think, I just do. I close the See-Saw program immediately, then take the legs off the receiving station and hide them in the loose metal paneling behind my bed. I shove the body of the receiving station and my laptop into a backpack.

"The schematics," I murmur and rummage through my desk drawers. I stuff every diagram of the See-Saw into the backpack.

I grab my phone and text back.

*Tower falling.*

I put the phone in my pocket and hoist the backpack around my shoulders. I walk to the door, then remember the charging pad. I grab it and stuff it on top of everything else and come to a dead stop.

Dad.

I hesitate for a moment then turn the door handle. Dad is still at the kitchen table. He looks up at me briefly, then back to his laptop screen. The schematics of Galileo are pulled up. Dad is inputting notes. The dishes are still on the table.

"Getting some air," I mumble. I walk around him and out onto the screen porch. I'm sad. I've been scared to love him too much because he's the only parent I have left.

But I can't think about that now. I look at the sea hole then down at the water. I fight my fear and take a deep breath. At least I'd had a trial run. I crouch on the floor and swing myself through the opening. I make it to the edge of the house bar by bar without a problem.

I press both feet firmly onto the Platform and duck so that I am below the sight line of the road. I run thirty yards along the side of the house, then sprint across the open area before the sea wall dips down below road level again.

Now it's easy going because I'm not visible from the houses or road. I put my hand on the sea wall to steady myself. The path is only three feet across. One wrong step and I'll be in the ocean swimming for my life, dead, or clinging to a Platform leg until I'm rescued.

The thought of my demise doesn't scare me so much as depress me. I've done nothing with my life, gone nowhere. I've only started to imagine what I want to do, want to discover. Who I want to be. I want more of everything. I slow down and continue on the path more carefully until I reach the wreckage yard.

Most of the strip-salvaged or broken-beyond-repair boats and cars are brought to the wreckage yard for storage. Twice a year, the PC sends ships to gather the metal. They melt it down on Hades, mold it, then send us back new metal sheets to make repairs and add to new projects. It's never enough, but some of the boats have always escaped major salvage because of lack of resources and time.

One of them is named *Eiffel*.

I continue in the shadows, but travel toward the left central area of the yard. I pass two small crafts—the *Nina* and the *Lover's Call*. I lean into the side of the *Some Of It's Magic* when I reach her. She's an old tugboat missing her engine, winch, and propeller. I know because Drayton and I stripped her parts one summer.

Hulls of ships seem to stretch into infinity, but after a few more minutes, I find the *Eiffel*. But no Drayton. "Where are you,

Drayton?" I whisper and tuck myself into the shadows beneath the leaning side of the ship to wait. The wind is brisk, and I wish I had brought one of my mom's thick sweaters. I've outgrown mine.

I hear a metallic screech on my right, like someone is scraping a piece of metal across the floor, and I tense up, hyper vigilant. A drone buzzes past the *Eiffel*. I hold my breath. The drone continues on, and I hear another screech. I don't have a weapon, so I drop to my knees and feel around for anything that I can use to defend myself.

A figure materializes from the neighboring wreckage. It's too tall to be Drayton. It backs toward me, and I grab a rusted piece of metal piping and hold it firmly in both hands. I count one, two, three, then strike out.

The metal connects with something hard.

"Hey, ow," I hear.

"Chanko?"

"Man, that was a solid hit." Chanko rubs his bicep. "That's going to bruise."

I drop the metal pipe and shove Chanko into the shadows. "Why are you sneaking around? I just saw a drone."

"I'm still in pain. Only Drayton's girl would know how to hit like that."

"I. Am. Not. Drayton's. Girl."

"Oh, sorry. I thought you were."

I give Chanko a drop-dead look. "No. What are you doing here?"

"Rescuing you before you knock me down or maim me. Come on."

I stand my ground and cross my arms. "Not without Drayton. Where is he?"

"Not his girl, huh?"

"Nothing to do with it. This has to do with friendship. Ever heard of it?"

"I've heard of it. So let's be friends. And leave."

"Not without Drayton. I can rescue myself if I need rescuing."

Chanko's face turns serious. "Fine. Because the tower is falling. The *Eiffel* tower to be exact. Satisfied?"

Drayton wouldn't have told anyone the second part of our secret code unless it was absolutely necessary. "What's the password?"

Chanko looks at me blankly. "He didn't say anything about a password."

"Right answer. Let's go."

I follow Chanko down the winding, shell-paved path between the wrecks. When we come to the edge of the yard, he turns away from the road. We weave and climb through rows of stacked recycling. It's dark, but I recognize piles of driftwood and usable barge trash. It smells like ten-day-old fish.

"Why are we in the recycling plant? It's smelly."

Chanko puts his finger to his lips and points to the water. He stops short a few steps later and intones a long, low whistle. He crouches on the Platform lip. "Follow me. We're on the same team."

"I'm not taking another step until you tell me where Drayton is. Seriously. And as far as teams go, I'm on my own team, not a team with you. What the hell is—"

"Drone!" Chanko tumbles forward, right off the edge of the Platform.

I gulp. The ocean stretches before me, empty and churning. I don't look down. I'll never jump if I look down. Time slows. *Tower falling* echoes in my mind. Drayton's smile. The way he never lets me have the last word, ever. How his eyes are the color of the sky some days, the color of the sea the next. I see the drone.

I move my backpack to the front of my body and jump.

# Chapter Fourteen

I LAND IN A PILE OF OLD TIRES. It doesn't hurt, but it knocks the breath out of me.

"Joe!" I know the voice before I see Drayton's face hovering above me. He has on a bright headlamp.

I'm alive. And I'm mad. "Why'd I have to jump, you idiot? For all I knew, it could've been into the sea like at my house!"

Drayton helps me up, and I check to make sure none of the bones in my back or butt are broken.

"It got real," Drayton says. He slips a headlamp with a strap on my forehead. "We had to move."

I adjust the strap to fit more comfortably over my pile of hair. "Where'd you get the headlamps?"

"Dad's night supplies for trash salvaging with his salvage group. I took ten. Looks like we may need them."

I touch the headlamp. The tiny solar panel sticks up like an antenna. "For what?"

"I'll explain inside. Did the drone spot you?"

"It's not here, so obviously not." I look around. The pile of tires is actually in the forward part of a medium-sized liftboat. Three spires push up to almost Platform height. The captain's quarters stick up from a completely flat surface the length of a three-story building. Stacks of tires are tied together with ropes and latched to the deck. "Why couldn't I just climb down?"

"Because the leg jacks are sheer," Drayton says and motions me forward. "Let's go inside. Please."

"Inside," I mimic, but I cross the deck and enter the captain's quarters.

The captain's quarters has been refurbished to be a living space and command center. The controls and steering mechanisms look new. Pots and pans line the wall to the right in a haphazard fashion over a stove. Two sleeping bunks made from double shower stall doors are bolted on top of each other. Several chairs are pulled into the center area, and closets and cupboards make up the other wall. "Whose vessel is this?"

"What is beauty, I ask you? Better yet, where is the eye that sees it?"

I blink my eyes, and Flox appears, leaning against the wall. "Flox?"

Flox makes an elaborate bow. "Welcome to *The Fluddery Doo*, my lady."

It's like a line from every bad movie that Drayton and I watched on the pads, and we've watched all the ones stored on Nod's Land resource link. Except now I'm starring in one of the worst of the worst.

I turn and look at Drayton. "*The Fluddery Doo*? Who names a liftboat *The Fluddery Doo*?"

"It's a solid vessel. The controls and outside hull are retooled. I checked them. She's a beauty of a ship, never been salvaged. She'll get us there."

I look from Flox to Drayton. "Get us where?"

Chanko closes the exterior door and smiles. "Well, we only need to rescue one more, and we'll be on our way."

"On our way where, Chanko?" I ask, although I know exactly where we are going. I just want to hear someone say it.

"Land. Didn't Drayton tell you? He said he was going to tell you."

"No, he didn't. And that's funny, because I don't particularly want to go to Land. I'm perfectly content right where I am. Or where I was. Up there with my See-Saw and Dad."

"Was just getting to it," Drayton says apologetically. He finds a life vest in one of the stuffed closets and hands it to me. "A transport ship with important cargo is coming in tomorrow. Two members of the PC will be aboard. You know what that means."

I do know what it means. It means trouble. PC members never travel in pairs unless it's a trial or a removal—too many Platforms to cover. "And you know this…"

"Flox heard about the ship. Chanko was notified that his cousin was coming for a visit two days ago. Chanko needs to check his messages more often."

Chanko smiles sheepishly. "I don't usually open messages from the PC."

*The Fluddery Doo* is rolling. So are my stomach and my head. "How does all that information combine to mean that we have to go to Land? Right now, at night, in the dark, on choppy water. It's a recipe for shipwreck. The PC couldn't have heard about your speech yet. The visit isn't connected to us, I bet. I could continue, but I'll let you answer."

"The water is always moving, lady," Flox says from behind me. "It's the sea. If it were still, we'd be in trouble. That's when the days turn into hours until death."

Drayton adjusts knobs on the control booth. "You're so poetic, Flox. The PC raided my house. Took the telescope. Pretty sure I'm going to be relocated. It wasn't the speech. Looks like I don't hack as well as I think I do."

Fear grips me. "How did you escape?"

"Mom," Drayton answers sheepishly. "She is one persuasive woman. She made Gramble and Fristhe disinfect before entering her work area, which is where I was. Gave me time to jump and run. Literally—I jumped out the window and swam to Mr. Neiri's pontoon. He saw me but didn't let on. Climbed up to the Platform from there. Ran to Flox's."

Chanko adds, "I didn't even make it back to camp. Saw more drones over my work area, headed to Flox's."

"I am a destination," Flox sings.

Only yesterday, things were normal. I woke up, I ate, I went home, I went to sleep. Everyday, normal stuff. I didn't know how much I liked normal until now. "How does all this translate to *me* having to go to Land right now?"

Drayton points to the antennae on the front of the boat. "Scanners. You're involved. So is Lisette. Flox. They'll eventually connect the dots even though Flox jams his scanner signal. You can stay and be rounded up, or come with us."

I think about my dad, alone, working on *Galileo*. Then I picture PC Gramble and Fristhe tearing our house apart. "Dad. Stupid scanners."

Flox slaps his thigh. "Don't worry. I jammed the antennae on this sweet lass. Zip, zip and tally ho! We go!"

The vessel begins to move through the water.

"Well done, Flox," Chanko comments. "It slices the water like a sharp knife through a dead fish."

"Beauty is all in the ear of the listener," Flox says and sits down next to Drayton at the control booth. "Don't worry about your speech. Had to be said."

I can't stand it. "One, that's gross Chanko. Two, the quote is about eyes and beauty, Flox. And three, aren't we a little too close to the Platform? Can you control this vessel so near the tension legs?"

"Flox knows what he's doing," Drayton says. "His navigation skills are the best of the best. It's nice to see this beauty finally in use. It was a crime to have it tethered."

I feel sick from the top of my head to the bottom of my feet. "Wait. This is the liftboat that was in the dry dock by the moon pool?"

"One and the same," Drayton responds sheepishly.

"You stole the Platform Complex's liftboat?"

"They stole it from me," Flox says. He shakes his finger at the ceiling. "Technically, I reclaimed it. She's been very bored in that dry dock."

"You are talking to a vessel, Flox," I snap. "Don't you think they'll notice it's missing? Like soon?"

"Curfew," Chanko says. "No one's out except the PC and the drones. I doubt they'll notice. It's below eye level."

Drayton interrupts us. "I need your help, Joe. What's the best way to get Lisette out of her house?"

"Fire always works!" Flox shouts. "Set the light, see them run!"

"Settle down, Flox. No fire," Drayton says. "Joe?"

The boat rolls, and I grab Chanko for support. "I was going to say fire."

"Not helping," Drayton says. "What would Lisette come out for? Did you ever talk about having a girl's night?"

"Don't be ridiculous. Why can't I just text her to come out?"

"I bet the PC is listening. Those drones have receivers."

"Right. Maybe a rare plant? Maybe they aren't tracking all frequencies. I can set up a closed channel."

Drayton nods thoughtfully. "I brought a spare receiving station from Flox's."

"I brought mine, too." I realize my backpack has been on the front of me this whole time. I take it off and put on the life jacket. "And everything referencing my See-Saw. They'll have a time trying to get info from it."

"I knew you'd be on task," Drayton says and opens my pack. He takes out my laptop and sets it up on top of the stove.

"I can do that."

"Take a minute to catch your breath. Get used to the roll of the ship. I can help."

I stare at Drayton. Something has definitely shifted in our friendship. And I don't know if I like it. "I can do it. I'm not made of glass. I'll let you know when I start throwing up. Better yet, I'll throw up on you."

"Let the lady have her laptop," Flox says. "Come help me look for stray buoys. I can smell them, but I can't see them."

Drayton steps aside, and I start the set up for the new receiving station. "I'd rather use my receiver going forward, since I know exactly how it operates. But it's good to have a backup." I wait for my laptop to process my set up commands. "Speaking of backups…what's the backup plan here for getting to Land if this vessel sinks?"

"Swim," Chanko says at the same time Flox says, "Don't drown."

"Great." I get the receiver on line. The connectivity looks good. "Everything should be linked in. Can you check the receiving station, Chanko? There should be three rows of blinking lights."

Chanko looks at the side and top of the receiver. "Check. It's working."

"Okay," I say and pull up the address for Lisette on my phone.

**Lisette. Nice visit today. I saved what I think is a new plant species.**

I wait. The reply is swift and typical Lisette.

**Ooh! Water or soil bound?**

"Water or soil bound? She's asking." No one responds, so I decide for myself.

Water bound.

"Is she biting?" Drayton asks.

"Patience. You can't rush conversation with Lisette. I'm hoping that water bound is more interesting to her than soil bound."

**Cool. Keep it hydrated. I want to see it.**

I type quickly. **What about now? I'm afraid I will kill it somehow. I know it would be happier with you.**

"Weak," I say and shake my head. "She knows I wouldn't care this much about a plant."

"Drees needs to be with her," Drayton says. "I hacked the communication logs from Flox's. PC Gramble has her marked for the institution on Salem Platform. They're transferring her tomorrow."

I shake my head. "That's so wrong. Lisette isn't answering."

"Then try something different," Chanko says. "We'll be on the other side shortly, and we need to get out to open sea. Someone is bound to notice a liftboat sailing past their house. They'll hear us. Watch the wake, Flox."

"Get moving or get caught," Flox sings. "Drown with the fishes, the fishes, the fishes."

"Let's not do that," I mutter. I decide to go epic.

**Code red. SOS. Big news. Drayton is on his way to pick you and Drees up.**

"I went all in. Drama like I've never spouted before in my life. Waiting for a response."

Flox begins to sing again. His voice is strangely beautiful, and I recognize the tune. It's a sea shanty about Davy Jones' locker. I swallow. I have no interest in firsthand knowledge of Davy Jones or his locker.

**All right. We'll leave here shortly. We'll wait outside.**

"How long before we reach her house? I'm worried about drones. Chanko, how are you going to do this?"

Chanko smiles. "Five minutes. Memie dumped me, not the rest of the family. I'll be nice."

*The Fluddery Doo* shudders. I hold on to the stove to keep myself steady. "As tragic as that is, I meant how are you going to get them here? Drees is in no condition to jump."

"Her parents receive transports all the time, so their receiving dock is perfect," Drayton says. "Chanko can climb up to it easily. Small jump down. Tell her to go out the back and stay away from the front yard. I have to tie off. You're with me, Chanko."

Drayton and Chanko secure the door behind them. I type.

**Five minutes. Avoid your front yard. There are—**

I pause a moment and try to think of what could be dangerous in Lisette's front yard.

**—holes and it's dark.**

"So unimaginative." I'm disappointed in my lack of creativity. Lisette doesn't reply. "Well, it's 50/50 she told her father. And it's 50/50 that we're going to be caught and expelled from this Platform."

Flox appears next to me, and I almost scream. He puts his fingers on top of my lips. They smell like burnt fish. "Lie low and feel the vessel speak to you. Let her murmur you into relaxation. It's rough on this side of the Platform."

I step away from Flox. "Right."

Flox lies on the floor of the cabin. He crosses his arms over his body and closes his eyes. The boat rolls, and I grab my laptop. After another roll, I flatten my body on the floor next to Flox and close my eyes, too.

I name every star in the solar system I know. I make up names for the ones I don't know. After that, I name all of the elements in the periodic table. I start on the names of great mathematicians when I hear a series of thumps on the deck.

Flox sits up. I sit up, then lie back down as my stomach is even more upset than before.

"Any second now," Flox says and stations himself by the cabin door. He has a wrench in his left hand. That makes me feel better.

"Chanko," Flox says when the door opens. "Success!"

"What happened?" Drayton say immediately after. "Did she fall down?"

I groan. "I'm seasick, you idiot, if you mean me."

"Joe."

I recognize Lisette's voice and make a real effort to sit up. "Lisette. I'm sorry about the—"

Lisette's arms are around my neck before I can finish the sentence.

"I was about to run away with Drees. I don't know where we were going to go, maybe to your house. They want to send Drees to Salem! And Father is acting strange. He keeps saying we need to purge the garden. We've never purged the garden. I mean, how can we purge the garden? Everything is alive in the garden!"

I look over Lisette's shoulder. Drayton is supporting Drees.

"Good. I'm glad. About Drees and you, not the garden. Now let me lie here and die a slow death."

Drayton motions to Flox. "Get her going."

Flox raises both hands over his head in a strange salute. "To the Land. To the shore. To the island of Nevermore."

"To the Land coordinates Joe has is far enough," Drayton says. "I'll go untie us."

The ship rolls, and I hear a loud thump.

"What was that?" Chanko asks.

"Who was that is the better question," Drayton says and opens the cabin door. Chanko and Drayton run outside.

*The Fluddery Doo* pitches to the left, and I clamp my lips shut to hold down vomit. I imagine real ground underneath my feet.

# Chapter Fifteen

DREES RAMBLES ON about genetic sequencing. Lisette tries to comfort her. I attempt to concoct a plausible explanation for the PC about where we are, what we're in, and the equipment we have with us and fail. Drayton and Chanko are outside apprehending whoever jumped aboard. Flox starts the motor, picks up his wrench, and waits by the door.

"Is that Flox?" Lisette whispers to me as she strokes Drees' back.

"In the flesh." I turn over so that I am face down on the floor of the boat. My insides feel like a three-day-old, uncooked sponge. "Have him tell you his story later when we're all cellmates on Hades. He's quite the misunderstood ladies' man."

Lisette stares at me. "He…"

Drees screams. Lisette wraps her arms around her and rocks her like a child. "PC Fristhe ran all kinds of tests on her after you guys left. Now she's in shock. All she talks about is genetics and the virus. She hasn't slept since she got home, and now she's babbling incoherently."

"Stop that screaming," Flox demands. "Or we'll all go down with the ship. I refuse to see fish at night. They're more attractive during the day when you can appreciate their coloring."

From the floor, the scene is skewed and almost funny. Screaming woman, crazy old man, poor Lisette ministering to everybody on a stolen ship full of kids wanted by the PC—but I don't laugh. This is real.

"Lay her down on the bunk, Lisette. Flox, do you have any calming Illegalities on board?"

Flox opens a cupboard and takes out a flask. "I may have brought along a flask to restore my constitution. I'm recovering from a nasty illness."

"Can Lisette have it for Drees? She's delirious."

Flox looks at the flask then at Drees. He sniffs and hands the flask to Lisette. "Sparingly. Many spirits are bottled within."

"Thank you," Lisette says and hurries back to Drees' bunk. She opens the flask's cap and puts it to Drees' lips. "Drink. Just one little sip."

Drees swallows and coughs. Lisette's face is pinched and worried. Some strands of dark brown have escaped her braid, and she looks wild and strange in this new setting. So must I. I'm a fugitive on the floor of a decommissioned, stolen liftboat trying not to puke my guts out. I grimace so I don't actually throw up.

"Rough seas means a good voyage," Flox says when Lisette returns the flask. He takes a swig, then returns it to the cupboard. "Always one for luck. It comes in waves, on waves, through waves."

"Give it a rest, Flox. I can't take verse right now. I'm dying here."

Flox spins the wrench in his hand like it is a drumstick. After several seconds he begins to laugh hysterically, then coughs, then cackles. He opens the cabin door and peeks out. He shuts it and has another coughing fit.

The suspense is killing me more than the sea sickness. "What's happening?"

"A captive, no less, no more. A damsel in distress on the high seas."

Someone flings open the cabin door. I examine the figure that stumbles inside. Not PC Gramble or Fristhe. I relax until I recognize the shape in the dark brown janitor's jumper. My stomach lurches. "Harriet?"

"The PC will drown you all. You'll serve time on Hades. Then what? Then you'll just be like…like…"

"Like me, missy?" Flox asks and smiles.

Harriet takes one look at Flox's teeth and faints.

"Well, that's convenient," Drayton says and walks around Harriet's limp body. "Steer us out, Flox."

Disbelief fills me from the tips of my toes to the top of my ears. I push myself up to a sitting position. "You're bringing Harriet with us?"

"She jumped onto the boat. I told you, she's stalking you. What am I supposed to do?"

"Leave her on the Platform leg. Someone will eventually find her."

Chanko snickers. "That's cold."

"So is she," I say briskly.

"I can't do that. She's passed out now. That would be murder. And we don't have time to leave her someplace safe. We need to move."

I lie down on my stomach and moan. "You could *tie* her to the Platform leg."

Drayton doesn't respond.

"Look at it this way, Joe," Chanko says. "We have a prisoner now. A good one, in case we need a calling card to get back on the Platform."

"Prisoner?" Lisette says. "Calling card?"

"Don't call her that," Drayton says. "We aren't criminals."

"Aren't we?" I flip onto my back. The ceiling of the cabin is cracked and flaking. It looks like my life at this moment. "I think you're breaking every rule the PC ever instituted, Drayton Coleman."

Chanko leans against the cabin wall. "Everyone's still breathing. Let's not break that rule."

A sense of dread fills me. "There's no way out of this, is there?"

Drayton kneels beside me. "I'll bring you back home if you want to go, even if it means getting caught. Just say the word."

I stare at Drayton. Dad is on my mind—our future, the dreams I had about engaging in challenging research with peers who respect me. Reconnecting with my mom. But I can't abandon Drayton. "Damnit."

Drayton returns to the steering console. "I'll take that as a vote for Land."

I hate feeling caught. "I'll tell you where you can take it."

Chanko claps his hands. "Nice show, all. Let's move on. What do you want me to do with her?"

Flox answers, "Put her in the loo. There's adequate space for her in there, and it locks from the inside for privacy, on the outside in case of high seas. It's not decently clean, but there's nothing dead in there, I'm sure of it. There's another loo in the engine room for our usage. Or the great outdoors."

Chanko shrugs. "Fine by me. I've slept in worse places."

He picks up Harriet and walks over me. He opens the door in the back of the cabin with one hand. I get a glimpse of a dark hole with red walls and white fixtures. Chanko deposits Harriet on the floor, closes the door, and locks her in.

"She's going to be furious," Lisette says. "She's never slept in anything so uncomfortable."

"She'll survive," Chanko says. "How's your sister?"

Lisette looks at the bunk bed. Drees must be lying down, as I can't see her from the floor. "She's sleeping. Which is good.

She hasn't been sleeping at all. Flox shared an illegal drink with her."

"Whiskey," Flox says from the front of the cabin. "A little love in every drop."

"Solid medicine. Had it once or twice myself. Great-grandfather Chanko brought some with him from Land. Good stuff, until it hits your stomach."

I shut my eyes. I had no idea anyone I knew on the Platforms had Illegalities, let alone whiskey. I'm not exactly sure how whiskey is even made. But thoughts of Illegalities can distract me from the roiling in my stomach for only so long. I sink into a pit of negativity.

Lisette slips off the end of the bed and sits beside me. "Well, this is something."

I manage a gurgle. She halfway unzips my life jacket. Lisette to the rescue. "Maybe you can breathe better like this. Do you think it's wise? For us to go to Land, I mean."

I shake my head, then nod.

"That's how I feel, too. Excited, but…worried. I wouldn't choose to go like this, but now that we're going, why not look forward to it? Think of the plants—real foliage. Where exactly are we going?"

I hadn't calculated our exact coordinates. "Good question. Get my laptop, would you? It's next to the stove."

Lisette disappears from my frame of view, then reappears with my laptop. She puts it on my chest.

I open the screen by tapping my password in, then go to the last set of pings I received. I glance at the Morse code results.

JOE.

I gag and the laptop slips off my chest.

Lisette retrieves it. She puts it back on me. "Deep breaths. We'll get through this."

"No," I whisper. "Look."

Lisette reads the screen. "That's your name."

"I know. Why is it being sent in Morse code to me from Land? Call Drayton. I can't take a deep breath."

Lisette yells, "Drayton! Joe has something odd to report."

Drayton leans over us a few seconds later. I point to my name on the screen. "That's the last message from Land."

It isn't often that Drayton has nothing to say. The silence stretches for so long, I think he isn't going to say anything. "I can't explain this."

"Neither can I."

Drayton puts his hand on my cheek, then stands. "What are the coordinates?"

I triangulate the location of the pings and export the data into longitude and latitude. "Here."

Drayton memorizes them, then returns to the control booth.

Lisette grabs my hand. "How do they know your name?"

"I guess we're going to find out," I whisper. I must look really ill, because Lisette lifts my arms several times and then my feet.

"Good circulation is key," Lisette says. "Can I get you anything?"

"A lobotomy."

"Okay. When we get back to the Platform, I'll check into it for you. Maybe they will resurrect them specifically for your case."

When we get back to the Platform—if we get back to the Platform—we will be blacklisted. Expelled to Hades. I don't say it, but I know Lisette is thinking the same thing. She holds my hand and squeezes it every so often. At least we'll be neighbors for life.

Eventually, Lisette returns to her sister. The boat banks hard to starboard, and I shut my eyes and imagine a life without scanners.

# Chapter Sixteen

"WAKE UP, JOE. We're anchored. Flox dropped the jacks."

I feel woozy but open my eyes. Lisette is right in my face. She's so close her nose is out of focus. It feels like she is about to dissect my eyeballs.

I push her away. "What do you want? You're freaking me out."

"Sorry. I was worried you weren't breathing. I put your laptop back in your backpack and you didn't even notice. Then you were asleep for a long time. We've been sailing for hours. The light is coming, but we've hit some shallows. Flox is worried he'll tear off the jacks. Drayton's going to use the daylight to map out the shallows with the dinghy. It's too far to row in from here."

"Thanks for the update. Now leave me alone."

Lisette's voice drones on. "You have to get up. Harriet's awake. She's spitting mad. I'm terrified of her."

"Let her be mad. Drayton can deal with her."

"Drayton and Chanko are getting the dinghy prepared, and Flox just talks in circles. She's been banging on the bathroom door and screaming for like fifteen minutes. It's going to wake Drees up, and she really needs to sleep. Joe, please."

Lisette's voice is strained, and I'm a pushover for the word *please*. Besides, now that I'm awake, I hear one hell of a racket coming from the bathroom. "All right, all right." My stomach tightens as I move, and I swallow hard. "Focus," I mutter to encourage myself, and try to stand.

I sit down quickly. "Not all right."

"I can help you…"

"No need," I say and scoot myself on the floor to the bathroom's door. Harriet is wailing and banging what sounds like the toilet seat up and down. "Harriet," I whisper furiously.

Silence.

"Listen, Harriet. For once, can you not be a selfish ass? Lisette's sister is ill and sleeping. She's been through some serious crap. I am also seasick as a caught fish and should technically be sleeping. Yet here I am, talking to you. Can you suck it up and shut it for now?"

Silence.

"Harriet?"

Silence.

Lisette wrings her hand. "Do you think she hurt herself? She was banging around in there. She could have hit her head. She could be drowning in her own vomit."

I rest my forehead on the bathroom door. All I wanted to do was build a better communications system for the Platforms and avoid water and Harriet as much as possible. "Harriet. Answer me, please. Can you confirm that you understand the need for quiet and that you are—"

Lisette cuts in. "Breathing?"

"Yes, breathing. Harriet, are you breathing?"

Silence.

"We should check on her," Lisette says.

I stop Lisette from opening the door. I know that Harriet is conniving and smart—a dangerous combination. "Doesn't matter. If she's dead, we can just leave her in there when we abandon the vessel. No one will know she came with us. They'll think she jumped off the Platform in despair over her lack of creativity in developing a senior communications project that would compete with mine."

I hear a gasp from inside the bathroom. I nod at Lisette and make the thumbs-up sign. Lisette returns the gesture.

"You can't do that!" Harriet screams.

"I'd be quiet if I were you," I say in a monotone voice. "I didn't ask you to follow me, and no one asked you to jump on this vessel. You did this to yourself. Think about that." I wait several seconds, but Harriet doesn't reply. Satisfied, I crawl back to the center of the boat. I push my back against the stove and look at the tips of my shoes. The world isn't spinning as much.

"Time to get to work." I open my backpack and fish my laptop out. "Turn on the receiver over there, please," I say to Lisette.

She does, and I type a series of commands. "Since we're going to Land, I need to set up a functioning network. Whoever stays with the vessel may need to communicate with the away team in case all hell breaks loose."

Lisette sits down next to me. "Like if the drones find *The Fluddery Doo?*"

"Not possible," I respond. "We're out of range of the Platform Complex's wireless network. No drones, and our chips are inactive. The only way they can find us is if they sail here themselves. This new network won't be traceable even if they do."

"Wow," Lisette says. "That's impressive."

"Thanks. Put the gel charger on the deck, would you? Protected but in full sunlight. I don't want to lose power before I have to. You said it would be daylight soon, right?"

Lisette takes the yellow, hand-sized gel charger and walks to the cabin door. "Yes. Be right back." She knocks on the door three times then disappears through it.

I continue working on the set up until I need the receiver I brought with me moved. Lisette hasn't come back. I look at Drees. She's still sleeping. "And Harriet's in the toilet—not that she'd help me anyway."

I put my laptop on the ground and twist to face the stove. I grab the corner and heave myself up. "Like a mountain," I say and steady myself. I've never seen a mountain, but I imagine it would feel the same way if it tried to move itself.

I inch my body toward the cabin door. I reach for the handle right when the door opens, and I fall forward. "Oof!"

A pair of arms and a chest catches me. "Hey, what's happening? You didn't knock, so I thought you were Harriet escaping."

I push myself away from Chanko. "No. Definitely not Harriet."

"Course not. Sorry."

I push my hair away from my face and reconstruct my dignity. It smells fresher on the open sea—less like fish—which is nice. Without the jacks towering above us, the vessel looks like a lily pad floating on the ocean even though it's standing on the ocean floor. "I'm looking for Lisette. I need help setting up the receiver. It's a two-person job."

"You aren't so steady. Hitting Flox's stash?"

I look at Chanko like his head is three sizes too big for his body. "Motion sickness and me—we have a long and sordid history. Where's Lisette?"

"Aft. That girl has skills. She's a serious multi-tasker—spouting off scientific names of seaweed and everything else inanimate out here while making us food."

"Life goes on while I'm locked up with Harriet."

"Yeah. Giving my breakfast time to digest before I convince Harriet to get on board with the plan. She's still in the loo?"

"Yep. Since I can't walk without falling down, can you help me to Lisette before you begin the convincing Harriet process?"

Chanko puts his arm around me. "Sure. You need to get your sea legs. Envision your body moving, and it will move."

"I don't want sea legs. I just want my muscles to work when I ask them to."

"Ah, so you like me hauling you around," Chanko says and smiles brilliantly. "There's better ways to get close to a guy. I could show you a few tactics."

"Tempting," I say sarcastically and continue flailing alongside him. "There's seaweed in your teeth. Large chunks. Not attractive." A whistle alerts me to Drayton's presence on top of the cabin adjusting the solar panels. I whistle back then focus on moving my legs.

"Joe!" Lisette says when we round the cabin's corner. She is standing in front of a makeshift table comprised of a piece of rope netting tied across two tires. The vessel's flat surface stretches out before her like a silver ribbon. She is sorting sea creatures onto different plates. "You have to see this!"

Chanko drops me against a pile of tires next to Lisette. "Thanks. Very chivalrous of you. I wish you luck with Harriet."

Chanko mock salutes me. "At your service."

Lisette raises her eyebrows. Then she pushes three different green and tan squishy objects in my hand. "Look at those."

All three are so gross and sticky that I want to drop them. But Lisette looks expectant and excited, so I don't. "I'm looking. But I don't know what I'm seeing. Or feeling. What are these?"

"Edible jellyfish and a different variety of seaweed than what we get out at sea. This is a dream come true. I can't believe I'm really seeing these species in their natural habitat."

"Which is not normally Joe's hand," Drayton says. "Solar panels optimized. Thanks for preparing breakfast. We wouldn't know what was edible and what would kill us without you."

Lisette blushes. She's so happy that I smile. "When you're done here, Lisette, can you come and help me finish the communication setup?"

Lisette takes the seaweed and jellyfish back. "Sure. Is Drees still asleep?"

"Yes. For now, anyway. Chanko said he was going to talk to Harriet, so who knows how that will go. I'm hoping they'll clear out of my work area so I can get the system up and running."

"Did you eat?" Drayton asks.

Before I can answer, Harriet slides to a stop in front of us. She has a clear, heavy weather jacket two sizes too big over her janitor's suit. She looks like a windsock. "*You,*" she directs at me in a snarl. She looks at Drayton. "*And you.*"

Drayton makes a beeline to the ballast area and ducks beneath deck. Coward. I decide to kill her with kindness. "Hello, Harriet. It's a lovely day, isn't it? Not a speck of rain."

Harriet puts her hands on her hips. "Hello, Harriet? And weather comments? That's what you're going to say to me after leading this ridiculous kidnapping and attempted murder escapade? The PC will send you all—"

"To Hades. Yes, I know. You've mentioned it," I say in a chipper voice.

"We checked to make sure you were breathing," Lisette pipes up cheerfully.

I give Lisette a stern look, and she goes back to separating slimy stuff from less slimy stuff.

"Did you? Because I don't remember that. Murder is a banishable offense on any of the Platform Complexes. So is criminal negligence. You'll do solitary."

"Be sensible, Harriet. We aren't criminals. And there's no PC out here."

Chanko opens the cabin door, then rubs his neck sheepishly. "It isn't nice to hit a person when their back is turned, Harriet. Especially when they are getting a jacket for you. I had to pick up everything that fell out of the closet."

She doesn't answer him.

Chanko steps beside Harriet and takes her arm. "I think we should take a little stroll, perhaps without the sneak attack."

Whatever else Harriet says gets lost in the open space as Chanko leads her away.

"Maybe he'll throw her overboard." I totter forward and clutch the side of the cabin. My legs feel like two sticks of squishy stuff, and it's annoying. I crouch down, put my hands behind me, and move across the deck like a crab. "A whole new way to travel."

"You look great!" Lisette yells.

I look like an idiot but appreciate Lisette's support. "Come help me when you can." I round the corner and reach the cabin door. I stare at the door handle and feel overwhelmed and really weak for almost a full minute. Defeated.

I lie down and kick the handle open with my right foot. At least my legs work when I'm closer to the ground.

# Chapter Seventeen

OUR COMMUNICATION STATION is set up, thanks to Lisette and Drees. Besides helping me, Drees volunteered to clean the deck earlier in the afternoon with Chanko. It's a good sign that she is interacting with us and taking an interest in our plans.

"What's the situation with our course?" I ask Flox.

"Situated," Flox sings. "Right as rain, or fins!"

"Right as rain," Harriet mimics.

Harriet has been pure evil all afternoon. She tried to lift the jacks, then attempted to damage the solar fuel cells, so Chanko tied her to the stove. Loosely of course, as we all feel bad about it, but she has to be contained. "One more sound, Harriet, and I will personally stick a gag in your mouth. A dirty one."

"Ooh, threatening. Especially from a moron who can't even walk properly."

I grit my teeth. "Lisette."

"Yes?"

"Can you move the receiving station to the furthest point aft that you can and lash it down? Make sure it won't get dislodged. Put a raincoat over it, or a spare tarp."

"Sure," Lisette says in a perky voice. She picks up the receiving station and takes it outside.

When she's gone, I look at Flox. "Grab the whiskey."

"Aha. What'll it be? Dirty sock?"

Harriet gasps. "You wouldn't dare."

I point to the cupboard then to the sheet on the bunk bed. "I'd say two swigs of A, and then a strip of B would do it."

Flox nods. He takes the flask from the cupboard. Harriet talks a blue wave, threatening everyone and everything. She squeaks when Flox approaches her, but I'm already tackling the next challenge: walking

"I have to get over this," I mutter and push myself up. I hang onto one of the bunks and practice bouncing up and down in place. It feels like octopus appendages have replaced my normal legs. I envy the ease with which Flox moves around on the boat without his cane.

"That Harriet is a weasel of a girl," Flox says. "Perhaps a lady, perhaps not. Too soon to tell. Looks can be deceiving."

"Thanks for handling her, Flox," I say and step away from the bunks. "Now tell me what's wrong with my legs. Why can't I function like everyone else on the sea?"

"It's your ears. Poor equilibrium. Or water in them. Were you dunked as a child?"

"I don't even know what that means. So I'm going with no."

Flox coughs, then holds his pointer finger up. "How about looking at the ceiling and trying to walk?"

"What would that do?"

"I have no idea. But it would be better than you crawling all over my ship like a sea spider. I do not like sea spiders."

"True that." I look up at the ceiling, but my body starts to careen to the right as soon as I take a step. Flox puts his hand on my shoulder and rights me to center.

"Bend your knees. Feel which way the deck is rolling and bend the opposite knee. Imagine that you are a liquid changing shape to stay within your container."

Lisette opens the cabin door. I bend my knees and walk toward her with both arms outstretched.

"She's got it!" Flox says and returns to the control panel. "She rises from the dead. Or she has become the sun. Perhaps both."

Lisette grabs the back of my life vest and walks the perimeter of the room with me. "Hey, that's a lot better!"

"I'm liquid."

"Is Harriet…"

"Don't look. What's going on outside?"

Lisette hesitates, then answers me. "Drayton wants to make landfall when we are least visible. He and Chanko mapped out the reefs with the dinghy so he can navigate them in the dark. He's solar charging the headlamps, and Drees is helping him prepare low lights near the jacks. We'll be able to see the vessel from Land if the lights are on."

"Let there be light!" Flox starts to whistle. It's a catchy melody, but I can't place the song.

Lisette can't stop glancing at Harriet sprawled in the bunk. "Shouldn't we…"

"No. Harriet is fine. Just taking a nap. Leave her alone." I waddle back to the bunk and slide down to the floor. I imagine what I would feel like if technologically advanced people suddenly appeared on my Land after bailing centuries ago. I wouldn't feel good about it. In fact, I'd probably run them off. No—I'd understand their technology first so I could better my situation, then I'd run them off.

Lisette joins me on the floor. "We get to walk on real Land. Aren't you excited?"

I stretch my legs in front of me. I'm emotionally exhausted and far from excited. And I'm worried about my dad. "Depends on what's on it. What condition everything is in."

"You mean who's on it, right?"

I recognize Flox's song. It's "Ring around the Rosie." I picture Land. Pestilence. Disease. Some of the old zombie films Drayton and I laugh at. "That too."

❦

The tires beneath me are comfortable. I rest my head against a rim and scan the horizon.

The sky seems more beautiful forty-four kilometers from Land—two-thirds closer than Nod. The ocean reflects the colors more brilliantly. The cloud outlines seem sharper, more in focus—like a perfect painting.

Flox is dressed in camouflage and has what looks like black ladies' underwear on his head. His goggles hold it in place. I don't want to ask, but I have to know. "Is that underwear?"

Flox's face dissolves into a million creases as he makes a disgusted face that reminds me of dried fish jerky. "No indeed. This is an aviator's cap."

"Oh. I've never seen one."

"Of course you haven't. You live on a Platform, not on a plane."

I can't fault his logic. Lisette comes out of the cabin and joins us. "Drees is settled, Flox. You'll take good care of her?"

"That one I like," Flox says and shuffles away from us. "We can talk about splicing, cutting…recreating the universe."

Lisette crinkles her forehead. "Is that a yes?"

"I think so."

She sits next to me on the tire stack. "Who do you think's out there? I know you're thinking about that message. Your name."

I'm actually thinking about Dad eating dinner alone. But Lisette is looking for reassurance. "It could be a machine that reactivated because of a power arc. It could be a new species of human. It could be the old species of human wanting their technology back."

Lisette leans forward on the tire. "Are you scared?"

"I guess so. It all seems so…"

Lisette sighs. "Unreal."

"Yes. Yesterday, we were at school with our light boards."

"That was two days ago."

I'm already losing count. "Right. And now this."

Lisette makes a sour face. "We'll miss graduation."

"I can live with that."

Lisette moves to the boat railing. She seems more relaxed than she was at school. Her posture is looser, and she laughs louder and more often. She looks pretty and full of life. "Drees really doesn't think the virus will still be active if there is a population. I trust her. She's the smartest one in my family."

"That's good to know. Our organs won't clot over and lead to our premature deaths. I feel better already."

"Ha ha. But really. It's comforting to know."

"I guess. Though something else less unpleasant could kill us. A wild animal. A bee. We have no immunity to anything on Land."

"All right," Drayton says and steps between Lisette and me. "We are ready to go at dusk."

"Are *we*?" I ask.

"*We* are. Harriet has agreed to come with us. She doesn't want to stay with Flox anymore than I want to leave her with Flox. She'll drive him crazy."

"I think he's very nice," Lisette interjects.

Drayton smiles at Lisette. "He is. And Harriet has calmed down. She likes Chanko."

This is news, as Harriet has never liked anybody but herself and her inner circle of friends, Kay and Darby—nice girls except when they're with Harriet.

"Kudos to Chanko. Go team! So what's the plan?"

"The plan is to sail closer to Land, then drop the dinghy in the water and paddle to shore," Drayton explains. "*The Fluddery Doo* will return to open water. We follow the coordinates to the SOS signal. Then we will—"

I interrupt Drayton. "Follow them how?"

"Thought of that. Chanko brought his pocket compass, so we'll use it for navigation. If we meet hostiles, we'll try to get a message to Flox on your communication network and let him know to pull the jacks and get going. Otherwise, he'll wait for one week."

Hostiles. Hearing the word makes me shiver. "We need a plan for hostiles."

"Flox brought his cache of Illegals, varying degrees. We'll use them to defend ourselves once I figure out how to work them."

Lisette pushes away from the railing. "You mean weapons? Second degree or first degree? I can help with second degree. Dad taught me to use my grandfather's pistol and rifle. I don't know how to use automatic weapons. There's a reason those are first degree."

Drayton and I both look at Lisette in surprise.

Drayton speaks first. "That's amazing. Flox's are all second degree."

"Those are easy to use. I can show you."

"Wow," Harriet says and snaps her fingers. "Really well done, Lisette. There you go, saving the day. And without a plant in sight."

Lisette colors, and I grit my teeth. Harriet's voice is always annoying. It's high and whiny and everything a sixteen-year-old female voice shouldn't be. "And then there's Harriet. Appearing randomly and saving nothing."

Harriet fake smiles. "I needed some air to clear my head. Seems I had too much to drink."

Lisette looks at me accusingly. I put on my best innocent face. "Maybe not enough."

"Chanko?" Drayton calls. "Don't provoke her, Joe."

"He had to go to the bathroom," Harriet says. "He wasn't taking me with him, and there's really nowhere else for me to go on this floating flat piece of metal since you've locked everything down."

I look around, then pointedly at Harriet. "Plenty of water for you to swim around in."

"Sharks. Ever heard of them?"

"I have. And I think they'd like you. All of you."

Drayton coughs. "All right. Maybe you can wait for Chanko near the cabin door, Harriet?"

Harriet gestures something rude to us with her right hand and walks away. Drayton fake laughs. "How about that training session?"

"Sure," Lisette says and follows Drayton to the stern.

I restack the tires so I am standing more, but still secure. The water isn't as rough this evening, and it's almost pleasant. I notice more birds this close to Land, and they circle the vessel searching for food. I'm fascinated by the way they glide on the wind. I've read about planes and space travel but can't imagine actually sitting in a plane or shooting off into space. I'm not sure I'm brave enough to try either.

A stiff wind comes from the west, and I relish the feel of it across my face. It's like a caress from Land. Tonight, I will do something that hasn't been done by a member of my family in over one hundred years—walk on Land. I wish I could tell Mom about it, or have Dad here with me. In a perfect world, I'd have them both with me.

I hear a series of super loud pops and sit down hard on the tire stack in surprise. Lisette runs from the back of the boat toward me. "We have a means of defending ourselves! Come on, your turn for training!"

"No running on the vessel," I caution.

"Yes, I know. I'm just excited." Lisette puts her arm around my waist. We weave-step our way to the stern. "You really are improving."

"Just in time," I mutter. The liftboat thins out like a waistline without any legs. Drayton points one gun after the other toward the open water, away from the glare of the sinking sun. Chanko and Harriet stand on the other side of him.

Drayton picks up a small gun from a bag made of carpet samples lying on the deck next to him. "You're next, Joe."

Now that I see the gun, I don't want to touch it. "We're going to shoot at these people? Isn't that why their whole society fell apart in the first place? We'd be repeating history, but backward."

"Only as a last resort. We need some means of protection. You said so yourself."

"No. I said we needed a plan, and I meant a peaceful one. Like running."

"We would never—or I would never—kill someone. Just because you swim with sharks doesn't make you a shark."

"No," I reply. "It makes you dinner."

Drayton shrugs his shoulders. "You don't have to learn if you don't want to."

"I don't want to."

"Okay. Chanko?"

Lisette shows Chanko how to load and shoot the weapon of his choice. I hate the sound of the gun even more than how it looks. It sounds like the lift on Nod when it gets stuck, except faster and louder.

"What about me?" Harriet asks.

"She'll shoot you in the back," Flox says and moves his index finger across his neck like he's slitting his own throat.

"Where did you even come from, you old—"

Drayton talks over Harriet. "Let's sail, Flox. Harriet, we'll teach you to aim with an unloaded gun."

Harriet seems mollified and pays attention to what Lisette teaches her. This time, I don't feel so sick when the boat moves. I stay where I am and watch Lisette, Chanko, and Drayton try out more weapons. Eventually, they all choose the weapon they feel most comfortable with.

I feel a hand on my shoulder some time later. I know it's Flox as the fingers are long and bony, the fingernails hooked and filthy. He puts a small metal object in my hand. "I do not care for guns either. Too much kick. Take this instead. First class grenade. Pull the pin, throw, and boom."

"Thanks, Flox." I slip the grenade into my shirt pouch. I don't look at it, as I hope I'll never need to use it.

# Chapter Eighteen

I'M EXHAUSTED, but I manage to stay upright for the rest of the sail. We have five kilometers to row to Land. Harriet is watchful but isn't hindering anyone's efforts. She gets into the dinghy without argument.

"Ready, Joe?" Chanko calls.

I step off the side of the liftboat and push my legs down on the steel ladder rungs one at a time, awkwardly moving myself with the strength of my arms. It's a hard climb, and I have to force my muscles to react. I keep my chin up, willing myself to ignore the water churning below, waiting to swallow me.

I finally make it into the dinghy without tumbling into the ocean. The dinghy is a small, red watercraft complete with two benches and two oars. Chanko sits next to me. We sit across from Lisette and Drayton.

Harriet sits straight as a stingray tail in the well of the dinghy by our feet. I wish she'd relax a little instead of looking like a proper martyr. As a natural sloucher, I've always admired her posture, though I'd never admit it to anyone.

"Ready?" Drayton asks. "Keep the headlamps off until we are ashore. Now row."

We all—except Harriet—coordinate our efforts and row the dinghy toward shore. No one talks. I don't know how much time passes until I start to pick out the shapes of trees on the beach. Huge rectangles on tall poles line the sky above them. Rows of houses with sunken porches and ripped screens line the beachfront. Giant arms with saucer-shaped light sources curve above a roadway, though none of the lights are on.

Seagulls and sandpipers circle above us. And the smell—I don't even know what I smell. It's a heady mixture of sweet and salty at the same time, sort of like Lisette's garden, but with distinctive metallic and spicy elements.

The bottom of the boat scrapes, and we stop rowing. I see the seafloor through the water. Land. I take my shoes and backpack off and scramble out of the boat. The water is cold around my ankles and between my toes. Land is beneath my feet—solid, firm. I scoop a handful of sand and let the fine granules sift through my fingers.

I wade onto the beach, one foot in front of the other, and switch my headlamp onto low light. Sand squishes around each step, and when I look back, there are footprints following me. I feel tall for the first time in my life. I am strong.

I dig my heels into the sand and run, right first, then left. I want to laugh and shout, but I know I can't. Lisette takes my hands. We skip in a circle and dance. The Land feels like a dream beneath my feet.

"Joe, Lisette," Chanko whispers. "Nice dance moves, but everyone has to chip in to move the dinghy."

I throw a fistful of sand at him and miss as I follow him back to the water. Drayton picks up the rear of the dinghy, Chanko and Lisette the middle. I put my arms underneath the front. Harriet sits on the sand.

"Now," Drayton commands.

We drag the dinghy across the beach and into the treeline. Harriet trails after us. I grab my backpack from the dinghy and put my shoes on, surveying my surroundings as we walk. I see power lines beyond the trees. A long, thin building is to our right. The roof is gone, but different-sized surfboards are still stacked behind a metal counter. Several doors are bolted together on our left to create a wall. The paint is weather worn, but they were bright red, orange, and yellow at one time.

Chanko and Drayton turn the boat over and hide it in a bush that looks like waves on the sea in plant form. I marvel at how many different shades of green and brown there are.

"I'll let Flox know we landed."

"Good idea," Drayton says. "Everyone, keep your headlamps on low power. We need them to last."

A gust of wind hits my face, and I hear rustling. The trees and bushes move gently, and I notice a cement barrier buried in vegetation. I investigate and realize it is the edge of a ramp. The ramp rises up like a gigantic U.

"Tidal," I whisper and climb onto the flat surface. I open my laptop, select the new program, and activate *The Fluddery Doo*'s point to address. An ant crawls across my hand, and I watch it, fascinated. "The pads don't do this justice. Drayton, come look at this."

Drayton sweeps his arm across the U's surface and removes several vines. "This is a perfect spot for our camp."

"I thought so, too." I sync my phone to the laptop. "What should I send to Flox?"

Drayton lays his hand on my shoulder. I don't pull away. I like how reassuring his fingers feel.

"Something significant."

"The Eagle has landed? That one was famous."

In the dark, Drayton's face is softer, and he looks even younger than he is. The corner of his lips raise, and I know he gets my joke. Then I notice something move through the foliage behind the U. I recognize the hair.

"Do it. It seems apt."

I send the message. "Cool. I'll double check the Land signal coordinates, too. But you may want to track Harriet. She's on the move."

Drayton mutters under his breath.

"She went right through the trees over there. Pretty slow, like she was having trouble with the undergrowth."

Drayton darts into the bushes, and I giggle. Poor Drayton. I pull up the coordinates from the Land signal beacon. Lisette and Chanko are collecting vines to drape over the dinghy. I motion for Chanko to come to me.

He walks over slowly.

I smirk. "Having problems walking?"

"Yes. My legs feel weird."

"Not mine. I finally feel like I'm walking right. Did you bring the compass?"

Chanko digs in his pocket and produces the compass.

"Brilliant. 30.2543° N, 88.1124° W."

Chanko marks the coordinates on the compass. "Got it."

I check my laptop, and there is a return message from Flox. I read it out loud.

*Chicken eggs are good for breakfast.*

Chanko reads the message aloud a second time. "What's he talking about? I've never eaten an egg. None of us have."

"He means don't lay an egg," Lisette says. "That's a good one."

"Hilarious," I mumble and shut my laptop.

"What are we going to do now? I wouldn't mind staying here. I could guard the dinghy. There's so much to learn. I want to put my nose on the ground and study it inch by inch so I don't miss anything."

I understand how Lisette feels. I would love to walk around and follow cables and wires to their sources, but we have to stick with the plan. "We follow the compass to the signal coordinates and find what there is to be found."

A high whistle breaks the silence.

"Or we follow that whistle," Chanko says. "That's Drayton. Nine o'clock."

Lisette, Chanko, and I walk in the direction of the whistle until we reach a tan, brick building. Huge plastic pieces of what was a sign litter an overgrown cement parking lot with eight robotic machines with rubber tubes and screens arranged in rows of two. Several cars in various states of decay are lined up next to them.

The front door of the building slides open. We all jump, then realize Drayton moved it. "Check this out. It's a gas station."

I pick my way to the front door. A huge bin labeled "ICE" is on my left. To the right is a wire cage with small tanks in it. "Propane?"

"Probably still good," Lisette says. "We should bring this back to the Platform. Propane would really light up the fish fries."

Chanko, Lisette, and I walk into the building. Our headlamps are like long fingers cutting through the dark inside. Everything is doubled in shadow. Rows of metal shelving stacked with merchandise stretch to the back wall. To the left is a plexiglass-surrounded area with more shelves and merchandise. I pick up a colorful plastic bag. "Cheetos."

Drayton puts something in my hand. I recognize the shape and color. "Twinkies?"

"For later," Drayton says. "This is amazing. Everything we need to survive all in one store."

Water is dripping from the ceiling. Part of the ceiling tile has caved in, so I walk around the mess. Then I notice the glass walls. There are doors every two feet or so and the shelves inside are full of water and other beverages. The end door opens into a bigger space and…I swallow and back away. The room is full of piled clothes and human remains.

Harriet blurts out, "Everyone is dead in there." She is holding a bottle of water and a thin, yellow package labeled "jerky."

I cringe but stay logical. "Which is what we all expected."

"Probably used it for cold storage when the bodies stacked up," Chanko says. "We need water, so load up. Lighters, anything canned. Wow. Toilet paper. I thought that was a myth."

Drayton and I fill two plastic bags with practical supplies like bungee cords, shampoo, charcoal, and disinfectant. Lisette and Chanko help us. Harriet opens bags of chips and pours them on the floor.

Everything is so available. I'm overwhelmed and don't want to be inside anymore. There's a door behind the plexiglass area, and I walk out of it. The back of the store opens into a field dotted with discarded items—a bathtub, a stove, several cars on blocks and three rows of metal shelving. A huge mound in the center of the field is flanked by two smaller mounds on either side. They're made of shells. A sign on a stick is next to one of them. The text is still legible, so I read about the Mobilian shell people culture. "This was a sacred sight," I say and back away from the placard. Then I realize the third mound isn't listed on the informational map. It's made of human bones.

"Joe!"

I recognize Drayton's voice. Since I don't know any religious words, I bow my head and back away.

"What are you doing?" Drayton asks.

"Nothing," I say. "Looking around, that's all."

"Stay with the group. This isn't like the Platforms. You can get lost."

"Got it," I say and follow him back to our group.

Chanko and Lisette have made slings from beach towels they found in the store. I pick up one of the plastic bags and carry it in front of me. Harriet dumps out anything we ask her to carry.

Drayton hoists a bag made from a beach towel. "Let's go."

We walk along the main roadway, Chanko leading our procession. After a while, I forget about Harriet and the bone mound. Even though it's dark, we are surrounded by a myriad of colors and textures highlighted by an almost full moon, a sprinkling of stars, and our headlamps. I hear bird calls—owls, I think—and small animals rustle in the foliage around us. A flying insect buzzes close to my ear. There are abandoned, decaying cars and buildings everywhere. Signs are stacked on top of signs—everything's labeled. The few huge signs that are still readable advertise for health care, food, or entertainment. Trash cans line the roadway. We pass several bicycles lined up in racks near larger trash receptacles. Vegetation grows over everything like green wrapping paper. Land is a recycler's dream.

Chanko stops suddenly, and I run into the back of him.

"Chanko! What—" I stop speaking when I see what stopped him.

A chainlink fence is in our pathway. Machines built in the shapes of mythical beasts and spiders tower over it. One machine has cups with spooky faces hooked to a wheel, another an octopus with individual cabs attached with ball-and-joint hinges that allow them to spin. There is a dragon with chairs attached to its open mouth and an enormous shark with cabs along its spine. In the dark, the machines look almost real. I read the sign. "Adventure Land."

"Theme park," Drayton says. "They were common at the time. Those machines are rides. For fun."

"Our destination is through there," Chanko says.

"We could go around," Harriet says snidely.

I take the lead. "We go through."

Everyone follows me beneath the Adventure Land sign. We push through a series of spinning metal barricades. Rust makes them difficult to turn, and noisy. Inside is a wide field. Booths with crude, hand-painted words like "$1" and "Free Throws" are placed every few feet near the entrance. Pieces of machinery that were part of rides riddle the walkway. Eventually, we come to a long, brightly painted building missing some walls and most of the roof. Mirrors line the inside, and as we walk by, I see grotesque images of us. I'm fat, then tall, then super thin.

"This is eerie."

"Not attractive," Lisette agrees. She touches my arm and pulls me to stop. She points to a large, yellow mass to the right of the exit. It has four legs and a tail. "Wait. Is that a…"

"Dog," I whisper. The last domesticated animal died eighty years ago on the Platforms, so it's like seeing a mythical creature. "It looks like he's waiting for us to exit."

Chanko walks forward cautiously. The dog doesn't bark or move from the gate. Chanko skirts the dog and walks away from the exit. The dog follows him, tail wagging.

I stumble over a ball of fencing wire. There are clothing remnants, bones, and a shovel near it. I shiver at the thought of someone burying themselves in the fake shadow of Adventure Land. Reality has a new meaning for me.

"Watch your step," Lisette cautions.

The vegetation is suddenly gone, like a large pair of scissors cut out the edge of it. The Land is covered with four lanes of cement. Sprigs of grass and vines have overtaken pieces of it, but traffic lines are visible, white and yellow, and I recognize tar. Large green signs indicating direction and place names hang like flags from thirty-foot-high metal posts. Some have fallen to the roadway. "A major highway."

We are easily visible walking down the highway. I pick up my pace and catch up to Chanko. When I get close enough for him to hear me in a normal speaking tone, I say, "There's no cover here. Let's get back to the treeline."

"Can't do it. You're looking at our SOS signal."

A massive, beige, two-story building sprawls across the Land before us. Several smaller buildings are connected to it in a star formation. Blinking lights crown the top. The moon is right behind it, large and luminous.

I turn to tell Drayton, but he's already right next to me.

"I heard him. What's your analysis?"

I examine the blinking lights on top of the two-story building. "It's a beacon for ships to navigate the rocks. It has to be linked to an underwater buoy transmitter, which is how I picked it up. Someone must have reactivated it. Or it reactivated itself. Joe could've been the name of the last ship that passed through."

"Reactivated itself?" Harriet asks. "Great. No people, no food, no bed to sleep in. This is tragically un-tidal."

"We'll see," Drayton says.

"Let's keep moving," I say. "We're too exposed."

A ten-foot fence topped with razor wire surrounds the building. Signs on the fence warn that it is electrified. Cautious, I throw one of my shoes on it. Nothing happens. "Not anymore," I mutter and retrieve my shoe.

The dog jumps through a hole in the fence thirty feet away, and Chanko follows him. He reaches the side of the building, then signals the all clear. We duck through the opening, then run together across the fifteen feet of exposed grass.

The wall of the building provides shelter, so we relax for a minute. Harriet sulks and sits on the ground, Lisette combs through the grass. Chanko and Drayton study a schematic on an elevated post. I study the building. Black letters with circles and dashes are spray painted near eye level.

*The Plague is upon us.*

*God is watching.*

"The Moralists," I say and show Lisette.

Chanko points to the front of the building. "The only entrance to the main building is up those steps. I'll go first with the dog."

"I think we should all go together," Drayton says.

I agree. "We'll be weaker if we get separated."

"All right. I just wanted to be a hero."

Harriet grimaces. "So not cool. Weaker if we get separated. Want to be a hero. This is just sad." She sticks her tongue out at me.

I look away. "Let's go."

We run single file down the length of the building then approach the steps. They are nearly twenty feet long, and big chunks are missing from some of them. But the grass is tended, and there is a tilled garden near a working fountain. I catch my breath. Evidence of habitation.

Chanko takes the steps two at a time. Drayton and I flank him. The dog is next to Chanko's left leg. Lisette and Harriet climb the steps slowly. I look back and count the steps—eleven.

Chanko turns the round doorknob. "Locked."

"Is there a scanner? If there is one, I can jam it," Harriet says. "For a price."

"Is that how you climbed into my bathroom?"

Harriet smiles slyly at me. "I could tell you the frequency…"

"No need," Drayton says. "No scanner."

I put my plastic bag of supplies down and pick up the pineapple knocker attached to the door.

Drayton hisses, "Don't knock on the door!"

I stop mid second knock. "Too late. Already committed with the first one."

"If someone is in there, they'll know we're here."

"That's the point of knocking."

Drayton doesn't laugh. "This is not the time to be fearless. Abort, back to the side of the building!"

Chanko and Harriet follow Drayton, and Lisette moves a few steps away, but I stay on the porch. I'm not going to run. I already knocked.

Lisette calls my name, then Drayton, but I ignore them. I look more closely at the door. Something about it seems familiar to me. Almost like home.

I read the sign on the left side of the door. The Estuary. I have seen this sign before. The Estuary—I can't think where or how I'd come across it before, but I have. Even the door knocker is familiar, the pineapple motif—which is why I'm not scared, just nervous.

But no one is answering. The lights flash on top of the building. Maybe I *am* scared. Drayton pulls on my arm, and I turn to follow him back to cover, but then I hear a noise from inside. I face the door.

It opens, and an angel smiles at me.

"Mom?" I step forward quickly and my right foot hits something hard. I'm falling. The world explodes in color then goes dark.

# Chapter Nineteen

LIGHT FALLS ON MY FACE. Something smells odd—fresh and salty at the same time. I rub my eyes and squint at the ceiling. There's a ceiling fan, but no hum of electricity. I'm lying on something soft, with a pillow. I flail my legs.

"You're all right," Mom says. "Don't struggle."

"Mom." I rub my eyes again, but she's still there. I look around. There are curtains on the window and artwork on the wall. The floor has a rug, and the furniture is made of wood. Real wood. Mom is standing at the foot of my bed. I feel overwhelmed and confused. "Am I dead? If so, why does dead smell so weird?"

Mom laughs her happy laugh, and I smile in return. I didn't realize how much I missed that laugh until now.

"Very much alive," Mom says and sits on the side of my bed. She's wearing a white jumper with a zipper up the front. TE is stamped in blue script on the left lapel. "That's a bit of menthol and smelling salts. You tripped over an iron boot scraper and hit your head on the doorjamb pretty hard. You've been out a few hours. We'll monitor you for a possible concussion."

I touch a sensitive lump on my forehead. "That explains the ache." I don't feel too bad. My head's sore but okay. I look around the room. No Drayton. Panic creeps into my voice. "Where is—"

"They're exploring the facility because they couldn't sleep," Mom interrupts. "It was good to see Drayton again. And

Lisette. You can catch up with them later. It was selfish, but I wanted to have a little mother-daughter time."

I touch Mom's hand shyly. "Mom. It's really you? I feel like I'm back on the Platform dreaming really vivid, really smelly dreams."

"No. It's truly me, in the flesh." Mom pats my hand. "It's so nice to touch you. I am thrilled that you are here. How is your father?"

I'm about to cry, and I haven't cried in a long time. "Lonely. He works a lot. He misses you."

Mom sighs and keeps patting my hand. "Does he know you're on Land?"

I shake my head. I swallow my tears. Mom's here, and everything has to be all right now. I take a deep breath and prepare to tell Mom just how glad I am to see her, and how great she looks. Instead I say, "Why didn't you write? They said it was extended PC business, but that doesn't explain why you never wrote." I bite the inside of my lip. I sound pitiful. I wish I'd said something smart, or at least funny.

Mom puts her hand on the side of my face. "I wasn't on a PC assignment. I talked to Drayton while you were unconscious. You and I ended up here for the same reason. The PC forcibly removed me from Nod."

I lean forward. "What do you mean?"

Mom holds both my hands. "I had questions about power usage activity I noticed on Land and filed queries about it. The PC didn't like the questions, so when I received the temporary assignment order, I knew I was in trouble. I asked Duritz to smuggle me out."

"Duritz?"

Mom hugs me tightly. "I wanted to tell you and your father. But I couldn't, for your protection. Duritz stuck his neck out for me. I scanned on to the transport ship, then bailed mid-route next to buoy 162. Duritz picked me up from there a few hours later in his bass boat. He's been trading with the black marketers for years."

I feel relief. Mom didn't abandon us for her career. But I can't imagine Duritz bringing Mom all the way to Land. He'd be missed on the Platform. "Duritz brought you here?"

"Goodness, no. Duritz is scared of Land. Petrified, actually." She stands up and walks to the window. "He radioed a constituent who makes Land trips to the outer islands. He participates in some of their transactions, from afar of course. He's procured a few things for me over the years."

I drop my jaw. My mom has participated in the black market. "Like what?"

"Like spare conduits, splicers. Nothing Duritz couldn't handle."

"So Duritz is a smuggler."

"He's just a distributor. The actual smugglers call themselves entrepreneurs."

"But how did they know to bring you here?"

"I gave them the coordinates and rowed in just like you did. They don't sail to Land. Too dangerous for their boats."

It all makes sense, but I feel like I'm missing something. "Why didn't you bring me with you?"

Mom makes a scoffing sound. "Your last semester at school? And not knowing if I would make it to Land safely, or what I'd find here? No way. You're too important."

"I wouldn't have minded. I hated school."

"But I would have. I'm still wondering how Drayton convinced you to sail here. I taught you to be more levelheaded."

I feel like I'm ten again. "Mom. The PC was getting weird. We've been living a lie on the Platform. There was all this evidence about stuff, bad stuff."

"I know. The evidence is true. And I am happy you are here. But I worry about your career. Your life. That's what moms do."

We smile at each other. Then I realize that Mom has been alone all this time. "Didn't you go mad here? I mean, you're all alone, but you still managed to send us signals."

"Not all alone. There are many who live on this island. They reactivated the navigational beacon that you and Drayton discovered years ago, not me. The PC hasn't told us yet."

"What? Why?"

"It's a threat to them. They don't want mass panic."

"You didn't send a message in Morse code of my name?"

Mom laughs. "They've been sending every name for years. Coincidence. Enough—let me show you the facility."

I look at my feet. Someone took my shoes off.

"I took them off. They were so worn and filthy." Mom grabs a pair of shoes from the floor and hands them to me. "These are for you."

My eyes almost pop out of my head. "Trainers? For me? Where'd you get them? These are awesome!"

"Plenty of them available here. We'll have to go to the mall soon. It's in town. Now come on."

I smell the inside of the shoes. They're new, never been worn. Delighted, I slip my feet into the trainers and tie the shoelaces carefully. I've only had one pair of trainers in my life, and when I outgrew them, I was devastated. I'd cut holes in the tips just to wear them longer. I rub my head. "That doorjamb did a doozy on me."

Mom looks thoughtful. "It was quite an entrance for our reunion."

I give Mom my best hurt look.

"Please, don't even try it. That look never worked on me."

I grin. "I missed how we joke around. That and everything else."

"Me too." Mom takes my hand and kisses the palm. She's done that since I was a kid. "We have all the time in the world to catch up now."

I follow her through the door and down a long hallway. Large windows line one side. Everything is alive inside as much as outside. Plants with trailing tendrils hang from the roof in front of each window. I am walking through a different world. Land.

"It's so green. Everything looks like it's waiting to be smelled, picked, or admired."

"All the time," Mom replies.

We pass a man painting the hallway. He's dressed in a white jumper like Mom. Mom greets him, but he doesn't reply. He just stares at her.

"Hard to make friends?" I ask.

"Josiah's not a talker," Mom responds. She opens a door at the end of the hallway, and I enter a laboratory. The inventory is impressive. Medical supplies, computer monitors, lots of wires and plastic goods line long metal tables. An odor is prevalent.

"What's that smell?"

"Vinegar," Mom says. "It's a safe cleaning liquid. They have a huge supply of it, so you'll smell it everywhere."

We enter another hallway. There are rows of cabinets and lockers and all kinds of safety paraphernalia. Some of the suits look like space suits. Buckets are piled on top of the lockers. Several mops and brooms are propped in the corner. Two bins labeled "soiled" and "clean" jut out of the wall.

"Mom. The sign on the door. I've seen it before, but I can't remember where."

Mom leads us through an arched opening, then down a shorter hall to another door. The doors are all the same—white painted metal with a pull lever and button locking mechanism.

"It's by the stove. It was your great-grandmother's. She worked here."

Wow. Now I feel like I'm walking through my ancestor's life. "She did?"

"Yep. She was a sustainability engineer. That's how she ended up on the Platforms. She was the most respected in her field at the time, and they needed her expertise for long-term Platform habitation. She didn't want to go, but in the end, she left Land. She was pregnant with your grandmother and wanted to ensure that her child would survive."

Tidal. "Why didn't you tell me about her before?"

"I did. You weren't interested. Too stuck in that laptop of yours."

"And the pineapple?"

"The knocker?"

"Yes. It was familiar, too."

Mom chuckles. "I sang you a song about pineapples when you were a baby. Besides that, I don't know."

"Oh. Maybe I dreamed it."

We enter a large room with black overstuffed couches and chairs stacked with comfortable-looking pillows. The walls are bright orange and yellow. Large bay windows line the eastern side of the room. Sunshine spots the beige rug. I turn around in awe and think of my monochrome tin can room. Then of my great-grandmother. "She didn't have anything to do with the virus release, did she?"

"No. Thankfully, we don't have that legacy to bear." Mom sits on a sofa and pats the space next to her. "Come sit by me. The director will be with us shortly. He wants to meet you, and he's making his rounds."

"The director? Of what?"

"The director of this research facility."

"Okay." I sit. The sofa swallows me up. It feels like it's made of air. This room smells more like the spices at Lisette's house. Minty. Portraits line the walls, and I recognize many of the last names common on the Platforms. This place is like a time capsule. I shiver.

"Are you cold?"

"No. I'm adjusting. This chair doesn't have any structure. It's strange."

"Lean back to get the complete feel of it. I did the first time I sat in one."

I lean back and close my eyes. The luxury is ridiculous. Like the pre-packaged food from the store we found last night.

"What Platform is he from?" I finally ask.

"None." A deep voice fills the room.

I open my eyes. I sit up slowly so that I don't look foolish.

"I'm from Land. This is my home."

I locate the source of the voice. A medium-height man with a broad, muscular face and curling, dark hair is standing in front of the windows. His features are even and not unattractive. A long scar runs from his eye to the corner of his mouth. His eyes are singular, golden-brown in color.

The director motions to my mom. "May I join you a moment? I am passing through to the research laboratories."

Mom stands up. "Please. This is my daughter, Josephine."

I rise as well and offer my hand. "Call me Joe."

Mom laughs. "I was hoping for Josephine, but I guess it's Joe. A mother can dream."

The director crosses the room. He takes my hand and shakes it firmly. "Director Vraise. Glad to have you here. I have heard a lot about you. Your mother is an invaluable asset to our rebuilding program."

I look inquisitively at my mom then back at Director Vraise. "Rebuilding?"

Mom sits down. "I haven't shared the Institute's purpose with her."

Director Vraise sits across from us, so I happily sink back into the luxury of the cushions. He smiles at me, but his eyes are calculating, like PC Fristhe's.

"We are rebuilding here on Land."

"Rebuilding from what? What happened here exactly?"

"Humanity wasn't wiped out," Director Vraise says matter-of-factly. "That's a good place to start the story. In fact, the humanoids left on this continent grew stronger. Their immune systems adjusted, and they quickly overthrew the Moralists. Unfortunately, the infrastructure was already destroyed. Surviving was a struggle for the first generation."

"It's still a struggle," Mom says quietly.

Director Vraise nods. "The first generation scraped a new life from the wreckage. The second rebuilt in new locations. My group—part of the third generation—was lucky to find this facility in nearly pristine condition."

Director Vraise's accent becomes clipped the more he speaks. I have to really focus to understand him. "Congratulations. How many were originally left, Director Vraise?"

"After the genocide or the Moralists? Both took a toll on the human population."

I look at my trainers. An overwhelming feeling of guilt presses me. My family had escaped all of this and left the others to die. "Sorry. After the genocide. Or both, I guess. The total."

"Several thousand in the States. After the first generation, records are less certain as groups didn't communicate with one another, but the best estimate is one thousand. After the second, a little over five hundred."

The scientist within me kicks in. "Why the drop off in population if the virus was no longer a threat and the Moralists overthrown?"

"Lack of females. Many believed it was the end of the human era on Earth. But, by the third generation, our numbers here began to grow again."

"But only here?"

"We are one group on an island, so we don't know. That is where your mother and others like her are helping us. It's why my group reestablished this research facility. To answer questions and move forward with our brothers and sisters of the Platforms and Land."

I look at Mom.

"There are three of us who made it here from the Platforms. We all noticed the signs of life on Land and followed them. One has been sent to the Mainland, and the other works in the sustainability department. We were all removed by the PC."

I say some bad words in my mind about the PC. "What's the sustainability department?"

"We are no longer focused merely on surviving as a species," Director Vraise explains. "Our focus is on the future. We have the time and energy to cultivate non-survival programs like plant and animal research, technological innovation, communications, and long-term sustainability."

The Platforms are in sustainability mode, so I understand. "Why try to contact us?"

"We need to connect to others of our kind, begin to explore our Land world again, and develop our societies. We don't have time to reconstruct technology we should have never lost, so we need Platform help. A new life awaits us all, one of equality and friendship."

All of this equality and friendship talk sounds great, but at the end of the day, he needs Platform help to rebuild technology quickly. "But the PC said—"

Mom interrupts me. "They lie. I know they've said no one survived, but the rest of the staff are all from Land."

Director Vraise nods. "Those with me here are interested in research and the resurrection of connective technology so that we can make first contact in the four cardinal directions. We'd like to reach other continents, eventually, and repopulate the earth."

"Are you sure there are others?"

Director Vraise takes out a handkerchief and puts it to his forehead. "Others are mentioned in records the first generation kept. But we really don't know. They may have survived, as we have."

"Probably near the equatorial locations. Not too hot, not too cold."

"Indeed," Director Vraise says and chuckles. The sound reminds me of a shell scraping against metal. It's not pleasant, and definitely not full of humor. "We hope you will choose to work with your mother in restoring our communication capabilities. But no more history lessons for today, young lady. Please, explore. Not only within, but without. It is a remarkable thing, this Earth. It is long past time for the healing of all its people."

"Thank you. My friends…"

"I have met them, and they are roaming the facility. The only member of your party we have had to detain is Harriet. Fortunately, Apollo notified us when she tried to leave."

I raise my eyebrows.

"The dog's name is Apollo," Mom explains.

I narrow my eyes. "Are we not free to leave?"

Director Vraise raises his hands. "Not with several key pieces of lab equipment in your pockets."

I wish I was invisible. Harriet has self-imploded since we left the Platform. "She didn't. Tell me she didn't do that."

"She did," Mom says. "Her parents would be disappointed in her."

Director Vraise sighs wearily. "We will keep her detained until she proves herself trustworthy. On Land, we are innocent and help each other remain innocent. We watch, we wait, and we thrive."

"Okay." The directive seems fair but intrusive. I don't want anyone to help me remain innocent.

"You will learn our ways. I must attend to my duties. Mignon."

Director Vraise bows to my mom, then strides across the room and leaves through a tan, wooden sliding door. The use of my mom's given name startles me. Dad always called her Em.

"Are you hungry?" Mom asks me.

I shake my head.

"Are you sure? You should eat. Something small?"

Mom sounds like Mom. "I'm too excited to eat. I will later."

Mom relents. "All right. I have to get to work. Go explore, but don't wander too far. There are still things we don't understand about Land and many malfunctioning machines since power was restored. Plus, we need to check that lump on your head. Come back for lunch."

Mom has never told me not to wander too far. There was no such thing as too far on the Platform. This new idea of space is heady and strange. "Okay."

Mom kisses me on the forehead. "Have fun."

"I will." I have a new world to explore.

# Chapter Twenty

I PUSH OPEN the nearest set of double doors and stop beneath a canopy laden with sweet-smelling, flowering vines. The flowers look like pink and white bells. Sensory input comes at me non-stop in long, colorful slices. Everything is in the process of becoming. I can't distinguish one scent or sound from the next one. My senses have to learn to process data more quickly.

A gigantic dome of glass and plastic soars over an organized garden in front of me. To the right and left are trees and wild space. I decide to bypass the covered garden in case Lisette is digging around. I want my first walk on Land to be solo.

I'm already damp as the humidity clings to my skin like a moist rag. My toe hits something that rolls, and I step gingerly around a small animal skeleton. Various wires and poles dot the landscape, and empty metal trash cans line the walkway. One of the poles says "Emergency Call Box Only." I stop and examine it. The box is fused shut, but I wonder what was inside of it and about the people who once used it.

I notice an electric cable spool several poles away. New electrical distribution wires connect a utility pole constructed of a composite material hewn into the shape of a traditional wood pole. I follow the line, and it looks like electricity is being siphoned away from the Institute and over the edge of the fence. "To re-electrify the town?"

I don't expect an answer, as I'm alone, but when I turn back I see a classroom of twenty-five children walking from the domed garden area to a separate, circular building near the open space. They're all dressed in the same white jumpers I've seen on all the Institute personnel. I guess they range in age from three to maybe ten years old. But they aren't playing or running or causing havoc like Platform Complex children. They are walking in perfect lines. And they're all boys.

I watch until they disappear into the building. I read the lettering—Aquatics Center.

"Don't judge," I say and look away. "Explore the space." I return to the Emergency Call Box and travel in the other direction. I feel powerful walking on Land. A light breeze ruffles my hair, and grass tickles my ankles. Clumps of weeds with delicate white flowers bloom every few meters. A bird with brown-and-black markings flies overhead and lands in a tree. Bushes clump together in the most impractical places. And the trees are tall and strong, lithe.

I want to climb a tree. I pick out the perfect one—not too tall or wide—and put my hands on the trunk. The bark is coarse like dead coral. It smells alive and tiny ants climb in its rivulets. I press my face against it, hug it, then reach for the nearest branch and hoist myself up. A caterpillar runs across my hand as I reach for another branch and climb higher. It tickles. I can't reach the next tier, so I sit on the tree branch I'm on and look around.

Land stretches out before me. A fence surrounds the whole Institute. There are no gates, but several sections are missing. I see clusters of taller buildings to the east and the remains of several bridges to the north. Highways connect everything like arteries on a flat body. The air hums with life. A butterfly drifts in front of me, and I reach out to touch it.

"You'd definitely break something if you fell now. So don't fall."

"Ah!" I scream. I grab onto the tree's trunk and steady myself. I don't recognize the voice and search for where it came from. There's no one beneath the tree or above me. I have never heard voices, but there's a first time for everything. I gulp.

"From this height, it'll be a fracture. I know from experience."

I look around again, then at the tree.

"Up here. Eight o'clock."

I shade my eyes. There is a boy dressed in brown jeans and a long sleeve green shirt sitting in the branches above me. He has on gloves and a backpack. He blends in so completely that I'd missed him when I glanced up.

"I'm Ulster. And you are…"

I stammer out, "J-joe." Ulster doesn't move. I hold on tighter to the tree trunk. "Umm…is this your tree?"

"No, it's the Estuary's. I'm collecting samples. Some of these trees are dying, and I need to figure out why. It's one of my missions at the Estuary."

"Oh. You work here." Ulster has dark, straight hair. His smile is genuine and takes up the entire bottom half of his face. He looks similar to Director Vraise—same angular cheek bones and muscular neck—but his eyes aren't golden. They're dark brown. And he has beautiful skin. "You aren't in the white jumper, so I didn't know."

"Field work," Ulster replies.

His teeth are very white, his voice soft and disarming. I realize that I'm staring and look away. "Well, I'll be going then."

"Wait. You're one of the Platformers, right?"

"Platformers? Is that what you call us?"

"Yeah. What do you call yourselves?"

"In school we called ourselves refugees. But I don't think that's applicable anymore."

"Oh, right. Hang on."

Ulster swings down the branch, then slides his arms around the tree's trunk. He lands neatly on the branch across from me.

"Ulster," he says and offers me his hand. "A proper introduction. We aren't savages here on Land."

"Joe," I say and put my hand in his. His accent is also short and the vowels clipped, but he's not as hard to understand as Director Vraise. He doesn't take off his gloves. "I didn't say you were."

"Want me to show you around?"

Something about Ulster makes me want to say yes, but I did want to take my first walk alone. "I don't want to put you out. You have work to do."

"No problem. It's nothing that can't wait. Things on Land don't move around. It'll be here when I come back."

I stare at Ulster. His eyes are captivating now that I can really look at them. They are dark, but one has a lighter gold portion rimming the iris.

"That was a joke. Seriously, I don't mind."

I laugh shrilly, and I would kick myself if I could. "The samples for your work. Are they time sensitive?"

"No, not really." He reaches around to pull his backpack to his front, and I notice several small bark pieces and leaves in his other gloved hand. He deftly removes a test tube from the backpack and uncorks it with one hand, then gently pours the samples into it with his other. With the cork back in place and the tube securely stored in his backpack, Ulster takes off his gloves and puts them in his pocket.

He looks at me expectantly, and I realize I've watched the whole efficient procedure with my mouth open. I close it. "Well then, okay."

Ulster flashes me a huge grin. "Great. I'll climb down first in case you get into trouble."

"Why would I get into trouble?"

"I assume you haven't climbed a tree before. Climbing up is one thing. Climbing down is quite another. I still haven't mastered it."

Ulster climbs expertly down the tree. I mimic his motions with no problem, but I'm definitely less graceful.

"Not so bad."

"You were great! One minute." Ulster kneels and takes out several test tubes from his backpack, checking to make sure none have broken. Satisfied they are whole, he returns them to his backpack.

It looks like something Lisette would do. "You have to meet Lisette."

"I have. She's great. I couldn't sway her to leave the garden—not even to work with the trees. She knows a lot about plants."

I like Ulster. "That's Lisette."

Ulster stands and brushes off his pants. Small pieces of grass fall from the material. He points to the campus. "Now, for the tour."

Ulster is easy to listen to. He's very informative and describes the trees and plant in the area. It's obvious that he loves what he does. He recounts what the Estuary looked like five years ago before active restoration and points out the new trees and gardens he has personally planted from stored seed supplies.

"We are now beginning to study marine vegetation."

"Why? I thought technology was your priority. Reconnecting to the greater land masses. The world."

"That's Dad's priority. Not mine. I stick with living things of the root variety."

I examine a patch of pretty yellow flowers on the edge of the pathway. "Dad? You mean Director Vraise is your dad?"

"Yep." He points to the flowers. "What you're looking at there is a waxflower. Wildflower, very common. And tenacious."

I didn't picture Director Vraise having a family. He seemed so focused on his mission. "What about your mother?"

Ulster doesn't look at me when he answers. "She went back to the Mainland years ago. I don't remember her much. She didn't like island life. It's not for everyone. Lots of communal work and planning."

"I'm sorry," I say. I can empathize. "I understand. I didn't like Platform life. I hate living on the water."

A long, piercing whistle sounds. I've never heard anything like it, and it hurts my ears.

"What does that mean? I know it's a whistle—we have them on the Platforms, but not as loud or as high pitched."

"It means lunch, and I'm starving. Let's go."

I can't deny that I'm hungry, so I follow Ulster.

"Watch your step. We haven't thoroughly cleaned this segment of the grounds. Some of these wires may be live."

"Is there a functioning substation? You don't use fossil fuels, do you?"

"Course not," Ulster responds. "Fossil fuel technology was antiquated before the Moralists came to power. The solar generation infrastructure was already in place and easy to repair. There are still almost a hundred unused panels in the Estuary's storage. We've spliced the lines and built our own substation. We worry about new materials, though. All the manufacturing plants were on the Mainland."

Ulster's worry sounds familiar.

"But you can access the Mainland from here."

"Yes, but it's tricky. The Mainland is a disaster. Shells of homes, craters where industries used to be. This facility wasn't too damaged because of its island location."

"It sounds like the Platforms. An island so close to other things, but so far away really."

"Exactly."

"But your mom's there?"

"Yeah, she's there. Duke, Edward. Thanks for fixing the leak."

We pass two gentlemen in white jumpers carrying a large piece of plastic tubing. I don't make eye contact. "What leak?"

"One of our in-house water tanks blew an elbow."

"Bad for water pressure."

"But easily repairable."

I pick up a feather in the grass and put it in my pocket. I want to save something from my first Land walk. We come to two wood thatched structures that smell like earth and excrement.

"What's in these?"

"This is where we hold our livestock."

"Livestock?"

Ulster cups his hands around his mouth. "Bok-bok-bok."

Several round mammals with thin legs strut from the structure.

"You have chickens?"

Ulster takes a bucket hanging from the side of the structure and throws them some golden colored seeds. "Yep. We gather eggs in the morning. You'll have some for breakfast tomorrow. They're decent animals, long as you feed them."

The chickens peck at the seeds, and I prevent myself—barely—from squealing. Their feathers are smooth and creamy white, and their beaks look sharp.

"Is that corn?"

"I think so," Ulster replies. "I confess, I don't usually work with the farm animals." Ulster leads me into the other structure.

"We have goats and cows here as well. They provide our milk. We're lucky to have them."

"Milk," I say slowly. The concept is so foreign to me that I don't feel any way at all about it. "To drink?"

"Breakfast will be interesting for you tomorrow—eggs and milk. You'll love them both."

I'm not as comfortable around the goats and cows because they're bigger and their cries scare me. And they stink.

"You don't eat them, do you?"

Ulster shakes his head. "Too valuable as a continuous food source."

"Good thing," I say. I pet one of the cows. She looks at me with disdain. I may not like them, but I don't want them to be slaughtered and eaten.

"We'll miss lunch if we don't get a move on," Ulster says.

"Right. Sorry!"

We reach a set of heavy metal doors, and Ulster opens one side for me. I mutter, "Thank you." Six rows of benches attached to long tables crisscross the room. Thirty people could fit on each row. I estimate there are almost one hundred people inside, including my friends. Lisette and Chanko are focused on eating and don't see me. I catch Drayton's eye, and he salutes me. I lift my hand in a "one minute" gesture to Drayton because the food smells delicious.

Two metal carts are set up against the far wall. Steam rises from one. There are stacks of plates—actual plates. Not signs made into plates, or pieces of plates. Best of all, there is no meter to scan for distribution.

"We serve ourselves from what is here," Ulster explains and grabs a plate. "Everyone shares. We harvest daily, so it's fresh. Take as much as you want."

There are at least twenty different food items of various colors and textures with serving utensils placed in them. I can tell some of them are vegetables, as they are firm and sliced and look starchy. One dish is soupy, and I recognize cucumbers in it. Another is frothy, like it's been whipped.

"What is all of this? I've never seen so many non-slimy things gathered in one place."

"Salad from the garden. Lots of great vegetables today. Take some of each, you'll like them. That is mashed potatoes. This is pea soup."

I sample one scoop of everything Ulster lists. I take a little extra of things that aren't green, like the mashed potatoes and what Ulster tells me is sweet corn.

"There is a water tap here, so drink your fill," Ulster says. "Glasses below this shelf. The water is clean, as we have reconstructed the solar filtering system. What's left of your food goes to compost."

"Compost," I whisper. I look at the plate of food, then back to Ulster. We don't even think about managing waste food on the Platforms. We never have any. "This is totally different. Like flood and drought."

"We still eat the same way, put our clothes on the same way. It's not hard to get used to. Give yourself a day or two."

I feel like Ulster is waiting for a response, but I don't have one to give him.

"Go ahead and join your friends. I'll rejoin you after mealtime."

"Okay." Ulster leaves, and I feel stupid for not asking him to sit with us. Next time. I put a glass with pretty gold pressed designs beneath the water tap and watch as water flows and flows into it—as much as you can drink.

I head to the table where Drayton, Lisette, and Chanko are seated.

"Joe," Lisette says. "When did you get here?"

"Just now."

"How's your head?" Chanko asks.

"Still attached."

"We were worried, but your mom convinced us you were okay," Lisette says between bites of food.

"Wait until you taste this stuff," Chanko says. "We've been living on the low end of the diet spectrum."

I scoop a forkful of salad into my mouth and chew. My mouth explodes with taste and pleasure. Nothing is stinky, dried, or slimy, and the textures roll across my tongue, smooth and creamy. I move on to the warm items. Firm, sweet, and delicious.

"No words, right?" Chanko says and points his fork at me. "Inexplicable goodness. Eat up."

"It's all glorious," Drayton says. Something about the tone of his voice is off. He has dark circles under his eyes, and his hair is tousled. Drayton's hair is never tousled.

"What's up?"

Drayton shakes his head. "Nothing. It's just so glorious. Profoundly, perfectly glorious."

Drayton doesn't mean that it's glorious, and I don't want to ask him what he does mean in front of Lisette and Chanko. "Here's to glorious," I say and lift my glass.

Lisette lifts hers, and Chanko follows suit.

Drayton half raises his glass.

"Did your mom tell you about Harriet?" Lisette asks.

"Uh-huh," I say and chew.

"I feel sorry for her. She won't leave her room. She doesn't like the guard they set to watch her. She has to be lonely. She's so social on the Platform."

"Are you kidding? She's a nuisance on the Platform."

"She just wanted to keep up with you," Lisette says.

I consider Lisette's words. I feel bad. I never tried to be Harriet's friend. We were always rivals. "I guess."

Lisette smiles. "Always time for a second chance. I'll see you in the garden. I have all kinds of things to show you."

"It's a date. Especially since this stuff comes from it. I may get on my knees and eat it right from the ground. I've always wanted to do that."

Chanko pushes his chair back. "Director Vraise said I could create a map of working infrastructure in the old city. No one has done that yet. One of the Landers is taking me after mealtime."

"Cool," Drayton says. "See you."

Which leaves Drayton and me with an opportunity to talk privately.

"What's this glorious stuff?"

"They have me looking at their engines. They need help in power conversion. I'm not sure for what. I want to lay low for a while."

"Lay low? I plan on being as large as possible and learning as much as possible, not to mention walking on a surface that doesn't move as much as possible. I'm not laying low for a moment."

"Did you notice the new utility poles?"

"I did," I reply. "Why?"

Drayton rubs his forehead like he has a headache. "Don't contact Flox yet. Just trust me."

"Did you tell them how we got here?"

Drayton sneezes and wipes his nose. "I agreed with what they thought. Flox helped us, handed us off to smugglers. Then we rowed here. So keep it secret. Can you do that?"

I don't mind keeping it to myself. It's better to be safe than sorry. "Yep. Are you sick?"

"I think I have allergies. My head feels like it's about to explode."

"That's new. Did you ask if they have medicine for it?"

"I did. Don't trust Ulster."

"Why not?"

"Because."

I don't say that's a stupid reason because Ulster sits down across from us.

# Chapter Twenty-one

"ULSTER, THIS IS DRAYTON."

"We've met," Drayton says.

"How's the food?" Ulster asks at the same time.

"Unbelievable," I say. "I can't imagine how I ever ate sponge. Seaweed. Fish. *Dried* fish. Most anything I've always eaten."

Ulster laughs. "I don't think I'd like the cuisine at sea."

Drayton drums his fingers on the table. "Probably not. So you specialize in plant health? Trees?"

"I wouldn't call it a specialty. I work in reclaiming the ecosystem that once thrived here. This week, a mystery ailment affecting trees has my attention. Next week, I could be investigating bee hives."

"Bees," I echo. "How cool."

"Buzz, buzz," Ulster says playfully.

Drayton's voice is flat when he speaks. "How'd you learn how to care for the ecosystem?"

"I attended class in the next building over. We have records of what was here before the Revolution, so that was most of the curriculum. That, and normal reading and writing, math, science."

"At the Aquatic Center?" I ask. "I saw some kids going in there today."

"Exactly."

Drayton laughs loudly and stands. "Knowledge is power, isn't it? See you."

Drayton leaves the table quickly. His abruptness verges on rudeness. I'm embarrassed for him.

"He's not normally like that."

"It's okay. I don't mind answering his questions. Do you want to see more of the facility?"

"I'm going to spend some time with Lisette in the garden. Maybe later?"

Ulster bows to me and says, "At your service," which is totally weird, before he leaves.

I make a half bow and mutter, "Okay. Me too."

There a few white jumpsuit-clad individuals still in the cafeteria, but none of them are Mom. I want to show her my empty plate like I did when I was a little girl. And have her check my head.

"Hi."

A tallish girl appears at the end of the table—maybe ten or eleven years old. Her features are so similar to Ulster's, they must be related. Her hair is a glossy black, long and wildly curly.

"Hello," I respond politely. "Who are you?"

"Eugenie," the girl says and sits down. "My bones are intact."

"Eugenie. That's a pretty name." I ignore the second part as I have no idea what it means. "Are you Ulster's sister?"

She giggles. "Yes."

"I'm Joe."

Eugenie claps her hands. "You're a Platformer."

Eugenie sounds curious. I would be too. "Yes. That's where I'm from. It's like walking on a rolling piece of Land that never stays still. The food is bad and there is no space. Just viaducts and squares. Nothing green."

"Different. My bones are intact."

"It is different," I say. "Nice to meet you." I pick up my dish and place it in the bucket with the other soiled dishes then turn to look at the room.

Eugenie is right beside me. She touches my arm shyly.

"Oh, hello again."

Eugenie smiles.

"Come, Eugenie."

I recognize the voice as Director Vraise's. He takes Eugenie's hand. "Eugenie should be in school. She should not be mixing with the adults."

I like being called an adult, but I feel bad for Eugenie. "She wasn't bothering me. I was waiting around for Mom."

"Your mother is working through lunch. Good day." Director Vraise leads Eugenie away. Director Vraise doesn't seem like a fun dad. There are three people still eating, and since I don't want to meet anyone else, I head out of the double doors toward the garden.

It will be nice to listen to Lisette chatter.

☙❧

Lisette never stops talking, and after several hours of poking around in the dirt with her, I'm tired.

"Drayton says we can't talk about *The Fluddery Doo* yet," Lisette concludes. "I'm worried about Drees."

"They're fine," I reassure her. "Probably concocting new genetically improved jelly fish."

Lisette giggles. She looks like she is going to say something else, but then two researchers walk by. They stare at us.

We stare back. "Are they all attractive?" I ask when they're out of earshot.

"You've noticed it, too."

"Of course. Tallish, darkly handsome. Not a bad combination."

We walk back to the main campus entrance. Lisette describes several of the different plants that we pass and speculates about their viability on the Platforms. She helps me distinguish colors and shapes. Every bloom and leaf is singular, distinctive. I ring the doorbell when we get to the front door.

Eugenie answers it. "Joe."

"Yes. Good memory, Eugenie. This is Lisette."

Eugenie turns around and leaves us at the door.

Lisette says, "Nice to meet you," but Eugenie is already gone.

I shrug my shoulders. "Kids."

We enter the main lobby. Eugenie reappears with two envelopes in her hand. "For Joe and Lisette."

"Thank you," Lisette and I both say at the same time. We look at each other. I say "hook" first, but Lisette gets to "hook, line, sinker" before I do. We both laugh.

Lisette rips her envelope open. "Oh! Fun!"

I run the paper across my chin. It's smooth and smells like ink and vinegar. I finally open it and read.

PARTY IN HONOR OF THE PLATFORMERS. 21:00 AT THE WATER TOWER.

I don't particularly want to go to a water tower. I can think of only two things that we will do—climb or swim—but I'm going to be brave about it and go. No one's ever thrown a party for me before.

Eugenie pulls on my arm. "It's from my brother."

"I thought it was. Thank you for delivering it."

"I'm going, too. My bones are intact," Eugenie says and skips away.

"Okay," I say. I have to ask Ulster about the bones intact stuff. Lisette and I reach the stairway landing and several doors are to the right and left. Lisette spins around in the middle of the landing.

She strikes a dance pose. "A party! We can all go together. What's a water tower?"

"It's a reservoir of water on tall stilts."

"That sounds cool!"

"Ish. See you later." I open the door to my room and close it behind me, turning the lock with a *click*. A new set of clothes is set out for me on the bed. I would choose clothes like this—functional but not boring. I run my hand over the shirt. The fabric is smooth and dyed a true red. The pants are khaki with lots of pockets and cut with wide, loose legs. The material will be cool and practical on Land. Mom must have known about the party and taken her lunch to get me clothes.

Then I notice a door on the opposite side of the room. I'm curious, so I check it out. I gasp and do a funky dance move. A bathroom with a real sit-down tub. I perch on the rim then roll into it. I untie my shoes and throw them on the floor. I don't want to ruin them. I stop the drain and turn the spigot to the right. Water comes gushing out. I don't even take my clothes off. I just let the water rise around me until I feel buoyant and warm.

When the water is about to spill over, I turn the faucet off and float in the tub. I duck my head underneath the surface and hold my breath. I push up and laugh. I feel incredibly wasteful and relaxed.

I look at myself in the full-length mirror on the door—a wet mess. "Clean thyself," I command and take off my clothes, a challenge now that they're soaked. I toss them into the sink so they don't get the floor too wet. The soap in the dish smells like flowers and rain. I lather it between my hands and put bubbles on my nose. I've always wanted to make bubbles. I'm wrapped in warmth, and I love the entire experience.

I step out of the bathtub and dry myself off with the towel provided on the rack. It's soft and fluffy, so I take time to caress every part of my body with it. I have never felt so clean, so alive, in my life.

I hang my wet clothes off the side of the tub and slip into the new ones. Comfort wraps me, and I decide that a nap is in order. Just before I lie down, my door opens.

"What?" I blurt the question because I had locked the door from the inside.

"Joe," Eugenie says happily.

"Eugenie. How'd you get the door open? I thought I locked it."

Eugenie holds up a key and laughs. "I have all the keys."

"Eugenie. It isn't nice to open people's locked doors without permission. You should knock, then ask to enter."

Eugenie laughs harder, then points at me. "Joe."

"Yes. Will you give me the key?"

Eugenie looks at me, then the key in her hand. She shakes her head.

"Why not?"

"It's for Ulster," she says and winks at me.

"Ah, no," I say hastily. I reach for Eugenie, but she bolts down the hall. I stick my head out to yell after her, but she is gone. "All right," I mutter. I lock the door, then drag the only chair in the room in front of it and secure it beneath the doorknob.

I return to my bed and lie down. There are so many things to consider. A new life, a career. Mom. Land. Dad. Drayton. Ulster wants the key to my room?

Eugenie is probably just playing matchmaker. But I don't like that there is a key to my room floating around the Estuary.

༄ஓ

I jolt awake from a hard sleep. The whistle is blowing, and it is even louder inside the building.

"It must be dinner," I say after a few seconds of confusion. The room is darker, so I know it is dusk. I'm already dressed, so I move the chair away from the door and exit my room. I don't bother locking the door.

The hallway is deserted. I pass several closed doors but notice one open at the end of the corridor. It's a materials closet with blue and green lab coats stored inside. There are several boxes labeled "gloves," "scopes," and "disposables."

I open the next set of doors and realize that I've taken a wrong turn and I'm in the medical wing. It looks like a surgery ward. There's a buzz, like a light isn't fully connected, and several gurneys line the hallway. A large desk is in the center of the next room. Two tables with warming lights are close to it. Several open-backed surgery gowns hang on a nearby rack.

I shiver and back out of the doors. I need to ask Mom what kind of surgery they do.

"Josephine?"

I stop in my tracks. Director Vraise is in a surgical gown in front of one of the gurneys. He radiates tension, as if something is terribly wrong.

"Yes, I..." I struggle, then blurt out, "Joe. I was looking to get my concussion checked out."

"Of course." Director Vraise relaxes and presses a button on the wall. "Shallick," he says. "Please report to Surgery 1."

I don't hear a reply but before I can ask any questions, a shorter man I assume is Shallick arrives, takes my arm, and leads me from the surgery area and down a narrow hallway to a room enclosed by a plastic curtain. There is a table flanked by two rolling stools. A desk is against the only wall.

"Sorry," I stammer. "I wanted to have my concuss..."

I trail off as Shallick lifts me onto a table and turns the lights off.

I panic. "Umm—"

A bright light with four hand-sized plastic flaps around it descends from the ceiling and positions itself above my head. The flaps close until they are an inch from my face and turn counterclockwise. The light above my head pulsates and strange star-like patterns dot the flaps in front of my eyes before sharpening into one beam.

"Follow the light."

I follow the light. After several seconds, the flaps retract and the mechanism returns to the ceiling. "What is that?"

"Computed Tomography Scanner," Shallick says. A board lights up on the wall. Several images of what I realize is my brain flash onto the board. Shallick examines them and turns to me. He has the same sloping nose as Ulster and Eugenie. "Results. You are fine. The exit is to your right."

"Okay," I respond.

Shallick sits down at the desk in the corner of the room. He doesn't say goodbye, but I don't mind. I'm creeped out. I exit and find my way down the stairs and back into the main gathering place that serves as the Estuary's common room.

Chanko and Lisette are already at a table, so I go to the food bar and put slightly less on my plate than I did at lunch. There are labels on the food choices this time, and I pick squash, pumpkin, and peas. No one speaks to me, and I still don't see my mom.

Lisette beckons to me, so I take my plate to their table.

"You look so pretty," she says.

I slide in next to Chanko. "Thanks. I took a bath and got my head scanned."

"Oh! How was that? Head okay?"

I flash an okay sign with my hand and dig into the food. I'm hungry, probably more because the food is so good and less because my body needs the calories. "But really creepy. We thought the PC doctors had bad bedside manners. Where's Drayton?"

"Took a plate of food to Harriet."

I feel a twinge of guilt. But not for long.

Chanko continues. "You need to see the city, Joe."

"Why?"

"Communications holds court. Co-axial cables, telephone wiring, electric couplers all hooked up for quick service. You would find it fascinating. Darwin, one of the researchers, and I had a close call with a sinkhole due to water leakage beneath the ground, but besides that, it was awesome. I could resurrect that city. I want to."

"Sounds like you enjoyed it. Are you going again tomorrow? I need to understand how the existing grid is set up if I'm going to hook up network communications."

Chanko smiles. "Yes. That'd be cool. You and me. Alone, in a deserted city. We can bring snacks. Pretend the moon is up."

"Don't forget about Darwin," I say and stuff more food into my mouth. The pumpkin is delicious.

"He doesn't let me. Can't go anywhere without him by my side."

"Sounds like a handler."

"Speaking of," Lisette whispers.

Ulster walks by our table. I expect him to join us, but he walks past us. I elbow Lisette. "How is that speaking of?"

Lisette's face gets red. "I don't know. He could handle me. Any day."

Chanko laughs. So do I. I push away my plate. "I get it. He's all yours, Lisette."

Drayton sits next to Lisette and eats the peas off my discarded plate. "Who's Lisette's?"

"One, that's my food—disgusting. And two, none of your business."

"I don't feel like getting a plate. You didn't eat half of this."

One of the Landers sits at the end of our table. Lisette and Chanko slip off the bench. "We both want seconds," Lisette explains.

"Good for you," I say.

Drayton scrapes my plate with his fork then points to the Lander at the end of our table. "The genetic similarities are uncanny."

I look around the cafeteria. There are three or four women, and the rest are men. Same face shape, nose type, similar eyes and heights. I think about the children I saw earlier. It is odd, but maybe I'm being paranoid. "Dominant traits. Going to the party?"

Drayton nods. "Wouldn't miss it."

"Is there a lights out time here?"

"Ask Ulster. He seems to be waiting for your attention."

I pretend that I'm stretching. "Do you have to be so obvious? And loud?"

"Does he? I'll see you tonight. Think on Eiffel."

Drayton finishes off the last bites of peas on the way to the food bar, then puts the plate and fork in the bucket. The hair stands up on the back of my neck. Drayton never drops our safe word for no reason. Two seconds later, Ulster sits across from me.

"I was waiting for him to leave."

"You didn't have to. We're all friends here, right?"

"Right. But this is personal. Eugenie told me she visited with you today." He looks very uncomfortable, and his voice falls over the words like he doesn't want to say them.

"It's okay."

"I wanted to explain. She likes you, and she has a very active…well, it's like she has this other fantasy world, a play world she lives in. She thinks that you are a princess of sorts."

Now that is one thing I have never, ever thought of myself as. "What, and you're the prince?"

"Yes. I apologize."

Ulster looks like he is about to melt into a puddle on the floor. I sympathize with him. "No problem. There are worse things than being a princess in someone's fantasy world. I could be the wicked witch. Or a goblin or something. She's a kid, it's normal."

"Thanks. She doesn't understand privacy or boundaries. Let me know next time she barges in on you."

"Better a barge than nothing at all. My dad used to say that—barges mean supplies, but they're really hard to sort through. They stink."

Ulster looks at me quizzically. "You miss your dad?"

"Yes. It's funny, I've missed my mom so much that I didn't think about how it would feel to miss my dad. It's like the missing never stopped, it's just flipped from one parent to the other."

Ulster snaps his fingers. "How about a trip to the long pier before the water tower? You can see the Platforms from there."

"I'd like that."

The smile Ulster gives me is even more brilliant than the previous ones. "Great. I'll meet you out front. We'll have to go on my moto some of the way. It's too far to walk."

"Sure. What about Eugenie? She said she was going."

"I can ask Dad to bring her."

"Okay." I have to ask. "Ulster, Eugenie always mentions her bones are intact. Why?"

Ulster looks at the floor. "Hypophosphatasia. Genetic disorder. It's rampant in the female population here."

I don't want to sound stupid, and I know I've heard of it somewhere before, but I ask. "What is that?"

"Soft bones. Meet you by the main entrance in a few." Ulster darts out of the room. There are a few people left eating. They stare at me or ignore me. And they do all look similar. I wipe the table with my shirt sleeve and leave.

Soft bones? Eiffel may fall sooner rather than later.

# Chapter Twenty-two

I'M EXAMINING THE PINEAPPLE door knocker when I hear the loud *pop-pop-pop* of an engine. I turn around as Ulster pulls up on a loud, red-and-yellow motorcycle. I'd only seen one on Nod, and it was in a junk pile. They're completely impractical on constantly wet Platform roads.

"That's your moto?"

Ulster runs his hand along the handlebars. "Restored it myself. Hop on. It's completely safe."

I climb on the back of the motorcycle. "Okay. This is cool. Frightening, but cool."

Ulster puts his hand on my right knee. "Hang on!"

We lurch forward, and I slide to the side.

"Hold on to me!"

I get a good grip around Ulster's abdomen and hold on. I feel a little out of control, but anchored. The motorcycle hums beneath me. I am very aware that Ulster is right in front of me, and that my arms are wrapped around him. He smells like the outdoors, and—

I scrunch my nose. Vinegar.

The ride away from the Estuary is a blur. Ulster slows down near the beach, then putters up to a three-story house built on five-foot stilts. He kills the motor. I jump off the motorcycle and stomp my feet on the ground.

"Well, we didn't die."

"Of course not. I'm an excellent driver. I have to stash the moto, then we'll catch a ride to the pier. It's clear tonight."

I follow Ulster up the steps to the front door. He pushes the motorcycle on the side of him, lifting the front wheel to clear each step. Vines cover every available surface, and part of the wood siding is falling off the porch. Two shutters are missing. The door used to be white, but now it is a dingy gray with scratch marks on the bottom. The sign says "Low Tide" in fading red paint, with the image of the ocean and the sun sinking below the horizon. I can still see the artist's signature.

"A. Belle," I say softly.

Ulster swings the door open. "Probably the former resident. Don't worry, we cleaned out the remains. Nothing frightening in here. Just a portrait of the past."

The interior looks like the vintage pictures we studied in school: sofas, televisions, seashells, and other decorative objects populate the rooms. The kitchen fascinates me. There's a blender and microwave on the counter, and hanging pots and pans above a stove. A silver refrigerator is in the corner. "Cleaned how?"

Ulster props the motorcycle up in the hallway. "We cleaned decaying matter and booby traps out of dozens of beach cottages. We found a whole family's bones in one down the block, dogs and cats included. The hardest part is always the carpet. You can't get the stench of death out of it. Or mildew. These houses are solid, built to withstand the salt and the humidity. Humans aren't."

Ulster's attitude is callous, which surprises me. "That's horrible."

Ulster look serious. "Progress can be. They're clean now, and usable. So we use them. Let's go. We'll miss the tram if we don't hurry."

"Tram?"

Ulster jogs across the beach, and I hurry after him. I struggle to keep up. I wouldn't have agreed to come if I'd known there was running involved. We jump over a gaping hole and avoid several stacks of cars. About a kilometer later I'm gasping for breath, but Ulster finally stops and announces, "Made it."

We are standing in a square in front of tracks. There are stores surrounding us, several with their windows busted out. One has a sign that says "Hardware," and another "Computer Repair."

Overhead cabling grabs my attention. "This is an electric tram?"

Ulster nods. "We run it three times a day for our staff working in the city. It's returning now."

I crouch and look at the tracks. They are cool to the touch. "How do we get back?"

Ulster indicates a white, round container on stilts another three kilometers or so from us. "Dauphin Island" is still legible in arched print across the body. It looks tall in comparison to the rest of the skyline. "We'll be near the water tower. We can catch a ride back, and I'll collect my moto tomorrow."

He has the details already planned out. Impressive. "Okay."

"Here it comes," Ulster says. "Get ready."

"For what?"

A red-and-white carriage the size of a pontoon rolls down the rails. It doesn't have a top, and two of the sides are missing. It's incredibly quiet. It stops in front of us.

"It isn't in the best shape, but it works. After you."

I step on the tram. There are metal rungs on the floor. "Slip your feet into these," Ulster says. "It doesn't travel over thirty kilometers per hour, but you need them to balance."

I follow his directions, and the tram starts moving again. He's right. The track takes a slow turn when it reaches the beach, and I put my arms out like I'm surfing. I bend one knee, then the other, and keep myself upright. It's exhilarating.

"The strip." Ulster indicates the massive buildings on the beach. Some are missing huge chunks. Others look like they've just been built. "They're all original hotels. We're fortunate—supplies galore. The tram connects them to the city center, the Mainland bridge, and the Estuary because it offered nature programs for tourists."

The tram slows, and Ulster steps off. I do too. "That was fun!"

Ulster laughs. "It's pretty tame, but fun I guess. The pier is behind this hotel."

The hotel was pink at one time. The entrance has ten double doors that look like a crooked grin. "Casino" is written in big letters underneath a word I can't make out. "What was it called?"

"The Imperial," Ulster responds. "We'll go around. The inside is gutted. Dad plans to make labs out of the ground floor rooms for a secondary campus."

"Why? It's so far away."

"Direct sea access."

"Oh." Being landlocked is a foreign concept to me. I yawn. So is not having a curfew.

"Careful," Ulster warns. "The walkway is broken here. We haven't connected the lights yet."

"Thanks." The walkway widens out into a large boardwalk, then a wooden pier. We reach the end of the pier, and Ulster invites me to sit on a bench. I rest my arms on the rail instead. There is a lovely breeze from the ocean, and the air smells wet and salty. Seagulls cry above us. It's the first time I've felt like I was back on the Platform since arriving on Land. I can make out the outlines of abandoned Platforms and maybe Nod. I feel homesick.

Ulster joins me. "Look at the moon. One day, I'm going there."

The moon is almost full and very clear. "To the moon?"

"Yes. I want to be the first post-Moralist Revolution person to stand on the moon. Ever since childhood, that's what I've dreamed of."

"That's cool, Ulster." I have to respect his goals, even though I can't imagine building a rocket in our lifetime.

Ulster puts his hand on my shoulder. "I knew you'd understand."

I feel uncomfortable, so I step back. Freedom feels a little scary, and not so free. "We all have dreams. They should be followed."

"Are you and Drayton a couple?"

I cringe and start to babble. "No. We've been best friends since we were in diapers in nursery school. Cloth diapers, by the way, hard to come by these days. Now people just use clothes that are no longer usable and potty train as soon as possible. We're running out of fabric on the Platform, and here you have whole malls full of it."

"So you aren't a couple?"

I take a deep breath and pull it together. "No. Shouldn't we go? I don't want to miss the party."

"Sure," Ulster says. "It's about a ten-minute ride. You do know how to ride a bicycle?"

"Yes," I say.

We walk back down the pier and to the other side of the hotel to a row of bicycles. They are red and have "The Imperial" painted on the side in white.

"Wow. So many."

"Take your pick," Ulster says. "We all use them. There are kiosks of bikes all over the city."

I pick out a smaller bike and get on it. "There's just so much *plenty*. We've already covered more square footage than Nod even has."

"Get ready for more," Ulster says and pedals down the walkway.

I'm not as quick on the bike, but after pedaling a while, I gain confidence. We cut across a grass area, then onto a paved path. Every so often there are faint white graphics of a bicycle or person. Lights are affixed to aluminum poles every twenty feet and turn on as we pass. They are powered by small, square solar panels.

I'm having a good time until I see the water tower. It's taller than the Empire on Nod. I brake when Ulster turns off the path. I step off the bike and approach the water tower slowly. In the moonlight, the tower looks like it's glowing. I park my bike next to Ulster's. The area is deserted. "Where's the party?"

Ulster is already climbing a ladder extending up the back of one of the legs. "Climb up!"

He disappears on a landing about forty feet above us. For the first time, I wish we were above water. Land is hard if you fall on it. I put my hands on an eye-level rung and start climbing. And climbing.

Ulster helps me onto the landing. It's the size of my house on the Platform. A flat piece of metal the size of a four-pack Platform solar panel loosely covers an opening in the center. The four corners are attached to a thick chain that extends up to the bottom of the water tower.

"Joe, meet Foad."

Foad keeps his hands on a small motor box with two buttons on it, red and green. His white jumper has red stripes on the sleeve.

"Hello," I say.

"Hello," Foad replies. He doesn't look at me, but his voice is soft and bears the same Land accent as Ulster's. "Have a nice time."

"Get in," Ulster says. "It's perfectly safe."

I doubt that, but I step gingerly on the metal lift. The motor cranks. It sounds like blades being sharpened. The metal sheet lifts off the tower frame in jerks. There are no edges, so I grab onto the chain above my head. The makeshift lift spins in the open space between the water tower legs and tips dangerously to the right.

"Hold on!" Ulster cries. "Almost there."

I'm not sure I'm going to make it. I feel dizzy. The metal sheet skitters to a stop when it reaches the highest landing. The base of the water tower is right above my head.

"We're here!"

I scramble off the still swinging metal sheet and hold on to the edge of the water tower. I look around. No people in sight, but I do hear a rolling sound. A piece of the water tower's surface is cut off where the landing joins the tower's wall. Ulster ducks through the opening. Nothing to do but follow him in.

I'm surprised to find no water in the tower. Wood scaffolding supporting crude, metal seating surrounds the rim of the tower. Several ramps curve around the inner circle. Forty or so people—more men than women, and no young kids—are on flat boards with wheels on them. I spot Lisette and Chanko rolling around. And Eugenie. I can't find Drayton.

"What is this called?"

"Skateboarding," Ulster says. "This is our ultimate skate park. There are a few other parks in the city."

"I saw one on the beach. A big U."

"Yes, exactly. Let's get you set up."

Ulster hands me a skateboard with orange wheels and shows me how to stand on it. He demonstrates how to kick and shift your weight so that you stay centered on the board. "Like this," he says and skates across the curved surface.

It looks hard. Some of the other Landers are doing flips off the water tower walls. "I'll work on that."

"Ulster!" A group of men with sticks beckon for Ulster to join them.

"Skateboard hockey," Ulster explains. "I'm an offensive striker."

"That's awesome." I have no idea what that is, but it sounds important. "Go ahead. I'll get this on my own."

"Are you sure?"

"Quite. Have fun!" Ulster skates away, and I relax. I prefer to attempt new things without a rapt audience. I give it a try, fall down three times in a row, then pick up the skateboard and walk to the periphery to find a seat.

"Not a fan?"

I recognize Drayton's voice before I see him tucked into the scaffolding's bracing arm behind me. "I tried three times. Failed three times. So no."

"Try again in a minute. It's not bad."

Eugenie falls off her skateboard right in front of me.

"Eugenie!"

She stands up. "I'm okay. Bones intact!"

She gets back on the skateboard and rolls away. And I remember where I know Hypophosphatasia from. It's Hermeneutic Lab's claim to fame. They fixed that as well as a slew of other genetic disorders with their splicing technology.

Drayton interrupts my train of thought. "Land to Joe."

"Yeah. Sorry, putting something together. What?"

"I asked you to come look at this."

"Okay." I scoot against the wall and follow Drayton through the exit. We walk around half of the water tower on a ring-shaped steel walkway. It's only a foot across in places, and I hold onto the hand holds on the water tower's body. "This is crazy scary. There should be a safety net."

"I know, but look." Drayton steps out of my way and I see the whole layout of Land. Roads intersect, houses are lined up in rows. Green spaces are geometric shapes, and tiny cars polka dot the entire vista.

I rest my back against the water tower. "That's spectacular."

"Agreed," Drayton says.

Something bothers me. By the light of the near-full moon, I can identify the centralized power plant by its cylindrical flue and cooling tower. There are three functioning electric power transmission tower lines stemming from the plant. They are linked by several substations. Tiny blinking lights are on top of each tower. "Notice anything off about the power grid?"

"I thought so but wasn't sure," Drayton says. "That's why I wanted you to take a look."

I recount. "One. Two. Three lines. Yep, that's odd. Ulster mentioned making the hotel a secondary campus. He didn't mention a third one."

"Maybe it's not on the official tour."

I follow the third line carefully with my right index finger. It runs east to the coast. A blur of lights surround the point where the line ends. "It's powering something, that's for sure. Something big."

Drayton sniffs, then sneezes. "I'm going to check it out."

"I'll come too," I say. "Did you find something for your allergies?"

"No and no. You can't come. You've got a tail." Drayton climbs out of sight.

"A tail?"

"Joe?"

Ulster. I side step back toward the door. "Yes? I'm here."

Ulster inches toward me. "I thought you were scared in the lift. This is way more intense."

"I am. I was. I just wanted to check out the view. The bird's eye view."

"It is magnificent. But it's not safe out here. Come back in and join in a game. Infection. It's like chase, but with skateboards and multiple chasers."

I inch back toward the opening. "Why aren't the young kids here? Wouldn't they like that game?"

"School night," Ulster says.

"But Eugenie is here. I saw her."

Ulster holds my hand when I jump from the walkway to the landing. "She's on a different track in school."

"Oh." It makes sense. It's the same way on the Platform. He escorts me back into the water tower. I play up my head injury, so Ulster stops trying to get me to participate. I watch the teams play Infection. When it's time to go, I ride home with my friends and Desiree, a golden-brown-eyed female researcher in power co-generation.

I know what Eugenie will look like in twenty years.

# Chapter Twenty-three

THE DOOR HANDLE JIGGLES. The metal is cool beneath my fingertips as I hold it still. "Who is it?"

"Mom."

I move the chair and swing the door open. Mom looks tired and has a wary look on her face. I hug her.

"I came by earlier, but you weren't here."

I recognize her mood—overworked and overtired. "They had a party at the water tower for us."

"Before that."

"Oh." I sit on my bed. "I had my head scanned. I'm okay."

"I know. After that. Something to do with a moto."

Mom already knows about the trip with Ulster. She's using her stealthy Mom fishing tactics to see if she needs to know about anything else. I sigh dramatically. "Nothing happened."

"I didn't say anything did. I only mentioned that you weren't here."

"Mom." I draw out her name in exasperation. "You want a play by play? Ulster took me to the pier to see the Platforms. We took the tram and rode bikes to the water tower. I suck at skateboarding. I miss Dad. I might miss the Platform."

"Thank you." Mom strokes my hair like I'm a kid. "You don't miss the PC?"

"No." Mom always knows how to put things in perspective. And I remember my new clothes. "Thanks for the clothes, Mom."

She looks startled. "They aren't from me. Must be Eugenie. She likes to give gifts."

"They're nice," I say uncomfortably. I don't have anything to give Eugenie. "I'll tell her thank you. Where does she find them?"

"There's stockpiles in the laundry from the malls and abandoned homes. They're all cleaned before use as a precaution."

"Great. I'm walking around in a dead person's clothes, but at least they're clean."

"If they're from the mall they've never been worn."

"But maybe they were tried on, right?"

Mom isn't listening to me. She's distracted and pulling on her eyebrows. "It'll be nice when you join me at work."

"Yes," I agree. "I'd like to tour the city with Chanko tomorrow, then start work. He said the communication infrastructure is amazing. I want to map it out so I know what I'm working with."

"It is definitely something to see."

"I had a good view from the water tower. Are there three campuses? I noticed a third transmission tower line—"

Mom cuts me off. "The vessel that brought you here. It sailed back out to sea?"

I hear Drayton's warning play in my head. *Eiffel.* I also hear Mom's voice telling me I should never lie to anyone, especially not to her. Guilt drowns me, but Drayton wins. "Yes."

"I see." She looks out of the window. "No, there's no third campus. Must be an old line."

"Okay. Probably inactive." Except it was active enough to power lights. "What about Hypophosphatasia? Ulster says it's genetically prevalent here."

Mom winces. "It is. Now, go to sleep and get a good night's rest. Keep your window closed; it's going to rain. I'll check on Harriet."

And just like that, Mom has avoided answering all my questions. I hate when she does that. I'm not ten years old anymore. "Check on Harriet?"

Mom bends over me and kisses me good night. "Yes. She's been under the weather. I'll see you in the morning. Be safe." Mom points to the chair then closes the door softly behind her.

I get up and put the chair under the doorknob. I consider Mom's words and behavior and Drayton's Eiffel reference. Something is definitely up. I climb back in bed, pull the covers over me, and try not to think about it.

But I think about it. Maybe Mom is trapped. Maybe Mom doesn't want to go back to the Platform and isn't telling me. Maybe Mom wishes I hadn't come to Land. Or maybe Mom knows something about the Estuary that I don't.

I click the small light by my bedside off. I really miss the Platform. Things at least made sense.

❧

"Did the rain wake you?" Chanko asks.

"No." I finish sketching the main power substation in town. "We could power three Platforms with what they have here."

"I know. It's ridiculous. Wait until you see…"

Chanko drones on, and I busy myself with making notes. Darwin's been driving us around in a solar-operated van for hours. We've had to go around flooded areas twice because of last night's rain. We climb back in the van.

I tap Darwin on the shoulder. "Can I see the central power plant? I want to be sure my calculations are correct."

Darwin nods. He drives a convoluted route to get around debris and water, but I know we're close when I see the vase-like cooling tower and cylindrical flue stack. We stop in front of several long, boxy, gray metal buildings. Darwin swivels to look at us. "Lunch."

"Oh, sure," I say. "Please, eat."

Chanko takes a box from the back of the car, then hands me a wrapped parcel. "May as well eat too. Picnic?"

"Okay." There are two square machines with faded advertisements for soda and snacks next to several wire benches and a table near the plant entrance. "Looks like a good spot."

Chanko and I leave the van and set up our lunch on the table. "Should we invite Darwin?"

"Nah," Chanko says. "He's already eating."

We take opposite sides of the table and open our parcels. There are stuffed sandwiches inside. I may never tire of eating real sandwiches with lettuce in them. They are delicious. But I'm thinking about electricity. "There's enough power running through the substation to generate a third campus."

Chanko unwraps his sandwich and takes a bite. "Third campus? I thought there was only one."

"Quick catch up. Saw a second campus myself in an old hotel. I saw three transmission lines from the water tower. They were all active. Why generate more electricity than you need if you are trying to save your resources?"

Chanko chews thoughtfully. "That's fishy. And I don't mean good fishy."

"Is there a good fishy?" I ask lightly and eat my sandwich. "And Harriet. There's something weird about that. She's many things, but not a thief." I remember seeing her in my room trying to figure out my senior project. "Maybe a cheater."

Chanko opens the second half of his sandwich paper. "Agreed. Fishy. What's really fishy is that they all look alike."

"That doesn't count. Closed groups tend to have the same features." A flock of birds fly over us. Bird poo lands on the table next to our sandwiches.

Chanko points to it. "What does that make you think of?"

"Migratory patterns. That would be something to study. Think of the applications for navigation. It would be possible if we had a Land base to work from."

"We could fly home. Chart the wind patterns, build wings, and put motors on them. Maybe not fly home, but something like fly home."

I eat the last bite of my sandwich. "You're talking in circles, Chanko. Like idiot grade circles."

"Sticks and stones."

We finish our sandwiches, and I thoroughly examine the central plant. Chanko follows me around while I type notes. I finally close my laptop.

"Is it good or bad?"

"Everything runs efficiently," I say. "It's all green. Turbines and pumps are in excellent shape. This is a workhorse plant. Where's all the power going?"

Chanko sighs. "I knew this was too good to be true. The food…"

"It may be fine," I respond. "Caution is the key word. We're giving them technology. Let's make sure we know what we're giving it to them for."

"Point."

"I think our time's up. Let's go."

Darwin is waiting for us. We begin the journey back to the Estuary. There are signs labeling everything—street signs, highway signs, store signs, billboard signs. It's information overload. Darwin slams on the brakes. He grabs for the tranquilizer gun he keeps in case we run into wild animals but doesn't pick it up.

"What the…"

Chanko slides open the van door and whistles. "He must have followed us. Dog!"

I lean forward. "And Eugenie?"

The dog jumps into the van. Eugenie runs around the van singing. Darwin harrumphs. The dog smells like rain and the outdoors. It isn't terrible, but it isn't nice. Chanko pets the dog and scratches its chin. "Dog, you were supposed to stay. I told you I'd be right back."

The dog looks happy and ridiculous. So does Chanko. He talks to the dog in baby talk. It's a little bit disgusting.

"You know he's the watchdog for the Estuary—Apollo. You may not want to get too emotionally involved with a stinky creature that doesn't belong to you. Or on the Platforms."

"His name is Dog, and that's what baths are for," Chanko says. "Isn't that right, Dog?"

"For the love of clam shells." I step out of the van. "Eugenie! You need to go back to class."

Eugenie sings her response. "I don't have class. I failed the test."

She runs by me, and I run after her. "Of course you have class. Come on. You shouldn't sneak out like this."

Eugenie stops running. I almost crash into the back of her. "I'm sneaking!"

"Yes," I say and take her hand. "Back to the Aquatics Center we go."

"That's for boys. I didn't pass the test. So, no class. Just bones until I'm twelve."

"Don't be…" Eugenie looks up at me with her beautiful golden-brown eyes, and I realize that she isn't lying. "Okay. Well, back to the Estuary. It isn't safe out here."

Eugenie jumps into the van. I follow her and slide the door shut. The dog runs back and forth across the seats. He doesn't bark, and every so often, he licks my arm. It's actually nice once I get used to the rough texture of his tongue.

Eugenie babbles to the dog, then to Chanko and me. I pretend to listen, but I'm really thinking about Eugenie. *It's for boys. Bones until I'm twelve.*

The landscape back to the Estuary is grim. The industrial corridor is completely deteriorated. Everything is gray and metal. Dismal. It's worse than the Platforms. Abandoned trucks dot the road, and several larger trucks block the refinery and sewage plant entrances. Eugenie calls out letters. She expects us to name things that we see outside with the same letter. Chanko and I play along. I have trouble finding the letter K.

Dog whines at me, so I pet him. "How about kaleidoscope? It's not out there, but it's the right letter."

"What's that?"

"A tube that holds magical worlds of colors and shapes," I say. "Drayton can make you one."

"Okay," Eugenie says happily.

When we finally reach the Estuary, I'm ready to get out of the van. I don't know what is worse, Dog wanting Chanko's attention, Chanko giving Dog too much attention, or knowing that Eugenie is not schooled because she is a girl.

"Bye, Joe!" Eugenie cries and skips into the Estuary.

"Bye. Thanks, Darwin. See you," I say and leave without waiting for a reply. I want to talk to Lisette about Eugenie.

I find Lisette in the garden. She is wearing overalls with a long sleeved shirt and mud is caked on her face. "Lisette. Can I talk to you?"

"Hey, sure. This is Carth. He works in organics."

Carth is an average-height older man with slightly darker eyes than Ulster. He doesn't look any particular way except normal. That makes me feel better. "Carth," I say and shake his hand. "I'm Joe."

"A man's name," Carth says and turns back to the garden. He moves slowly but gracefully, and his words aren't slurred.

"He's from the Platform," Lisette whispers. "Eden. Won't talk much about it." Her face changes, probably a reflection of my own. "What's wrong? Something's wrong."

"Lisette…"

Lisette raises her eyebrows. "Incoming, four o'clock."

I turn. Ulster has on a dark blue jumpsuit, and his skin glows. He unzips it and takes it off. The typical white one is underneath. Today, the arm sleeve has three blue stripes on it. He balls up the blue jumpsuit and puts it under his arm.

"Hi, ladies! Had to clean up the fertilizer spill, hence the hazmat suit. How was the city, Joe?"

Always where I am….a tail. I choose my words carefully. "Illuminating. I have lots of ideas on how to fix the communications grid utilizing the technology still in place. And Dog followed us. So did Eugenie."

"Loyalty is the dog's most cherished quality. There are several on the outskirts of the Estuary, but Apollo is definitely ours. They come pretty close to the perimeter. With a little persuasion and training, they stick around."

"What about cats?" Lisette asks. "Those were also popular living companions."

"We see colonies in the abandoned cities. They don't tend to come this way, even for food. I think Carth may have had one at one point. I remember a white cat lived here when I was young."

I decide to ask Ulster point blank. "And little girls who don't have school because they've failed a test? Where are they found all day?"

Ulster laughs. "Did Eugenie tell you that?"

I nod. "Pretty convincingly."

"We have school for little girls. We test *all* children and place them in classes geared toward science and math or basic survival skills. Eugenie is awesome, but not the smartest in math or science."

"So she's in survival skills?"

"Yes," Ulster replies. "She learns basic problem-solving skills and how to recycle efficiently, read, and write. No higher math or science. We have a shortage of teachers, so two different school periods."

I remember Lisette and Carth and turn to involve them in the conversation, but they have disappeared.

"I believe they returned to the greenhouse now that I've cleaned up. I repaired the roof's wind damage, too."

Ulster really is here on Estuary business, not because of me. And Eugenie didn't tell me the whole truth. I feel petty. "I slept right through it; I guess because I didn't feel it. I hate how the Platforms move with the wind."

"I'd hate that, too," Ulster says kindly. "I'm going to check on my hydrilla project. Want to come?"

"I really should—"

"First-class tour of the swamp. You can't say no."

I hesitate, thinking the worst. "Lisette will be super jealous."

"She and Carth are elbow deep in mulch right now, and I bet they're happy as Apollo when he gets table food. Please come. I rarely go in the swamp alone—safety first."

I am overthinking everything. He just wants company. "All right."

"Thanks. We have to go through the Aquatics Center."

The building is deserted, but I do see a classroom with desks and bright colors near the main entrance. Ulster walks purposefully down the hallway, then ducks down some stairs. "All the gear is already loaded in the boat."

"Boat?"

Ulster swings open a set of glass doors. Three flat boats with huge fans on the backs are tied to the dock. The fans are covered with protective wire casing. Large solar panels line the back of the casing like a stiff cape. Ulster throws me a life jacket. I put it on.

"Ever been in an airboat?"

I shake my head. This kind of boat wouldn't last two minutes in the open sea. Its flat design would fill with water or be overturned by the waves.

"Didn't think so. Get ready for some fun."

Ulster climbs into the raised driver's seat in front of the fan, and I sit in the flat area of the boat. He is about five feet above me. I look longingly at the dock. I can't back out now, but if I could…

The fan roars to life, and we skip across the water. It sounds like a monster is propelling the boat forward. I'm terrified and grip the boat rail with both hands. Ulster slows down to pass another boat, and I relax a little. It's half sunk, but there is a paddlewheel on the back and the name "Mississippi Queen" on the side. It's two stories, and the architecture is ornate.

"We'll resurrect her someday," Ulster shouts and puts the boat back into high gear. I hold on. We pass everything quickly, but I get the impression of abundant trees, Spanish moss, and turtles sunning themselves on exposed tree stumps. We stop right before a bend in the canal. I can see the ocean on the other side of a strip of land. I hadn't realized there was a canal that connected the Estuary to the ocean.

"This is the trouble," Ulster says and jumps from the driver's seat. The boat rocks, and I stop myself from gagging. He leans over and picks up vegetation from the water. "Hydrilla. Imported hundreds of years ago. Water weeds. It's clogging this turn."

I clutch my stomach. "Oh."

Ulster moves to the front of the boat and dumps out a bucket full of liquid. "Have to get the tubers. This natural herbicide will keep it in control. But it's not a long-term solution."

"Great," I say. My stomach has settled some. Ulster is intent on his conservation, and I can appreciate his passion. Dragonflies land on the water around us, their legs barely marking the water's surface. A water spider looks like it is skating nearby. The water is alive with minnows, and larger fish break the surface regularly.

"Make sure you notice the birds on the ride back," Ulster says. "Egrets, herons—they're really beautiful."

I'm glad he doesn't notice that I'm about to vomit all over his airboat. I close my eyes for the ride back to the Estuary, and when I step out of the flat boat, I feel shaky. Ulster secures the airboat. There are several orange submersible boats tethered on the connecting dock. Bright letters spell "FUN BOAT RIDES" in all caps. Not a phrase you'd catch me saying.

The dinner bell whistles shrilly.

"Hungry?"

I'm not, but I pretend to be. "Let's have dinner."

I follow Ulster to the food line. I take my time filling my water glass. I drink it down, then fill it again before joining Ulster at a long table. Lisette and Carth sit down next to us. Ulster shares details of the airboat ride with them then talks about invasive plant species.

Chanko joins us, and he starts a conversation about the resurgence of plant life in the city. He thinks it's only a matter of time before a large storm will obliterate several of the multilevel structures because plant roots have damaged their foundations.

Drayton doesn't show. And I keep thinking about Eugenie and her bones. What's so significant about year twelve? The word Eiffel keeps running through my mind.

"Good night," I say abruptly. Ulster seems confused, but I tap my head. "Headache. A little too much sun today. And I want to get an early start tomorrow with Mom."

Ulster stands and takes my food plate. "Of course. I'll take care of this for you. Good night."

"Thanks. Night all." I walk quickly across the common area and head for my room. I pass Eugenie in the hall. She shakes her finger at me, then disappears through an open door.

"Eugenie! You have school! Ulster told me!"

But Eugenie is gone. "Even if it's half-baked school," I say and open the door to my room. My window is open. I shut the door behind me before I notice the figure standing in front of me. A flash of heat engulfs my body before I turn back to the door and open my mouth to scream.

A hand covers my mouth. "It's me. Climbed the gutter," Drayton's voice says behind me.

I bite down, and he pulls his hand away quickly. "Ouch, Joe. That hurt. Man, you have sharp teeth, you know that?"

"My teeth are my business, not yours. What's with the Eiffel reference? It's messing with my head."

"You need to stay on guard. I contacted Flox. He's waiting for us."

"Good. Did you ask about Drees?" Drayton sneezes three times in a row. There are deep circles underneath his eyes, like he hasn't slept in days. "Are you okay? I'm worried about you. You don't look good."

"I'm fine." Drayton pulls out a handkerchief and blows his nose. "I ditched my handler. He still thinks I'm in my room sick. I followed the transmission towers. Rode a bike there and back."

I hate to see Drayton so physically down. But I'm interested in what he found. "And?"

"It's powering a slipway. Front half is all metal. Back part is open air. They're stockpiling boats."

"Boats?"

Drayton nods. "I'm not worried about them so much. They haven't figured out how to solar power them yet, and they can't access the oil reserves. Batteries don't last that long. What I want to know is what's in the front half. I'll bring Chanko tomorrow night."

"Bring me," I say.

"Too risky," Drayton says. "The girls are being watched more closely than the boys. Especially you."

"Speaking of girls...I don't think Eugenie has real school. Ulster explained it, but now I'm wondering if there's more to it than just testing. She keeps talking about her bones. Ulster says Hypophosphatasia is prevalent here, but Hermeneutic Labs eradicated this particular genetic disorder. And there's the number twelve."

Something jingles in the hallway. Drayton pulls me to him and kisses me. I kiss him back, but he pulls away and dives out the window. My hands are shaking at the unexpectedness of Drayton's lips on mine. I haven't seen him much since we landed, and now he's kissing me and jumping out the window like we've always been together.

I wait by the door, my fingers resting on my still warm lips, staring at the door handle. It doesn't move. After several seconds, I run to the window, but Drayton's already gone.

# Chapter Twenty-four

"AND HERE WE ARE." Mom inputs her code into the electronic panel by the lab door. I peek around her arm but can't see the numbers.

Our conversation has been stifled because Darwin had breakfast with us and walked us to the lab. "What about my code?"

"Later. Let's just get you started for now."

I belch. I ate too much at breakfast. Boiled eggs are my new favorite thing in the world. They taste so rich on the inside, smooth on the outside. I don't like the milk, though. The consistency is too thick. "Sorry. Excuse me."

Mom pats my cheek. "Thank you for minding your manners. You're with me." I follow Mom into the lab. Darwin doesn't accompany us. I put my laptop on the nearest workstation and look around the room. Various pieces of communications equipment are in different stages of development.

"Your offspring?" A large man with curly hair studies me. He has on a loose fitting robe that shimmers like sunlight on the water when he moves. He's the first person I've ever seen that is over the standard weight amount issued by the PC.

"Yes. Joe, this is Zarath. My research partner."

I extend my hand and Zarath takes it. His hand is twice the size of mine, but he doesn't exert much pressure.

"We begin," Zarath says.

Zarath's features are different. He has a sweetheart-shaped face and a distinctive widow's peak. His hair is heavy and arranged in an intricate design that reminds me of neatly coiled rope. "Are you related to—"

Zarath cuts me off. "I am not. I am the last of my kind. Free and alone. Some are born, others arise."

"Oh, okay. That's tidal."

Zarath returns to his workspace. I look around for Mom. She's in the adjoining room. A pane of glass separates us, and she pulls blinds down over the glass. I feel abandoned but take a deep breath.

"Do I have a designated workspace, Zarath?"

Zarath looks questioningly at me. "Mignon says to me that you are of intelligence. Now be so, and ask me no more questions."

I have no idea if that means set up wherever, or don't set up. I stare at the back of Zarath's head. Since that doesn't help me, I look around the lab. I spy my backpack. "Oh!" I squeal and hurry across the room. I open it, and everything I packed is still in it and dry. "And hopefully operational," I mutter. I pull out my battery pad and receiving station. "Just like home."

I glance around the room. Spare parts of every variety are organized in an ellipse of large, tubular steel bins. "Okay, not exactly like home." I rub my hands together. Junk diving at its finest. I happily tear into the nearest bin.

"Treasure," I comment when I find a sophisticated speaker buried in mounds of circuits and wiring. There are plenty of functioning receivers in the room, and I instantly know how I can solve the Landers' communication problem. I decide to create a small model of how we could use the existing transmission towers to make a powerful broadcasting network.

I set up a station at an empty desk. I make my laptop the center, then create a network of salvaged pieces around me. I'm the sun, and all the components are planets. I start wiring and programming, wiring and programming. Checking power. Checking connectivity.

"This is good."

I scream and whirl around with one of the wires in my hand. Zarath is standing right behind me. His nose is like a butterfly in the center of his face, and I find myself staring right at it even though I try to look away.

I mumble, "Sorry. I didn't hear you walk over."

Zarath studies my work, then me. "One from the lost tribe, indeed." He strides back to his workstation.

I don't know why Mom has left me with super serious Zarath. He weirds me out. "You are a grown up," I whisper, giving myself a pep talk.

I keep working. It's tedious, and I know it will take some time to get even a small model of the system I imagine in my head running. Once a full-scale model is built, I could contact Dad.

Dad. The longer I'm away, the worse I feel about leaving in the night, just like Mom. I hope the PC hasn't questioned him now that I'm a renegade.

"Stop," I mutter. Dad would want me to succeed. I close my new program and tap into the network like I'm a new user. It isn't very sophisticated, but better than what they have now. Anything is better than nothing.

"No lunch break; we were late," Mom says. She puts a sandwich in front of me, then brings one to Zarath. "Enjoy the bread. Fresh baked. Water and glasses are in the corner."

"Thanks," I say and shut my laptop quickly. I smell the bread and know it's going to be delicious. It is. I chew thoughtfully. Dad would love this bread.

Mom unwraps her sandwich and stands in front of me. "Have you visited Harriet?"

"No."

"Perhaps you should. She isn't feeling well. It might cheer her up."

Me cheering up Harriet is doubtful, but I don't tell Mom that. "Sure."

"Are you still at odds?"

I chew my food thoroughly before I answer. "If you mean are we still rivals, then yes."

Mom looks at me thoughtfully. "A little kindness goes a long way, Josephine. Remember that. Tonight we'll have movie night!"

"Movie night?"

"There's a real theater in the Estuary. I have permission to use it for a girls' movie night. It's a treat!"

"What about the fellows?" I don't want to say Drayton's name, so I stumble over the word "fellows." I still feel the pressure of his kiss on my lips.

"No boys allowed at all," Mom says and shakes her finger at me. She finishes her sandwich. "Land or Platform variety. Agreed?"

"Okay. That's cool."

"Okay? Cool? It'll be a wonderful time!"

"A wonderful time. What about the other ladies on Land?"

Mom's face changes, and she tightens her hands into fists. "I'll invite them. They won't come, but I'll invite them."

"Okay." I slip in a reference to Eugenie's situation. "Still sexist out here, huh? Researchers can't be girls."

Mom folds her sandwich paper into smaller and smaller triangles. "Something like that. I'll come back when it's time for dinner."

A hand on my arm stops me mid-command. I turn from my computer and follow the arm up to my mom's face, feeling disoriented.

"Is it already time?"

"You're like your father. When you get wrapped up in your work, you forget everything. Time, food, people."

Zarath puts his hand on my shoulder. "She will work well with us."

I'm startled and babble, "She will. I mean, I will."

Zarath touches his fingers to his forehead and leaves. I take a deep breath and relax. Finally. "Mom. He's a total creeper. Does he ever make noise when he moves?"

"He has a peculiar set of ways. Be respectful and don't judge. I taught you better than that."

"Yeah, yeah, yeah." I power down my laptop. I place my backpack over it and check my workspace once more. "And no one will touch this? Like creepy Zarath who I'm not supposed to judge?"

Mom shakes her head and gives me a warning look. "It's safe here."

"All right," I say and follow her out the lab door. "If you say so."

I'm not sure if I know what safety actually is. The Platforms were never really safe—not with the decay and water always ready to drown us. So far, Land has been, but…

"Mom, did you know Eugenie doesn't go to real school?"

"It's real enough," Mom says and almost jogs down the hall. "Don't be a slow poke."

I hurry to catch up to her. Real enough? That's not a typical Mom answer. I catch up, but Darwin is with her.

I fall into step beside them. The research wing walls are a drab, non-descript color in comparison to the green outside. The hallways are warmer today, and the common room is buzzing with people and activity. Mom eats with Zarath and other staff members, so I find Lisette and Chanko and sit by them.

Lisette and Chanko are in a deep discussion about plans to rebuild the sports complex at the Estuary. I lose interest in the discussion after a couple of bites of food. It's spicier this evening, and I like the strong smell of it. I poke around with my fork and fish out the dark green leaves that are the tastiest.

"That's the new kale crop," Lisette says.

"What?"

"You are eating a new crop. Isn't that wonderful?"

"I told her I'd eat any crop as long as it wasn't swimming," Chanko says. "Or floating."

"It is a nice, crispy texture. Strong taste, but not bitter. Where's Drayton?"

Chanko looks around. "Weird. He was here earlier. He wasn't looking for you exactly, but he asked if we'd seen you. Where were you today?"

"Working with Mom. The components they have available make my head spin. Seriously. I could contact the next solar system if I had enough time. Did Mom tell you about movie night, Lisette?"

Lisette shakes her head. "What's that?"

"There's a real movie theater on campus."

"Cool," Chanko interjects. "Movies were a major part of Land life before the Moralists. There are several theaters in the city. What are we going to watch?"

"Girls only, Mom says. Go salvage your own theater."

Lisette giggles. "It sounds fun. And exclusive."

Chanko winks at us. "That's cool. I've got other fish to fry."

"Speckled trout or electric eels?" I ask.

Chanko presses his lips together. "The electric variety."

The theater is huge and has luxurious tilting seats made of a regal fabric Mom tells us is actual velvet. It's so sumptuous, I have to stop myself from petting it.

Lisette, Harriet, Mom, Eugenie, and I all sit on the first row of the second tier of seats. Harriet is quiet, which isn't the norm for her. She looks pale, and I feel bad that I haven't seen her since she's been sick.

Lisette is excited. "I've never been in a real movie theater!"

"Of course you haven't," Mom says. "There aren't any on the Platforms. Eugenie, don't bounce on the seat. Harriet, come switch with her and sit by me."

The movie theater goes dark, and Mom claps her hands. "I started the movie, so let's hope this works. I chose a classic for ladies. Get ready for *My Fair Lady*!"

The screen lights up, and images move across it. I'm immediately fascinated, as the screen world is four times larger than the real world. But there's no sound.

"What happened to the sound?" Lisette asks.

"I'll go check," I volunteer. Everything is dark, so I pick my way carefully to the sound booth thirty rows back. Long cables run from the ceiling like Man of War tentacles, and strange, diamond shapes dot the floor. I don't recognize the equipment, so I check all of the connections. "It's probably just a..."

Three little girls dressed in white jumpers are standing in the back of the sound booth. They look like triplets. They all have golden-brown eyes. One of them has the sound knob in her hands.

"Hello," I say.

They don't answer. The little girl drops the knob. They grab hands and skip away. Beyond eerie. I put the knob back where

I'm pretty sure it should go and twist it to the right. I hear the sound boom in the movie theater.

I leave the sound booth and weave between the chair rows. I sit next to Lisette. I look at Mom. In the dark, her face is young. She has barely aged over the years. I look sort of like her, sort of not. Lisette, Harriet, and I look completely different.

Harriet looks thin, and her face is hollow. She isn't watching the movie, so I lean forward in the seat and whisper. "How are you feeling, Harriet?"

"All right," Harriet says. "You don't even like me. Why are you asking?"

"We're friends, Harriet. Like it or not. Platformers stick together. So I want you to rest and get well."

Harriet smiles, then her face fades again. "Platformers."

"Shhhh!" Mom says.

I sit back in my seat.

"Bric-a brac," Eugenie whispers in my ear.

"Bones intact."

Eugenie puts her head on my arm, which is awkward. "Bric-a-brac," Eugenie half sighs.

I wish I knew what her words meant. I give her the answer she wants. "Bones intact."

☙❧

It is not a good morning. I didn't sleep well. I dreamt of horse races and large umbrellas stuffed with sets of identical crabs dancing within them. I was late to breakfast and missed the eggs. Darwin escorted me to the lab. But I don't have a code, so I bang on the lab door. "Hello. I'm late."

Zarath answers it. I walk around him. "Thank you."

He returns to his project. I open my laptop.

"Salvage the day," I mutter and run tests on my in-house network. Everything works. Next step—increase the distance between the radio waves transmission and reception. I need something to act as a wireless...

A tall, tree-like structure on Zarath's workstation catches my eye. It wasn't there yesterday. I squint my eyes. If it's a tower, then Zarath has already built my project. I edge closer to his workstation and pretend to sort through transmitters.

It is a tower, and from the looks of it, capable of broadcasting a long-range signal. I can think of only two explanations for it not being in use—it doesn't work, or it does, and Zarath doesn't want anyone to know that it does.

I return to my workstation. I don't panic, as I see Mom through the glass separating her workstation from ours. I consider confronting Zarath but decide that I shouldn't risk it.

I keep building what I started out to build.

☙❧

The lunch whistle sounds, and I put down the soldering iron. Even though I'm freaked out about Zarath's work, I'm enjoying the opportunity to use so many different tools. It's nice to have abundant power, materials, and room to work. Mom waves to me through the glass. She points to her watch, and I nod.

*Time to ask some questions*, I mouth to her, but she shakes her head because she doesn't understand me.

We meet at the lab door. Mom hugs me. "Good morning?"

"Ugh," I say and hurry down the hall.

"What's the rush?"

I almost run through the next set of doors then grab Mom's arm. "Trying to outrun Darwin. Mom. Zarath already built my project. He has the capability to communicate with the Platforms maybe, the Mainland definitely. He's tapped into the existing cell tower grid."

Mom stiffens, then puts her arm around my shoulders. "Not with just his little tower."

"You know?"

"Quiet, Joe. Let's be quiet."

"But it's already done!"

"Zarath is a friend. Be quiet."

"Mom…"

Mom starts to sing a strange tune, and I tear away from her. "What is going on?"

"Hush. Ulster, you look well today," Mom calls.

"Oh, oh," I stutter. Ulster is waiting for us at the end of the hall.

"Good afternoon!" Ulster says. "I was going to join you for lunch break. I have a new plant species to share with Lisette."

"She'll love it," Mom says. "That's very thoughtful."

Ulster joins us. "Dad said Joe was making progress in the lab, so I wanted to congratulate her on fitting in so quickly. It's not easy."

I flinch. Progress in the lab? I've only been in the lab a day. And my laptop isn't hooked into the network. "Thanks. It's a marvelous lab. It's got everything I need."

"Even though they're in ruins, some of the factories on the Mainland are quite amazing. You should visit there someday."

Mom laughs in a shrill voice. "But not soon. She's just started here."

"I wasn't suggesting that at all. I only meant someday. For me, too."

Mom puts her hand on his shoulder. "I hoped not. Thank you, Ulster. It's so nice to have my daughter near."

We enter the common room in an awkward silence. All three of us get plates and serve ourselves. Mom picks a table in the center of the room.

"I don't see Lisette," I say.

"I do," Mom says. "She's with Eugenie."

Ulster puts his plate down. "I'll show her the specimen. Start without me, please."

"Dive in," Mom says.

I taste the food. I'm pretty sure the main dish is tomatoes. There's another vegetable that reminds me of potatoes mixed with sweet onions and an interesting flavor I've never had. "Man, that's good," I say and take another mouthful.

"Polenta," Mom explains. "We don't have it on the Platforms."

"It fueled the Roman army," Ulster says and sits next to me. "At least, that's what I've read."

I shovel the rest into my mouth. "Good stuff."

"I like it, too."

"What did Lisette say about the plant?" Mom asks.

Ulster beams. "It could definitely yield medicinal value. She identified it as Hyssop. She's going to help me collect a sample with solid roots and transfer it to the garden before the weather rolls in."

Mom puts her fork down. "Weather?"

"There's a large storm brewing. I can smell it in the air. Can you? It may smell different on the Platforms."

I know exactly what Ulster is talking about. I could tell when rain was coming by the way the sky looked and the air smelled. Here, I'm lost. I can't focus on the rain smell. "It's not the same."

"We should have a scary story night," Mom says. "Eugenie would like that."

"I think tonight we'll be on lockdown. Big winds."

"What's lockdown?" I ask.

Chanko passes our table. He puckers his lips at me and points to Ulster. I give him my best drop-dead look.

"It's mandatory procedure in bad weather. All non-essential personnel stay in their rooms. Sometimes the bottom floor takes on water, or we have wind damage. If there is a tornado, take shelter in the nearest closet."

"Noted," I say and finish my plate of food. "I could eat more of that, but…"

"You can have some of mine."

I recognize Drayton's voice. Half of a polenta cake magically appears on my plate. "Thanks."

Mom pats the bench next to her. "Where have you been hiding?"

Drayton joins Mom. "Not hiding. Designing things."

"I saw the preliminary model for your modified solar amphibious car," Ulster says. "It's impressive. It would be really useful here."

"Thanks. That's why I came up with it."

We are silent for a moment, then Mom asks, "What kind of amphibious car? Like the ones the PC have?"

Drayton and Ulster start talking at the same time, and I finish the polenta. For a few minutes, it seems like everything is perfect. Everyone gets along. Then two researchers pass the table. They look cloned they are so similar. I think of the triplets. Hypophosphatasia.

It's too much for me to think about. I excuse myself, put my plate in the soiled bucket, then exit the common room and head toward the garden. I sniff. It does smell like rain.

I hear footsteps behind me. I hope it's Drayton. I want to know what he found out at the third campus, so I slow down. But it's Ulster. "Ulster!"

"Don't act so disappointed. Expecting someone else?"

"No," I lie. "I was just thinking maybe it does smell like rain."

"What's so different about the smell?"

"On the Platform it's heavier. Like wet socks. I could tell if it would be a little or a lot, too."

"I can feel it in my bones when it is going to be heavy. It's an ache. Like I'm an old man already."

I stumble, and Ulster grabs my elbow. I force myself not to flinch. "Thank you. How are your bones today? Is it going to be a downpour?"

"Yes."

We stop at the front of the garden. "Do you have a protective barrier for the plants?"

"We do," Ulster says and points to a switch near the entrance. "We have a mechanical lid, so to speak. It will pull a net tightly over the roof of the structure. The walls protect the plants from the wind. We collect the rain water in the large cisterns for future irrigation."

It's a brilliant, waste-free solution. "That's amazing. Are there many storms that come ashore?"

"Many. We are an island, after all. Most aren't so bad. I remember one that got out of hand, though. We had to start the garden over from scratch because of too much rain. The plants drowned."

I hear Lisette's voice. She's talking to Chanko but traveling in our direction. "That's my cue. It's plant talking time for you guys! I have to get back to radio waves."

Ulster hugs me. "I'm glad you're settling in."

He holds me a little too long, and I push away. "Yes, thanks," I mumble and jet out of the garden and through the common room at top speed. Settling in? I'm far from settling anything.

I notice a few familiar faces in the hallway and nod to them, but keep moving until I'm back to the Communications lab. I bang on the door of the lab, and this time Mom opens it for me. Zarath is within earshot.

"Nice walk?" She asks.

"Yes." But I mean no.

Mom picks up on my sarcasm. "What did Ulster have to say?"

Zarath stands on a table to connect a communications antenna to a light fixture. I can't talk to Mom. "It's going to rain."

# Chapter Twenty-five

LOCKDOWN ISN'T ALL THAT BAD. I'm alone for the first time in days. I realize how much I enjoyed the amount of alone time I had at home because Dad was never there.

The rain pelts against the window and the glass shakes in the frame. The sound makes my teeth hurt. I don't want to wake up to a shower of broken glass. I push against the bed frame. It slides easily, so I move it as far away from the window as I can. I jam the left edge of the headboard against the door.

I crawl into bed and turn the overhead light off. The window lights up, and I hear thunder soon after. The storm is close. I shut my eyes and think of what I've been told sheep look like. Nice, fluffy sheep with lots of wool. Curly haired sheep, straight haired sheep. Sheep.

One. Two. Three. Four…

I stop counting when I hear a series of clicks. My eyes adjust to the dark. The doorknob is moving.

"Who's there?" I whisper. Silence. "I'm sleeping in front of the door, so if that's you, Eugenie, the door won't open."

I hear giggling, so I know it's definitely Eugenie. "Eugenie. Go back to bed. We're on lockdown. You shouldn't be in the halls. It's dangerous."

The doorknob turns. "Eugenie!" I say in my best adult voice. I push the bed away from the door and open it. "You have to…"

I recognize Shallick, the man who checked my concussion, before he puts his hand over my nose and mouth. I start to choke. I kick and claw, but then everything begins to spin. I punch until my arms won't work anymore. The sheep are smothering me.

I hear a thump and Shallick's hand loosens. I stagger to the floor and turn, ready to fight.

Shallick is on the ground. His head is cracked open. Blood spills onto the tiled floor. Zarath is behind him, holding a piece of galvanized pipe in his right hand.

"You…"

"Explanations later." Zarath shoves a white jumpsuit into my hands. "Put this on and come with me."

I pull the jumpsuit over my night clothes and run back into my room to grab my grandmother's ring, Flox's gift, and my trainers. I put the trainers on while I'm walking. The rest I stash in the pockets of the jumpsuit.

Lisette and Mom are at the end of the next hallway with Eugenie between them. They're all in Estuary jumpsuits.

"They've taken Harriet," Mom whispers. "I thought they might with the storm."

"What?" I ask.

"Lockdown provided the perfect opportunity. Zarath took watch and woke me when they snatched her. They're after her ovaries. The girls lose them at twelve unless they test high in critical thinking. They started grooming Harriet, dosing her with high-level hormones for a quick extraction. That's why she's been so sick. Shallick came for you so they could get a genetic sampling, not your ovaries."

I feel violated. "My genetics?"

"They clone to create new children. All the females you've seen have been a result of this cloning. There is no natural female population."

I accept Mom's explanation. I'm not surprised. In fact, I'm incredibly calm. "Where's Drayton and Chanko?"

"I woke them first. They headed to the third campus to steal a boat. We need to get to the outer sewage pipe that runs from the chemical plant and wait for the flare. That's the rendezvous point for escape. We have to hurry—Harriet's already in surgery. I don't know how we're going to get her out."

I don't think, I do. I disconnect a plant from its ceiling hook and hold it in front of me. Bones, bones is all I can think of. I round the corner. Darwin is standing by the surgery entrance. He looks surprised when I swing the plant and hit him in the head. He slumps down quietly, and I push his arm out of the way with my foot.

"Wait," Mom whispers.

I don't listen. I throw open the doors and rush in. Doctor Vraise is standing over Harriet. I recognize Desiree, but not the other researcher. "*Stop!*"

Zarath is across the room before I throw the plant at Director Vraise. I miss, but hear two cracks. Zarath has taken out Desiree and her companion. Doctor Vraise reaches into his pocket and pulls out a gun. It is long and dark.

I don't duck. Instead I scream and charge him. I hear a pop. Director Vraise falls toward me in slow motion. I catch him in my arms.

"Mom!" I cry.

But Eugenie is next to me. She strokes her father's hair with her left hand. She has a small silver gun in her right hand. "Eugenie!"

"You're nice," Eugenie whispers. "You have bones. Like me."

"Like you," I say sadly.

"I have all the keys."

"Oh, Eugenie."

Mom takes over in her no-nonsense Mom voice. "Zarath, carry Harriet. Eugenie, hold my hand and give me that gun. Lisette and Joe, move."

I don't argue. I drop Director Vraise. Blood is all over my jumpsuit. I try to wipe it away, but it doesn't come off.

"Go," Mom says. I follow Zarath, who's carrying Harriet like a baby. I can barely see her around his bulky body. She's wrapped in a teal-blue surgical blanket, and she's very pale. We run down the stairs and out the front entrance. The rain is pouring in flat, gray sheets. Zarath leads us to the Aquatics Center, but the doors are locked.

"Around the back!" I yell and tear around the side of the Aquatics Center. I come to the dock and realize there is no solar boat tethered. I look at the orange submersible boats on the connecting dock. "Load in!"

I force open the hatch on the roof of the first "Fun Boat Ride" and make sure everyone is aboard before I untie it. I push it away from the dock, climb down the ladder into its belly, and bolt the hatch closed. I don't know how much time we have. Our added weight has submerged the fun boat, but I'm not worried about sinking. I'm worried about staying right where we are.

Zarath has already laid Harriet down along the wall farthest from the door and taken a seat in one of the four white, plastic chairs. He's breathing heavily, and she's unconscious. Bike pedals protrude from the base of each seat, and I know how to get out of here.

"Mom, Zarath, we have to pedal. Lisette, you too. Move."

Eugenie starts to cry as we get into position. I distract her. "Eugenie, you're the captain. Look out the periscope and steer us clear of the other boats and the dock. Grab the wheel and turn the…"

Eugenie stops crying. She grabs the wheel and giggles. "Steer the boat! Survival skills!"

She turns the wheel calmly to the left, then right. I'm shocked. Someone pounding on the door reminds me this isn't a pleasure cruise. "Get us out of here, Eugenie."

"Forward," Eugenie shouts at the same time I yell, "Pedal!"

The "Fun Boat Ride" moves forward. Once we start pedaling in sync, it's easy to keep the submersible moving. We glide beneath the water. Harriet moans. Mom leaves her post and kneels next to her. She rips a piece of material from her jumper and presses it against Harriet's midsection where the teal blanket looks black. "She's losing blood. They had already started the extraction process."

Eugenie leaves the steering wheel and kneels by Mom. "Bones intact."

"Eugenie, we need you to steer."

Eugenie puts her hand on Harriet's forehead. "Survival skills. Class three."

"This isn't play nursing," Mom says softly to Eugenie.

"Survival skills!"

We can't pedal blindly on. And Eugenie is in school mode. "Okay. Eugenie, take care of Harriet. We'll pedal with three. Zarath, we need you to steer us. You know this canal best anyway. Get us to the sewage pipe."

Zarath stands and takes the periscope. The boat rocks from side to side in the rough waters. "Let's hope the boat they steal is stout," I say lightly. Lisette looks like she is almost out of steam. "Keep pedaling!"

We pedal furiously until the windows are pressed in with Hydrilla. Pedaling gets hard as the propellers choke in tubers, and we all run out of energy. Zarath relieves Lisette, and Lisette steers us around the bend.

"If we do not achieve success, then we shall drown," Zarath says. "The sea has long fingers this night."

I do not feel like drowning. "Lisette, dig deep and pedal this final segment. Zarath, when we dump out into the ocean steer us close to shore. This fun boat isn't going to be fun once we hit real waves."

Lisette switches with Zarath, and I count aloud to keep our pedaling in sync. Zarath navigates us around the shoulder of the inlet and into the ocean. It gets rough, but we stay close to shore.

"We need to ditch."

"A little farther," Zarath says.

I feel the submersible's bottom run aground. "Nope. We need to ditch now."

Zarath wrenches open the door of the submersible and sticks his head out as water pours in. "The sewage pipe is forty feet to the west. Run."

I grab Eugenie's hand. Lisette is in front of me. Mom and Zarath lift Harriet. "Go!" I yell.

We wade through the water to the beach. Rain pelts us. It is cold, and I can barely see, but we run toward the huge pipe jutting from the land. A small sailboat could easily sail through the pipe. We reach it, and Lisette climbs in. I lift Eugenie up to her. "Get a few feet in," I say.

I look back. Mom and Zarath have Harriet between them. I can't even see the submersible. I hoist myself into the pipe and wait, legs dangling midair. I'll help lift Harriet when Mom—

A hand grabs my knee.

"Going somewhere?"

Ulster.

He is wearing a white wetsuit and holding a tranquilizer gun to my chest. The kind they use on wild animals.

"Ulster?"

"I was always nice." Ulster's voice is even, controlled, and very scary.

"Let me explain."

"That you're abandoning us? I saw you run aground—I was protecting the Least Tern habitat from the wind and rain, or I wouldn't have known."

I try to reason with Ulster. "We can't stay here."

"Why? We made everything available to you. Accepted you."

Maybe Ulster doesn't know. Ulster can't know—he is kind and smart and not his father. He's looking after birds in a huge storm. "Harriet was on the operating table. Your father wants her ovaries. They clone from them. Your sister is next! Come with us."

"My sister will be the mother of fifty children! Perhaps more. It's an honor! Harriet is disposable and can be cloned. You are not. You are our future."

I scream, but there is no sound. I replay every conversation with Ulster, every experience shared with him. And it makes me sick. "No. I don't want to be your future."

Ulster smiles. "It is not your choice. We will return to a freeborn population. You and Lisette will begin this transition. My father has mapped out the trajectory. I will take you both as wives."

I hear a guttural cry from my left, and when Ulster looks toward it, I whip my elbow around and strike him hard across the chin. I strike out again, and my wrist bone connects with a heavier bone. The dart gun flies over my head, deeper into the sewage pipe.

"Stop, offspring!" I hear, then another thud.

I fall down. My hand hurts like it never has before. Zarath is standing over Ulster's body, blood running down the side of Zarath's face.

"You fight," Zarath says. "This is good. But do not hit the wrong person."

"I'm sorry. I was aiming for Ulster."

"As was I. Help your mother with Harriet. I will tend to this."

Fear grips me. "Is he…"

"Tend to your kind," Zarath says.

"But how did you…"

"There are many accesses to this pipe. Go."

I crouch and peek around the edge of the sewage channel. The rain has turned into a wind-whipped, hellish side-slanting rain. Mom is holding Harriet in the shallows.

"Mom! It's safe now."

She drags Harriet to the sewage entrance. I sit on the edge of the pipe and lean over, grabbing Harriet under the arms. "Now!"

Mom lifts and I pull. We get Harriet into the pipe. I fall over backward but am careful not to roll over on Harriet. I push myself up and crawl to her. "Harriet."

Harriet moans. She is naked, and I cover her with the surgical blanket, but not before I see the cuts in her abdomen. "Mom! She's freezing."

Mom is beside me. "Hold her. Watch for the flare. We have to hide Ulster."

Mom is gone. I touch Harriet's face. "Harriet. Please, stay with me. We're going back to the Platforms."

Harriet is ashen. She's so cold. I hold her tightly. "Come on, Harriet. I don't even know you. I want to know you."

A streak of red lights the sky. "Flare!" I scream.

Mom returns with Lisette and Eugenie. Zarath picks up Harriet and brings her deeper into the pipe.

"Where are you—"

Mom interrupts me. "We have to leave her."

I follow Zarath. Harriet is so pale in Zarath's arms. He places her next to Ulster. "We can't leave her! She belongs on the Platform."

"We have to," Mom says. "They removed the dinghy you rowed in on. We'll have to swim. And—"

"No. We can wait out the storm. No one else knows we are out here."

Mom shakes her head. "We have to take this opportunity. There's too much at stake. I work for the Council. I know you think they don't have power, but they've been tracking the development on Land for years. We're not going back to Nod. Not yet. We sail for L'Esperance, a non-PC resurrected Platform in the reef off South America."

Another flare lights the sky. I recognize the outline of the boat—it's a Regulator, late model. The front half clears the water and points to the sky. It's almost fifty feet away.

"The Estuary knows where we are now with those flares. We have to leave Harriet. Her chances of survival are better here."

"Ulster will…"

"Care for her," Mom says. "She's a commodity."

I waver. "But Harriet…"

Mom cups my face in her hands. "Please, Josephine. We have to leave."

I finally nod.

Mom kisses my forehead. "Eugenie. You're with me. Go!"

I jump out of the pipe. The water is cold and tumultuous. The boat seems so far away, but I break the water's surface every other stroke to make sure I'm swimming in the right direction. Lisette is to my right. She's a better swimmer than I am, so I'm not worried about her. I'm worried about Mom and Eugenie.

I make out two figures on the Regulator—Drayton and Chanko. I'm almost there. I reach, reach…

I'm ripped from the water. "Drayton!"

Drayton holds me to him. He strokes my face. Dog rubs against my leg and barks wildly. Chanko pulls Lisette from the water. Zarath climbs the ladder next to the motor and helps Mom and Eugenie aboard.

The thirty-two-foot Regulator barely fits us all. Mom coughs up water as she tucks Eugenie inside the console area and stays there with her. Lisette joins them. Zarath and Chanko lift the anchor.

The outer area of the Regulator has been shaped into trenches. I notice cans and boxes tucked in them. And smell oil.

Drayton caresses my cheek. "I was so worried about you. Your mom had me bring your laptop and hers. They're safe. I brought a few Land things. I had to…that's not important. Joe, I want to tell you—"

"Are you running on gasoline?"

Drayton hugs me. "That's my Joe. Here I am, professing my undying devotion…"

I touch Drayton's lips with mine. "Yes, I know. I feel it, too. But are you running the motor on gasoline?"

Drayton leans forward and kisses me one more time. "Yes. It took a little water on. It'll crank back up. I added stabilizers and siphoned the gas from a home generator. They're fools not to realize almost every home here has a gasoline-powered generator. Supplies for miles."

"You're genius," I whisper. I shiver and lean into Drayton for another kiss. I never want to stop kissing him. It's not until this moment that I realize how much I've missed him over the past few days.

I think I've always known how I feel about him, but it's not until after he kissed me that I let myself realize how right it feels. How right *we* feel.

"Not if we don't get out of here," Chanko interrupts us. "I see lights."

The Estuary glows like it's the middle of the day.

"I see boats," Drayton says. "They're slow, battery operated, but we're heavy. Joe, man the motors."

The boats are small, personal fishing vessels, but they're coming fast. Drayton turns the ignition.

Nothing.

He turns the key a second time. The motor catches and sputters to life.

"Hold on," Drayton cries and he punches the motor. We pick up speed. The sea is choppy, the boat lurches unsteadily, and both my legs are cramping. I want to throw up, but I hold my station. If the motors go out, I will fix them someway, somehow. I push the hair out of my eyes and will my stomach to behave.

We lose two boats, but the third stays with us. It isn't a big boat, but it's fast and heading right for us. I flatten myself against the motor. Rain pelts me in the face. I think about going back to the Estuary and never seeing my dad again to tell him I love him. I think about life with Drayton. About being Ulster's forced wife.

I have a few seconds before the boat is on top of us. I wait until the front of their boat is almost parallel to us. I don't recognize the researcher about to board our boat, and I'm glad. I take out Flox's grenade, pull the pin and throw it as accurately as I can. It lands near the steering console. "Bank port! Hard port!"

Drayton hears me, and the Regulator careens to the left. The explosion happens when we are in the outside of the turn, and we almost tip over. Debris flies through the air, and I cover my head. Everything is on fire. The world is a low buzz. I put my hands over my eyes. I don't want to watch anymore.

※

"It's all you could have done," Drayton says for the fifth time. I've mentioned that I killed two men, maybe more, a number of times already.

I'm next to him behind the console, en route to *The Fluddery Doo*. Over the last few hours, Mom explained to us in depth about the Council, but I'm not sure I believe that the Platforms are capable of revolution.

Drayton is convinced. He wants to be part of it. I hate the whole idea of it—the change, the conflict, the lack of normalcy. Upheaval on a daily basis. Not seeing Dad.

But I want to be with Drayton. And Drayton wants to be with me. And L'Esperance is a long way away.

And I've always wanted to see a reef.

# Acknowledgements

A hearty thank you to Andrew, my ex-Thursday student, for sharing the beautiful ideas and worlds he imagines and keeping me on my creative toes.

Serious, earth shaking thanks to Emma and Hannah at Owl Hollow Press for believing in me, my world, and for the patience and care they have taken in the making of this book. My sincere thanks to Olivia Swenson, editor most glorious, for helping me sculpt my vision and language.

Props to the teachers who made me want to write more than anything—the late Judy Davis, Mrs. Hamner, and Mrs. Schaff. For my family and friends who are family—Sandra and Ronald, David, Jessica, Nanci—there are not thanks enough to give you. You allow me the gift of freedom to be who I am without constraint. My love and my gratitude to you are in every word of this book.

Katarina Boudreaux is a writer, musician, composer, tango dancer, and teacher—a shaper of word, sound, and mind. She returned to New Orleans after circuitous journeying.

Find Katarina at katarinaboudreaux.com

#PlatformDwellers

Printed by Libri Plureos GmbH in Hamburg, Germany